I0817816

THE YEAR OF FALLING IN LOVE

JESSICA SORENSEN

The Year of Falling in Love
Jessica Sorensen

ISBN: 978-1-939045-20-1
First Hardcover Edition: January 2016

For information: *jessicasorensen.com*

Cover Design by
Okay Creations

Photography by
Perrywinkle Photography

Interior Design and Formatting by
Christine Borgford, Perfectly Publishable

Chapter ONE

ISABELLA

It's been only minutes since Lynn told me Bella—my real mom—was a terrible person who's rotting in her grave. Only a few tiny minutes, yet it feels like an eternity, as if I've entered a time portal where time moves at half-speed.

It gives me too much time to think about my mom being dead, about how angry my dad was that I asked about her, about Lynn and how I shoved her after she told me. I ran out of my house right after without waiting to see her reaction. I was completely hysterical. But thank the damn stars Kai found me, otherwise who knows what I would've done. In the state of mind I was in, I wanted nothing more than to make the pain go away and would've done almost anything to make it stop.

But by some miraculous miracle—seriously, the guy is some kind of genius distraction wizard—Kai manages to calm me down. He takes me into the den of his house, tells me to sit down on the sofa, and puts on *Zombieland*. Then he gives me a bowl of popcorn and a box of Milk Duds and lies down on the floor.

I haven't explained to Kai what happened, at least not all the details, but I can tell he's wondering by the way he keeps staring at me instead of watching the movie. It's a zombie movie. No one is that distracted during a zombie movie unless they're deeply thinking about something. Or they're a total weirdo.

"I don't know what to do," I mumble through a yawn when the movie credits appear on the television screen. I roll onto my side to look down at Kai. His light blonde hair is flattened on one side and his cheek is red from where his face was pressed against the pillow. "I'm not sure if I can go home or if I can even call it home. After I pushed Lynn . . ." I shake my head. "I don't even feel bad. What kind of person does that make me?"

He rotates onto his back and cocks a brow at me. "You pushed Lynn? When?"

"Right after she told me about my mom." Reality crashes down on me. "I'm in so much shit, Kai. My dad was already super pissed I tried to find out about my real mom. He probably already changed the locks so I can't get into the house."

Kai nibbles on his bottom lip, contemplating. "Maybe that's a good thing. No more Hannah. No more Lynn. You'd finally be free of them."

"Yeah, I know." I twist onto my back, sweeping strands of my brown hair out of my tear-stained face. I'm sure I'm rockin' some awesome raccoon eyes right now and probably look like a real hot mess. Thankfully, it's just Kai here with me. After he apologized to me for what happened in seventh grade, and then I found out about how he told everyone that Hannah lied about me being in a mental institution, I know I can trust him. "I know this is going to sound crazy—it sounds crazy even in my own head—but part of me doesn't want to get kicked out."

When he doesn't respond, I slant to the side to look at him.

He's gaping at me like I just flew over the cuckoo's nest. "I'm going to chalk up your temporary insanity to the fact that you've been through a ton of shit in the last couple of hours and give you a piece of advice. If you can get out of that house, then do it. You'll be better off on your own than living with your psychotic, abusive family."

"They don't abuse me. Yeah, they're mean as hell, but they never hit me or anything like that."

Kai carries my gaze. "Isa, words can sometimes be just as harmful as actions."

I swallow the lump in my throat as I recollect how many times Hannah and Lynn have insulted me. How my dad ignored it. How crappy I felt, how small, how worthless. Then I think of Kai and how his dad treats him.

"You should take your own advice," I say with an insinuating look.

He shrugs indifferently. "I'm working on it."

I massage my aching chest with my hand, wishing I could get the tightness out. "I wouldn't be on my own if I moved out. I'd move in with my Grandma Stephy."

"Good. From what you've told me about her, she sounds pretty cool." He sits up and stretches his arms above his head, causing his black T-shirt to ride up just enough that I get a brief glimpse of his abs.

I try not to gawk like some band groupie ogling a

lead singer, but my gaze has other ideas. I blame it on my hormones. When they take over, I lose my self-control.

"Yeah, she's cool . . ." *Stop staring at him, Isa. You're such a weirdo.* "She's actually the grandma I went on that trip with this summer." I finally manage to tear my gaze off Kai's lean muscles and give myself a mental high-five for regaining my self-control. But then I cringe when I find him watching me with curiosity written all over his face.

He so just busted me.

I trap my next breath in my lungs, waiting for him to tease me, but strangely, he remains quiet. Maybe he's giving me a get-out-of-jail-free pass because he feels sorry for me. While I'm not a huge fan of pity, I'll take the pass.

"It'd still suck to move, though," I say. "I'd have to change schools . . . I know I don't have a ton of friends or anything, but I was just starting to fall into a good rhythm."

He frowns. "Why would you have to change schools? I thought she lived in Sunnyvale."

"She does but on the other side of town at the Sunnyvale Bay Community, which is a different school district." I sit up and lower my feet onto the floor. "It's a thirty-minute drive away from our school, so I'd have to transfer."

He props his elbows on the edge of the sofa only inches away from my legs. "It'll only take thirty minutes if you drive like a grandma."

"My grandma would have to drive me," I point out. "And I don't want to ask her to do that. And even if I did, I don't think she can. She lets Indigo borrow her car for work and stuff. It'd be way easier on everyone if I just transferred." I sigh, tucking my hands underneath my legs. "I just wish I wasn't so socially incompetent."

"You're not socially incompetent. You're just shy."

"Shy, socially incompetent, it still means I have a hard time talkin' to people." I flop back on the sofa. "I wish I could get over it, but I think I'll always be this way."

"Being shy isn't a bad thing." He reaches out to touch me, but then pulls back. "And we can get you over it."

"Not everyone can be a beautiful social butterfly like you," I smile for probably the first time since the madness opened up beneath me and tried to swallow me whole. "You're like a unicorn, dude."

His forehead creases. "A unicorn?"

I nod, patting his head. "All rare and majestic. Heads turn when you walk into the room because you're so pretty, and everyone wishes they could be as pretty as you."

He beams at me. "I am pretty amazing."

Yep. There's no use trying to deny Kai's gorgeous. He knows it. All the girls who go to my high school know it. Unicorn lovers everywhere know it.

His grin broadens as he pushes to his feet and plops down on the cushion beside me. "I have an idea."

I dramatically roll my eyes. "Oh no, here we go."

He presses his hand to his chest, pretending to be offended. "Hey, not all of my ideas are bad."

I snort a laugh. "Remember that one time you thought it'd be super awesome if I sat on your lap in that rusty swing set because there was only one seat and you wanted me to swing with you?" It was back in seventh grade during our fleeting friendship. When I think back to that time, I did a lot of risky things thanks to Kai. For some reason, I had a hard time saying no to him even when his ideas screamed *Danger! Danger! You just might die!*

He pulls a guilty face. "Yeah, that might not have been my best idea."

"*Might not have been.*" I gape at him. "The damn thing

broke when we were in mid-air. I almost broke my arm and crushed your manly parts."

He winces, his hand drifting to his lap. "Yeah, I remember that part too clearly." He considers something before twisting to face me. "What if I promise this idea won't bring you any physical harm. That the only thing you'll be in danger of is getting too attached to your sexy next-door neighbor."

"What does Oliver have to do with this?" I hold back a grin as I refer to one of my other next-door neighbors.

Kai narrows his eyes at me then gently tugs on a strand of my long, brown hair. "Let's get something straight. The only sexy next-door neighbor you have is me. Got it?"

The thought of Kyler Meyers, Kai's older brother, who I've had a crush on forever, pops into my head. I was supposed to be on a date with him tonight—our very first date to be exact—but had to cancel because I couldn't quit sobbing. I didn't tell Kyler that, though. I just told him something came up. He was really sweet about it and asked me out next weekend. Of course, I said yes. I just hope I feel better by then.

Not wanting to get into that with Kai, since Kyler is a touchy subject for him, I heave a dramatic sigh. "Fine, my one and only sexy next-door neighbor, what's your awesome idea?"

His eyes light up. "I was thinking, if you went to live with your grandma, I could give you a ride to and from school."

My heart melts like warm chocolate. That might be the sweetest thing a guy has ever done for me. Well, except for when he stopped the whole straightjacket rumor Hannah tried to spread about me. That one is pretty high up there. "You'd do that for me?"

"Of course. That's what *friends* do for each other, right?"

The way he says *friends,* as if the word is amusing, turns me into an overanalyzing, read-between-the-lines-way-too-much girl. Why did it sound like he finds it funny that we're friends? Or maybe I'm just over-thinking it. Why do I care?

Hormones, dude, hormones. Get a grip over yourself.

"While I appreciate the offer, I'm not sure I feel comfortable with you doing that," I tell him, even though I don't want to turn down his offer. "I mean, you'd have to get up like an hour earlier than you normally do."

"An hour isn't that big of a deal," he insists, picking up the remote and shutting off the television.

"You're not a morning person, Kai. You told me the other day that you hate waking up any earlier than noon. That you turn into a cranky monster."

"I didn't say cranky monster. I said asshole. And that's only on weekends. I get up at like seven-thirty on weekdays."

"Only when you go to school on time. You're usually late."

"Well, I guess I'll have to start being on time." He gives a casual shrug, pretending it's not a big deal, even though it is.

At least, it is for me.

"You really don't have to do this," I say. The last thing I want to do is force him to drive all the way across Sunnyvale to pick my sorry butt up and get himself on a schedule when he's clearly an I'll-do-what-I-want-whenever-I-want-to kind of guy. "It might be good for me to start a new school, anyway. It'll force me to make friends without your ever-so-awesome unicorn guidance." I press my palms together and bow to him.

He chuckles, shaking his head. "It's really not a big deal." He gives my knee a squeeze. "So just accept my offer."

My knee jolts from his touch and I hastily clear my throat, unsure how to respond.

While he keeps referring to us as friends, I'm not so sure our relationship is that simple. Yeah, Kai and I are friends, but we've drunkenly kissed once and almost kissed another time. While the kiss was brief, I swear to God fireworks and explosions burst through me. I felt like I'd stepped into one of those sappy rom-coms or something. According to Kai, though, he kisses everyone when he's drunk. But then he almost kissed me in our old hideout, a hollowed out tree trunk. And that was while he was completely sober. He hasn't tried to make up an excuse for that one. We're just pretending it never happen.

"So, what do you say? Will you please let me be your chauffeur?" he asks, drawing me back to reality.

His fingers are still on my knee, tracing delicate circles across my skin, his fingertips moving higher on my thigh toward the bottom of my skirt. I'm not even sure he knows he's doing it. I should probably wiggle my leg before he unknowingly feels me up, but I can't seem to move or breathe. Do anything really, except idiotically gape at his fingers.

Noting where I'm staring, his gaze drops to his hand. He stares for a second or two before swiftly withdrawing and coughing into his hand.

"Sorry, I . . ."

Awkward silence stretches between us.

Um . . . Can you say awkward?

Which is kind of weird since usually Kai just owns whatever he does.

My skin is on fire, and I clear my throat. "No worries."

"Besides, starting a new school your senior year would suck balls," he continues as if nothing happened. "Everyone will already have their own thing going on. It'd be better if you just finished here and then just started over in college."

"Are you sure you want to make that kind of commitment, though?"

"I never commit to anything aloud until I'm one hundred percent sure I'm down with it."

"Okay. I accept your offer to be my chauffeur." An ounce of weight lifts from my shoulders. Now if I could just get rid of the rest, life would be all cookies and vanilla sprinkle frosting. "But you know what that means, right? I get to boss you around."

His eyes narrow to slits, but it's a playful move. "I take back the chauffeur thing. How about just a *friend* helping another *friend*."

Oh, for the love of all zombies, why does he keep saying *friend* like that? Every time he does, it makes me think of our kiss and almost kiss, something friends don't do.

"Why are you blushing, Isa?" Humor dances in his eyes.

"I'm not." I duck my head, reaching for the stack of DVDs on the floor, and hiding my blush. "Can we watch one more movie before I deal with this moving out thing? I need to think about what I'm going to say to everyone."

His gaze practically burns a hole in the side of my head. "If that's what you want."

I nod, scoop up the DVDs, and straighten. "I'm avoiding going back to my house. I'm kind of scared."

"I don't blame you." He does that whole intense, smoldering, I'm-trying-to-burn-a-hole-into-your-head-so-I-can-read-your-thoughts look on me just long enough to make me squirmy. It's a breath of fresh air when he finally looks away, snatching the DVDs from my hand. "Which one are we watching?"

"I'll let you pick since you let me pick the last one."

He sorts through the DVDs and ends up selecting *28 Days Later*.

"You really want to watch another zombie movie?" I ask as he gets up to put the DVD into the player.

He feeds the disc in. "Sure. Zombies are cool."

My chest constricts again, but in a different, more welcoming way. "Kai . . ."

"Yeah?" He fiddles with the buttons on the DVD player.

My heart pitter-patters. "Thanks for taking care of me today."

"It's no big deal." He shrugs, but I swear to God I hear a smile through his voice. He presses play then returns to the sofa. "I mean, yeah, it's kind of a pain in the ass taking care of your sugar and zombie addiction." He sits down beside me and playfully bumps his shoulder against mine. "For a minute there, things got intense. I was worried you were going to turn into a Gremlin and bite my hand off if I didn't let you dump the Milk Duds into the popcorn, but I think I deflated the situation pretty well."

"They taste better together," I protest. "The heat makes them all melty, gooey, good."

"Melty, huh?" He drapes his arm across the back of the sofa and rests his hand behind me. "That sounds like a word that belongs in the Awesome Isabella Dictionary."

Smiling, I reach for the popcorn bowl on the end table beside me. I place it on my lap and stuff a handful into my mouth as the movie starts.

But around five minutes in, my mind is elsewhere, which is a first for me while watching a zombie movie.

But I let my temporary insanity slide since I have a lot on my mind.

I want to believe my mom isn't dead, that what Lynn told me was her sick, twisted way of messing with me. But even if my real mom isn't dead, I worry about why everyone thinks she's this horrible person. What could she have possibly done to make them think that? What happened fourteen years ago when I left the life I was raised in and came to live with my dad, the Evil Witch of the Anders home, and her Wicked Wench sidekick daughter?

Abruptly, Kai stiffens beside me. I think he's freaking out over the gory scene on the screen until I note he's staring at the corner of the room. The only thing there is a miniature gnome, so unless Kai's suddenly developed a fear of beady-eyed little creatures, I'm guessing he's stressing over something else.

"Everything okay?" I ask him.

He blinks at me. "Huh?"

"You were dazing off." I try to read his vibe, but Kai can be so mysterious sometimes. "We can change this if you're bored." I start to get up, but he clasps a hand on my leg, forcing me to stay put.

"Relax. I said I was cool with watching the movie and I meant it." He only releases me from his grip when I chillax. "Now watch the movie."

I do what he says, but ten minutes later, he's zoning off into empty space again, looking extremely bothered. Kai's in some kind of trouble with a guy who goes by the name T and I wonder if he's concerned over that. He won't talk about it, though. Trust me, I've tried.

I can't help thinking of a few hours ago when he hugged me in front of his house and winced, like I was hurting him. When I asked him about it, he cracked a joke about my tiny arms giving him booboos. Could T have hurt him?

"Isa, would you please stop staring at me?" His gaze glides to me, and he bites on his bottom lip. "You're giving me a complex."

"I know that's not true. No one could ever give Ego Man a complex," I retort, using the superhero nickname I gave him earlier today, trying to lighten his mood.

"That's not true." He steadily holds my gaze. "Every superhero has a kryptonite."

"You're saying me staring at you is your kryptonite?" I ask with skepticism.

He shrugs, but doesn't say anything, zoning off again.

"Are you sure you're okay?" I ask.

He nods then gets up and heads for the doorway like it's on fire. "I'm going to go make some more popcorn. I'll be right back."

I look down at the bowl in my lap, half full of popcorn. He obviously wanted to leave the room, but why? What is he hiding from me?

Chapter TWO

KAI

I wake up on the sofa with a warm body pressed against mine. At first I'm confused as hell. Then I catch the faintest scent of popcorn and the fogginess in my mind gradually lifts. Zombie movies. Popcorn. Milk Duds. *Isa*.

She's fast asleep with her head resting on my arm, her hand on my chest, and our legs are so tangled I can't tell where her's start and mine end.

We must've fallen asleep during the movie. I don't know if that's a good thing or not. I mean, sure, it's a fantasy come true waking up with her practically lying on top of me. But I'm supposed to be keeping this thing with us strictly a friend thing until I can get my act together, and she can get over this stupid idea that she's supposed to be with Kyler. Plus, her elbow is putting pressure on the ribs T cracked his knuckles against yesterday. I'm pretty sure one might be broken, but there's nothing I can do about it. I've broken a couple of ribs before in football and know the healing process consists of taking it easy and not moving the area much.

I'm deliberating what I should do when Isa lets out a soft moan and nuzzles closer to me.

Fuck it. This is definitely a good thing.

I rub my eyes with my free hand and relax, wondering what time it is. Sunlight is peering through the cracks in the curtains, so it has to be at least seven o'clock. I should probably wake her up and explain that we fell asleep. But it's too nice holding her, and I end up just lying there, watching her sleep like a creeper.

She looks so relaxed with her face resting in the crook of my arm, her lips parted as she softly breathes. I wish I could let her lie like this all day, but eventually, she's going to wake up and I'm going to have to tell her that her mom's alive but in a prison in Virginia for murder charges.

I tuck a strand of her hair behind her ear then graze my knuckles across her cheek. Her skin is so soft and warm—

"What the hell's going on?" Kyler's annoying voice cuts through the moment.

I let out a frustrated grunt. *Great. Here comes drama.*

I fire a shut-the-hell-up look at him. "Keep your voice down or you'll wake her up."

Kyler's face turns bright red. "Why is she here with you when she was supposed to be on a date with me last night?"

I hesitate. I'm not sure how much Kyler knows about what's going on with Isa. The longer I remain silent, the redder Kyler's face gets. I consider not uttering a word, letting him come up with all kinds of ideas about what Isa and I were doing last night. It's not like the two of them are officially together. They haven't even been out on a date yet. But I'm not sure Isa waking up to Kyler all pissed off at her is a great idea.

"Would you chill out?" I say, resisting and eye roll. "We were watching a movie last night and fell asleep. Nothing happened."

He crosses his arms, dumbfounded. "She blew me off so she could stay here and watch a movie with *you*?"

"No, you dumbass." I carefully slip my arm out from underneath Isa and stand up, wincing as my ribs groan in protest. "Something happened yesterday that upset her, so we hung out and I distracted her with a zombie movie marathon." When he continues to look irritated, I add, "Nothing happened." I want to add, *but it wouldn't matter if something did happen because she's not yours.*

His jaw ticks. "Why didn't she talk to me?"

I keep my elbow to my side, hoping to reduce some of the pain in my ribs "Huh?"

"When whatever happened that upset her. Why did she ask you for help instead of me?"

"She didn't come to me. I was just there when the shit hit the fan." It nearly kills me to say it, to tell him that Isa didn't choose me over him. I was just the who she ran into first.

For as long as I can remember, Kyler has gotten whatever he wanted whenever he wanted: from his choice in girlfriends, to positions on the team, to making everyone in our school worship him. He's always been better than me in sports and hooked up with girls I liked. I put an end to the sports problem by quitting, and it was a huge relief. I was tired of living in his shadow and wanted to find my own thing that didn't include being compared to my older brother. As for dating the girls I liked, sure it pissed me off, but I got over it.

Isa, though . . . She's different. She's seriously the sweetest, coolest, most beautiful girl I've ever known. I just wish I could've seen that back in seventh grade. But I was a stupid kid who wanted to fit in with the in-crowd. Still, I liked her way before Kyler did, before she started wearing makeup and dressing more like a girl. I know the only reason he likes her is because he thinks she's hot. He doesn't even know anything about her.

Kyler gradually unstiffens. "So maybe she would've talked to me if she hadn't run into you first." An arrogant smile rises across his face.

I want to punch him in the face, but I don't want Isa to wake up to a fight breaking out. Plus, more than likely, my dad would come in and chew my ass off. He can't stand me right now and is looking for any reason to punish me. I think he wants to kick me out of the house.

"You're eighteen years old," he said to me a couple of months ago after I came home trashed. "Maybe it's time for you to move out."

I wanted to argue that I wasn't ready to move out, but my pride got in the way. "Maybe I should."

He gave me the same condescending look he always gives whenever he's about to prove how much of a loser I am. "Well, you better start looking for places then." He slapped the newspaper onto the kitchen table in front of me. "Good luck trying to find a place when your dumbass doesn't have any money."

"Honey, watch your language," my mom intervened as she piled fruit into the blender. "Kai, what I think your father is saying is that if you can't clean up your act, we may have to take a more drastic route. We love you, but I'm not going to stand around and watch you throw your life away."

"This is so fucking stupid." I shoved the newspaper away as I rose to my feet. "Kyler got drunk all the time when he was my age and you guys never did anything."

"Kyler was also the captain of the football and basketball teams and was an honor roll student." My father looked at me with disgust. "You barely even go to school anymore. You're wasting your life, partying and coming home wasted every weekend. If you keep going down this path you're going to end up a dead-beat, pumping gas for a living."

"No one pumps gas for people anymore," I mumbled then left the kitchen before he could ream into me more.

"Umm . . ." Isa's startled voice yanks me away from the memory.

I glance over my shoulder at her.

She's sitting up, fussing with her hair, and her eyes are darting back and forth between me and Kyler. "What happened?" Her bleary gaze lands on me. "Did we fall asleep watching the movie?"

I nod. "Apparently even you can get tired of zombies."

She rolls her eyes like that's the silliest thing she's ever heard. "I'm not tired of zombies. Just tired." The second she spots Kyler she goes from playful to shy. "Hey."

"Hey . . . So, you canceled our date last night so you could sleep with my brother?" He winks at her. "I think that might be a first for me."

Isa's cheeks turn pink. "I didn't sleep with him. Well, I did, but not on purpose. We just sort of fell asleep while we were watching a movie."

Kyler chuckles then pushes past me and sits down beside her on the sofa. "Relax, I'm just messing with you. Kai told me what happened."

"Oh good." She looks away from him as she runs

her fingers below her eyes, trying to wipe away some smeared makeup. "Sorry I had to cancel our date, but a bunch of stuff happened and I would've been a downer to be around."

"It's okay." He brushes a strand of her hair out of her face. "Is it anything you want to talk about?"

I stand there, hoping Isa will duck from his touch, but I can tell she likes it by the way her eyelashes flutter.

I don't want to wait around to hear her answer. I don't think I can take it if she tells him about her mom and what's going on with her family, like she told me.

"I have to go." I back toward the doorway, tucking my hands into my pockets. "You two kids have fun. And don't do anything I wouldn't do."

Isa gives me a pleading look, like she doesn't want me to leave yet. I almost stay. But when Kyler puts his hand on her knee, I know if I stick around I'll lose my shit.

After I leave the den, I go into the kitchen to grab something to eat. As I'm pulling out a couple of Toaster Strudels from the freezer, I check the time on the clock. Shit. I'm supposed to be at Big Doug's place already. Last night I told him about the mess I've gotten into with T. He told me to come over today because he might have some work for me to do where I can make some cash fast and get T paid back ASAP. I've done some work for Big Doug before, but stopped when we almost got busted tapping into a bank's security cameras. To this day, I'm still not sure why we were doing it. But if we'd gotten caught, I could've ended up in jail. Which is why I hate that I have to go back into that world. But, at the moment, I don't see another alternative.

I shove the Toaster Strudels in the toaster, pop some painkillers, then head toward the stairs.

As I'm rounding the corner in the hallway, Isa walks

out of the den. The two of us collide hard.

"Aw, fuck," I curse, hunching over the pain radiating through my side.

"Oh my God. I'm sorry. I didn't see . . ." She trails off.

I glance up at her, wondering what she's doing.

Her furious gaze is fastened on me, and her hands on her hips.

"What the hell is that look for?" I try to keep my voice light, but I sound strained. I force myself to stand up straight and keep my arm at my side. "All right, what'd I do now?"

Her pointed gaze travels to my injured side. "I knew you were hurt. Why didn't you tell me?"

"Yeah, I'm hurt because we just crashed into each other," I lie, sidestepping to squeeze by her.

She sidesteps and blocks my path with her arms stretched out to the side of her. "No way. You're not going anywhere until you tell me what's wrong."

I bite back my amusement over how unintentionally cute she's being right now. "And what if I don't? What're you going to do?"

She mulls it over for a second or two then her arm darts forward. She grips the bottom of my shirt and lifts it up to peer underneath.

I should probably stop her before she sees the gnarly bruise on my side, but as her knuckles graze the bottom of my stomach, I get too turned on to care.

"Oh my God, Kai," she gasps at the sight of the purplish-yellow marks dotting my ribcage, reaching forward and tentatively touching the area.

My muscles constrict from the contact, and she immediately jerks back, but I catch her hand and hold it against my side.

Her gaze elevates to my face, uncertainty filling her

eyes. "Who hurt you?"

"It's not a big deal. I just got into a tiny, little fight." I wink at her. "But you should see the other guy."

"Was this . . ." She struggles for words, her fingers trembling against my side. "Did that T guy do this to you?"

I open my mouth to lie, but then I realize I don't want to lie to her anymore than I already have. "Yeah, and—"

"Hey, so I was thinking, since you didn't want to go home yet, that we could go get some breakfast," Kyler says, strolling out of the den.

Isa steps back from me. "Are you sure? I don't want to put you out," she says to Kyler.

I grind my teeth. If Kyler knows she doesn't want to go home, then does that mean she told him what's going on? Jealousy burns inside me, and I hate the feeling so much. I've spent way too many years carrying it around. It's part of why I decided to quit sports, change my life, who I was.

Muttering a goodbye, I haul ass to the stairway. I half-expect Isa to call out to me, but she doesn't. It's probably for the better. I need to focus on getting out of this mess with T right now before I even attempt to go down any sort of romantic relationship road with Isa. At least, that's what I try to convince myself, but deep down, all I want to do is go back, grab Isa, and kiss her. And for real this time, when we're both sober and can enjoy it.

As I enter my room, my phone buzzes from inside the pocket of my black jeans. I dig it out as I rummage through my dresser for a clean shirt.

> *T: If you don't get me my grand in three weeks, yesterday is going to seem like a fucking cakewalk.*

I swallow hard. A thousand! Mother fucker! I didn't

realize Bradon owed T that much. How the hell am I supposed to come up with a thousand bucks in three weeks? There's no way I can make that much in three weeks working for Big Doug. I have no clue what I'm going to do, but I better come up with a plan. And fast.

Chapter THREE

ISABELLA

Kai walks away from Kyler and me like we're carrying some viral disease and are about to infect him. I open my mouth to call after him, because I'm not about to let him leave until he explains what kind of trouble he's gotten into, but Kyler snags my hand and steers me in the direction of the kitchen before I get a chance.

Normally, I'd be all over the fact that Kyler Meyers is holding my hand, but my mind is on Kai and those bruises. They looked really bad, and he seemed in a lot of pain. I wonder if his ribs are broken.

"Just let him go," Kyler says. "When he gets like this, it's better you just leave him alone."

"Gets like what?" I wonder if Kyler knows what's going on with Kai.

Kyler shrugs as he leads me to the mudroom then releases my hand. "Pissy and upset. He's been like this since we were kids. He gets into trouble and then sulks about it and makes everyone miserable."

I start to slip on my shoes. "Do you know why he's upset?"

He sits down on a wooden bench to slip on his sneakers. "Who knows? He's been a real asshole lately. My parents think he's on drugs. I heard them talking about sending him to a rehab or something."

I shift my weight, feeling uncomfortable talking to Kyler about Kai, like I'm betraying Kai. "Kai's not on drugs, Kyler."

He peers up from tying his shoelaces, brushing strands of his light brown hair away from his forehead. "How do you know that?"

"He told me he doesn't do them." Anymore. But Kyler doesn't need to know about the anymore part.

"And you just believed him?"

"He's my friend. He wouldn't lie to me."

Kyler stares at me dubiously, seeming unhappy with my answer. But he pushes the irritation aside and rises to his feet. "Maybe you're right. Maybe he's not on drugs, but there's definitely something going on with him."

I keep my lips fused. It feels wrong to be talking to Kyler about Kai. Now, if I find out what's going on with Kai and it's really bad, then that's a different story. I'll do what I have to do to help him, even if it means getting help from his family.

"Where do you want to get breakfast?" he asks, grabbing a jacket from a coatrack.

"Anywhere works for me." I glance down at my wrinkled clothes. My breath tastes like rotten broccoli and I'm sure my makeup is smeared all over my face. "Can I go home and change first?"

"Of course." He opens the door and motions for me to go out first. "But I thought you didn't want to go home?"

Very true. I don't want to go home and honestly, I doubt I'm allowed to. Still, I should get my stuff. If only there was a way to get into my room without actually having to go through the house . . .

I dare a look over at the driveway of my house. Hannah's car is parked behind Lynn's and my dad's. They're all home, probably sitting around the kitchen table, eating breakfast.

Kyler joins me outside, closing the door behind him. "Isa, can I . . . Do you mind if I ask why you don't want to go home?"

I haven't told him anything, and I really don't want to. While I have a major, borderline-stalker crush on Kyler, I don't know him well enough to trust him that much. I want to. Like a ton. But establishing trust requires getting to know him as something other than the gorgeous, popular guy who lives next door, who talked to me a few times and gave me a rose once.

"I'm just fighting with my parents." I decide to go with the partial truth. I eyeball the banister of the deck attached to my bedroom. If only I had a Pegasus or fairy wings so I could fly right up there or perhaps Spiderman web fingers so I could scale the wall . . . Wait a minute . . ."Do you by chance have a ladder?"

He tracks my gaze and his expression plummets. "You seriously want to climb up there just to avoid your parents?"

I bob my head up and down. "It's better that way. Trust me." Yeah, it might be a little drastic, but it's way better than dealing with the drama waiting for me inside that house.

"If that's what you want, then you got it." He rubs his hands together, backing down the stairs and toward the garage. "One ladder coming up."

I smile at him gratefully then plant my butt on the railing and wait for him to return. A light fall breeze kisses the air, and clouds shadow the sky. It's the beginning of October and some of the neighbors have already pulled out the decorations, the Meyer's yard included. Inflatable pumpkins and plastic tombstones cover the front yard and a giant spider is perched on the basketball hoop. I remember all those times I sat out on my balcony, watching Kyler play basketball in his driveway, and wishing I was with him. And now I am over here. Funny how life changes. The thought gives me the tiniest drop of peace in the sea of depression swishing around inside me.

Optimism, I remind myself. Lynn may have said all those horrible things about my mom but, like Kai said, she's not the most reliable source. So, until I have the actual facts in front of me, I can't believe my mom's dead or that she was a bad person.

I just start to relax when the side door to my house swings open and Hannah walks out. At first, she's too busy texting to notice me sitting on the Meyer's porch. But when she drops her phone into her purse and reaches to open her car door, her eyes drift next-door and zero in right on me. A series of emotions flash across her face—confusion, shock, anger—and then her lips curl.

She strolls up to the fence, sneering. "You know stalking's illegal, right?"

I fold my arms around myself, starting to shrink away. But then I force myself to lift up my chin. *No. No more cowering.* "Is that the best you can come up with?"

Shock flickers in her eyes. "Have you looked in a mirror today? You look like shit. Then again, you always look like shit."

Anger boils inside me like lava. Usually, I bite my tongue and try to rise above or whatever, but after everything that went down yesterday, my willpower snaps. I'm furious. At her. At Lynn. At my dad for lying to me, for never sticking up for me, for letting me live with people who belittled my self-worth every day for years.

"What's your problem?" I hop off the railing and step off the deck, striding toward the fence. "I've never done anything to you yet, you've always hated me."

She barks a disdainful laugh. "Your mother almost ruined my parents' marriage. I have every right to hate you."

My muscles ravel into knots. How long has she known about my mom? How much does she know? "They're not just your parents. Your dad's still my dad, Hannah."

"If he had his way, he wouldn't be." She flips her blonde hair off her shoulder. "All you do is remind him of the biggest mistake of his life. No wonder he can't even stand to look at you." Her brows rise as she assesses me, her face pinching in repulsion. "But most people can't. You're worthless. I know it. My mom knows it. *My* dad knows it."

All the rage I've bottled up for nearly eighteen years explodes. Before I even realize what I'm doing, I lift my leg to climb over the fence.

Hannah's eyes widen in surprise and she trips back, causing one of her heels to get stuck in the grass. I'm not even one hundred percent sure what I'm going to do to her: slap her, push her down, mess up her hair, force her to watch me break her manicured nails off. But before I can get over the fence, arms wrap around my waist and gently pull me back.

"As much as I think you deserve to do whatever

you're about to do," Kai whispers in my ear. "She's not worth the trouble you'll get in for kicking her ass."

Hannah scoffs. "Like she could kick my ass."

Keeping one arm looped around my waist, Kai moves beside me and smirks at Hannah. "Then why do you look like you're about to piss your pants?"

Hannah glares at Kai. "You're such an asshole, Kai. Why are you even here? No one asked you to come over here and be a jerk."

"Why are you here?" He quips. "No one asked you to come over and bitch at Isa in that shrill voice of yours." When her eyes shoot daggers at Kai, he grins in satisfaction. "So, here's a thought: why don't you walk away before I tell Isa about what you did two summers ago and give her all the ammo she needs to make your life a living hell."

I have no idea what he's referring to but I'm so thankful that he's standing up for me that I want to turn around and hug him.

Hannah's expression darkens, her voice lowering an octave. "Are you *threatening* me?"

"Not so much threatening as warning you that I'll tell everyone your dirty little secret." He flashes his pearly whites at her. "But if you want to look at it like that, then go right ahead."

Steam practically shoots out of Hannah's ears. "No one ever threatens me. You're so going to pay for this." She spins around to leave, but then spots Kyler coming out of the garage with a ladder. She goes from the Ice Queen to cotton candy sweet, plastering on a sugary sweet smile. "Hey, Kyler. I didn't know you were home this weekend. I thought you said you were going on a trip with your friends or something."

Kai's hand falls from my waist, and he puts some

distance between us.

Kyler sets the ladder down beside the fence and dusts off his hands, his gaze skimming the three of us. "I . . . um . . . I was supposed to but my friends . . . bailed out at the last second."

I think he might be lying to her, and even though it might make me a little twisted, I find an odd sense of happiness in that fact.

"Oh." For a brief second, rage blazes in her eyes, but the look fades and an exaggerated smile returns. "Good, then I guess you can take me out today after all."

Kyler massages the back of his neck tensely. "Actually, I already made plans with someone else."

Her smile goes *poof*. "With who?" she snaps. "It better not be that slut, Carissa."

"It's not her . . ." Kyler shifts his weight uneasily.

I'm not sure whether to take his hesitancy personally. Is he ashamed he's going out with me? Or is he sparing me the hell that's going to follow when Hannah finds out?

Kyler gives me a sidelong glance, and his eyes carry a silent question: *what should I tell her*? I'm not sure. While I don't want to keep our date . . . hanging out . . . going to breakfast . . . whatever we're doing today, a secret. I also don't want to give Hannah more of a reason to torment me.

I never get to decide my answer, though, because Hannah notices Kyler looking in my direction, and Pandora's box flies open.

"Are you effing kidding me!" she shouts, her voice so loud the neighbor across the street looks up from watering his lawn. "Her! That . . . that loser!"

"What the heck is your problem?" Kyler says at the same time Kai warns, "Guess just threatening you wasn't enough." Me, I think about jumping over that fence again, going all ninja on her, and kicking her ass. Kai must sense this too, because his fingers fold around my arm and he holds onto me.

Hannah shakes her head, fuming mad. "Don't pretend like you two haven't thought the same thing. Up until she came back this summer, you both used to make fun of her all the time."

It grows so quiet I can hear Mr. Normbert's sprinklers turning on just down the street. I feel so small, like these tiny fairy statues my Grandma Stephy used to collect back when my grandpa was still alive. She kept them in front of her house near the tulip bed. I thought they were so cute and used to sit out there and pretend they were my magical friends who granted wishes. One day Hannah caught me, called me a freak, and stomped all over them until they were nothing more than broken glass.

"Actually, I never did." Kai inches toward the fence, getting close to Hannah. "You've always known what I thought of Isa, at least since *two summers ago*."

Hannah gives Kai the dirtiest look then, shooting one last glare in my direction, she turns her back on us, muttering something under her breath as she storms toward her car. She yanks the door open, revs the engine, and then peels out of the driveway, leaving tire marks on the concrete.

I start to let out a relieved breath when the door to my house opens.

My dad steps out and looks right at me. "Isabella Anders, get your ass over here right now. You and I need to talk. And that's not a request. Either get over here now or I'll call the cops."

Chapter FOUR

ISABELLA

I want to tell him to leave me alone, that we have nothing to talk about, but the threat of calling the cops scares the words right out of me.

"Fine. I'm headed over," I holler to my dad then turn to Kyler, feeling awkward. Unlike Kai, Kyler didn't deny that he called me a loser behind my back with Hannah and her friends. I'm not sure what to do with that. "I think I have to take a rain check on breakfast."

"I can wait for you," Kyler offers. "I don't have anything to do today anyway."

"Are you sure?" I ask. "It might take a while."

He nods, stuffing his hands into the pockets of his dark denim jeans. "I need to talk to you about some stuff, anyway."

"Okay. . . ." *Talk to me about what exactly?* "I'll come over here when I'm done talking to my dad." I wave at him then hike toward the end of the driveway.

Kai matches my steps, strolling along beside me. "Maybe you shouldn't go over there."

"I think I have to." I halt at the edge of the fence. "If for nothing else than to get my stuff before they decide to throw it away."

The wind blows strands of his hair up, and he runs his hand over his head to flatten them back down as he stares off across the street. "I don't like this."

"Kai, I'll be fine. I'm sure he just wants to tell me I have to move out."

Tension is set in his jawline as his gaze shifts to me. "I'm worried about you . . . that . . . that they're going to try to break you apart. I mean, why would he threaten to call the cops on you?"

"I'm sure that was just to get me to come over without a fight," I tell him, even though I don't quite believe the words myself. "It's not like I've done anything wrong. I'll be fine." I flex my muscles. "I've got skin made of steel baby," I attempt to joke but miss the mark, my voice falling flat like a deflated balloon. "I'll call you after I'm done talking to him, okay? I think we need to talk about some stuff anyway." *Like why this T guy beat you up.*

"Fine," he grumbles then shakes his head multiple times, mumbling something about having a bad feeling.

I start to leave but then pause as an overwhelming need surfaces. "Kai, thanks for everything you did back there with Hannah. For standing up for me. No one's ever done that . . . It means a lot."

"I was just doing what friends should do for each other." He doesn't use a funny tone this time when he says friends. He sounds dead serious and so is the intensity in his eyes.

I walk away with a hundred butterflies going wild inside my stomach and a tornado of confusion whipping through my mind. I feel like I'm tumbling into the unknown, down, down, down the rabbit hole into madness where nothing makes sense anymore. I have no idea who I am, who I want to be, what I want.

The feeling only amplifies when I enter my house, and my dad isn't in the kitchen. Instead, Lynn is sitting at the table with a stack of papers in front of her and an arrogant grin on her face.

"Isa, have a seat," she says, gesturing at the chair next to her.

I remain near the back door. "Where's my dad? He said he needed to talk to me, not you."

"Your dad's upstairs and he won't be part of this conversation because he doesn't want to have to deal with you. I've been kind enough to volunteer for the position, though." Her calm voice sends a chill down my spine. "So. Sit. Down."

I momentarily dither before taking a seat in the chair farthest away from her. I tuck my hands underneath the table so she can't see me fidgeting and wait for her to say something.

She drags the silence out for as long as possible, as if she knows it's driving me crazy. "Yesterday, after you put your hands on me, your father and I sat down to discuss how violent you've gotten."

"How violent I've gotten?" I shake my head. "I pushed you once, Lynn, and that's mild to the abuse you and Hannah have done to me over the years."

Her hard gaze narrows on me. "No one in this house has ever laid a hand on you."

"I'm talking about verbal abuse, Lynn. Words can

sometimes be just as harmful as actions," I repeat what Kai said to me last night.

Her fingers curl inward. For a horrifying moment, I think she's going to hit me. But she presses her knuckles against the edge of the stack of papers and shoves the paper across the table to me.

"After your father and I discussed your violent behavior," she continues on with her speech, "we decided the best thing for everyone is if you go to a boarding school that specializes with troubled teens."

My heart slams against my chest as I read the top of one of the papers. "You're sending me to *Montana*!" I shove back from the table. "No way. I'm not going."

She sits there with her perfect posture and a sickeningly pleased look on her face. "You're still a minor, and as your guardian, you have no choice but to do what I say."

"You're not my only guardian," I say then bolt from the kitchen. "Dad!" My feet stomp against the steps as I run upstairs. "Dad, you can't let her send me away." I hurry to his bedroom door and pound my fist against it. "Dad, please. Don't let her do this."

"I'm not letting her do anything," he responds through the closed door. "I agree with Lynn. You need to go, Isa. It's for the best."

"The best for who?" I grab the doorknob and jerk on the door, but it's locked.

I pound on the door a few times before giving up and running to my room. I try to call my Grandma Stephy, but she doesn't answer. I leave her a message then text Indigo, even though there's only like a one percent chance she'll read the text while she's at work. When she doesn't respond, I grab a few duffel bags from my closet and start throwing what I can inside: clothes, shoes, my sketchbook, art supplies, my computer. After I've stuffed the bags full, I dig my stash of cash out from the top dresser drawer and stuff it into my back pocket. Then I sling the bags over my shoulders and rush out of my room.

When I make it to the bottom of the stairway, Lynn is waiting for me, blocking my path to the backdoor.

"You're not going anywhere." She crosses her arms, her overly plucked brows arching. "You're staying here until tomorrow morning and then your father and I are driving you up to Montana. And if you so much as show any signs of getting violent, we won't hesitate to call the police."

I have an unsettling feeling she's hoping I'll try to push her again, give her a reason to call the police.

"I'm not staying here," I say in the calmest voice I can muster. "And I'm not going to the school in Montana. I'll be eighteen in a couple of months. I can live with Grandma Stephy until then."

"Until you're eighteen, your father and I tell you what to do, not the other way around. You won't be living with your Grandma Stephy. You'll be living in Montana, far, far away where you can't hurt anyone." Her lips curl into a smile. "And where you can't turn into your dirty whore of a mother."

I almost throw down right there, but at the last second, manage to see through the blindingly hot anger. She wants me to get mad. She wants me to hurt her. She wants me to be exactly who she's telling me I am.

"Is that why you've treated me so crappy," I snap, shocking her and myself. "Because my dad cheated on you with my mom."

Her lips curl into a malicious grin as her hand darts forward. She snags hold of my arm and her fingers dig into my flesh. "You ungrateful little brat. If you only knew what your mother did . . . How much she really ruined this family. How sick and twisted she really is . . . I could tell you too. Watch you break. But I'm not going to just yet. It's so much more fun watching you suffer. Watching your own father destroy your life. And he does it so easily because he secretly despises you and everything you represent."

My lungs tighten, sucking the oxygen out of my lungs. I can barely breathe. I see spots. If I don't get air into my lungs, I'll pass out.

Don't pass out. Don't pass out. If you pass out, God knows where you'll wake up. Just get out of here. Now.

Sucking in a deep breath, I wrench my arm away from her. Then I grip the banister and hoist myself over it like a freaking badass mofo hurdler. I'm on the bottom step, so it's not a far fall or anything, but my ninja move throws her off. She gapes at me in shock as I run toward the front door. It takes a second or two before I hear the sound of her footsteps chasing after me. I don't slow down, bursting out the front door. Then I sprint down the sidewalk straight for the Meyers house, crossing my fingers that Kai will be there to give me a ride to my Grandma Stephy's house where I know I'll be safe for now.

Dropping my bags on the back deck of the Meyers', I knock on the door while throwing a quick glance back at my house. Thank my lucky charms Lynn hasn't come out yet. Hopefully she'll give up and just let me leave. Although, I highly doubt it. Whatever happened between my real mom, my dad, and her, has caused her to set out on a mission to destroy me. I just wish I knew if Lynn's hatred stems solely from the affair of if there's more to it than that.

Every bone in my body excruciatingly aches as I replay her words over and over again. I've always known I wasn't my dad's favorite but to hear her say it aloud . . . So venomously . . . It stings, like poison in my veins.

I look down at my wrist where she grabbed me. Red marks dot my skin. How can she say that my violence is a problem after she did this? Knowing Lynn, though, she'll probably lie and tell my dad it was self-defense. When I really think about it, over the course of my life, she's done that a lot. Twisted stories to make me look like the bad one. And my dad believes them so easily.

By the time the Meyers' door opens, I'm tumbling into a hole of self-pity and loathing. But I claw my way out of it when I see Kyler in the doorway taking in the sight of me, out of breath, my eyes wild, and worry creases his forehead.

"Are you okay?" he asks.

I fight back my tears. "Um . . . Is Kai here?" I feel bad when he looks hurt, but I'd rather talk to Kai right now since he knows what's going on.

"He left just." He assesses me with concern. "What did you need him to do? Whatever it is, I can help you. Just trust me, okay?"

I stuff my hands into the pockets of my jacket. "Um, can you drive me to my grandma's? I really need to talk to her." It's the best I can give him for now.

He doesn't miss a beat. "Sure. Give me two seconds."

He rushes back into the house, leaving the door open. He returns two seconds later, wearing a blue hoodie and carrying a set of keys. Without saying anything, he picks up my bags and jogs down the back steps toward the garage. I follow him, repeatedly glancing over at my house. It's quiet. Too quiet. I worry Lynn might be up to something, like calling me in as a runaway. I consider going home but just the thought of doing so makes my stomach churn.

After Kyler and I get into his car, he backs onto the road and pulls out onto the main road.

"Do you remember where she lives?" I ask, clipping in my seatbelt.

He nods, cranking up the heat. "At the Sunnyvale Bay Community, right?"

Nodding, I recline back in the seat. "Yeah. And thanks for doing this."

He opens his mouth to say something, but my phone rings, cutting him off. I fumble to get it out my pocket. *Please let it be Grandma Stephy. Please. Please. Please.*

"Thank God," I say aloud when I see her name flash across the screen. I press talk and put the phone to my ear.

"What the hell did they do to you?" she asks before I can even say hello.

I briefly contemplate telling her I'll talk to her when I get to her house, when I'm not around Kyler, but then she announces she's out of town on a trip with Harry.

"Don't worry, though, hon. After I got your message, I hopped in the car, and I'm headed straight to the airport. Harry's on his phone right now looking for a flight home." Anger fills her tone. "Goddamn those two. I can't believe they're doing this to you."

"Me either." But as soon as I say it, I know it's a lie. I'm not surprised this is happening. In fact, when I look back at my relationship with my dad and Lynn, I'm surprised they didn't try to send me away sooner.

Tears well in my eyes as every painful memory and hurtful word come rushing back to me. Suddenly everything pours out of me in a jumble. I tell Grandma Stephy about how Lynn said my mom was dead and that she was a bad person. How I pushed Lynn and ran out of the house. How they'll call the cops on me if I don't go to Montana. By the time I'm finished babbling, I'm out of breath and highly aware that Kyler is watching me out of the corner of his eye.

"Damn my son and that stupid bitch he calls his wife," she says when I'm finished. "I'm not going to let them do this to you. They're not sending you anywhere. You're going to stay with me."

"But what if they call the cops?" I turn toward the window, not wanting to see the look on Kyler's face right now. If he didn't think I was a freak before, he probably does now. "What if they call me in as a runaway?"

"I highly doubt it." She seems pretty confident. "Lynn is all about appearances. That's probably part of the reason she took you in as her own daughter—to cover up your father's affair. I'm going to call your father and make sure his stupid ass doesn't let her."

"What should I do until then?" I ask, dabbing my eyes with the sleeve of my jacket.

"Where are you right now?"

"Um . . ." I sneak a peek in Kyler's direction. He's fiddling with the stereo, pretending to be oblivious to this crazy conversation going on right beside him. "Um, I'm actually with Kyler right now. Kyler Meyers. You baked cookies for him that one time."

"Oh, that boy you've been in love with forever," she says way too loudly.

My gaze flits to Kyler again, wondering if he heard what she just said. His hands are on the wheel, his focus straight ahead on the road, but I swear the corners of his lips twitch.

"No . . . I mean, yeah, that's him. But I'm not . . ." I bite down on my tongue to stop myself from saying anything embarrassing. Anything else, anyway.

"All right, I'll let you off the hook. But when I get home, I want the details," she teases me. "Can he take you to my house?"

"We're already heading there," I say, resting my head against the window.

"Good. There's a spare key under the welcome mat. Indigo will be there around ten, but send her a text to let her know you're there so she'll come straight home."

"What about Lynn and my dad?" I ask. "What if they show up there?"

"You let me handle them." The way she says it causes me to shudder. I love my Grandpa Stephy to death, but I pity the person who makes an enemy of her.

There was this one time she kept getting into an argument with one of her neighbors about the height of the shrubs in her yard. He kept threatening to call the police, saying they were hideous to look at and needed to be short enough that they were out of sight.

When he finally made an official complaint, she cut down her shrubs and then, in the middle of the night, snuck into his yard and whacked down all of the guy's prize roses. The dude was obsessed with his roses to the point where he would spend all weekend attending to them.

After she destroyed them, she piled both her shrubs and the roses into a barrel, put them in the middle of his yard and lit them on fire. He came running out of his house, freaking out and all my grandma said was, "There you go. Now both our problems are solved. You don't have to look at my shrubs anymore and I don't have to witness you fondling your rose bushes."

The man went livid and called the cops on her. The police wrote her up but I think they thought it was funny because they kept cracking jokes about rose bush fetishes as they took down notes.

"You'll call me after you talk to them, though, right?"

I ask her.

"Of course," she promises. "Give me a few and I'll call you right back."

After we say goodbye, I hang up and put my phone away. Then I remain quiet, unsure of what to say to Kyler. I kind of just want to remain that way for the rest of the drive to avoid telling him anything, but Kyler decides to break the silence.

"I've always known Lynn was a bitch to you, but I didn't know she was that bad." His grip tightens on the steering wheel as he casts a glance at me. "Isa, I'm so sorry you had to go through all that."

I shrug, acting all blasé, even though on the inside I'm a bundle of bouncy, hyped-up-on-sugar monkeys. "It's not your fault."

"I know but . . ." A deafening breath puffs from his lips. "About what Hannah said earlier, I want to be truthful with you, okay?"

Whoa. So, we're going there. *Now* of all times.

"I just want you to know I've never called you a loser." He pauses and I start to thank him, but then he adds, "But."

The cringe-worthy but, the word people use before they say something you might not want to hear.

"I never really tried to stop people when they said stuff about you." His voice is soft, conveying shame.

I'm not sure what to say. Part of my infatuation with Kyler came from the fact that I thought he stuck up for me, like when Hannah was teasing me and he stepped in. Or when his friends cornered me in the school, and he got them to leave me alone by telling them they were late for practice. Secretly, I always pictured him as this knight in shining armor who forced everyone to stop making fun of me even when I wasn't around to hear it.

"Isa." His cautious tone makes me apprehensive. "I've done some things in my past I'm not proud of, but I want you to know I'm not like that anymore."

Since when? Since I came back from Europe with my makeover? Since I became, as Indigo put it, "smokin' hot?" I want to ask him, but I'm afraid I'll have to watch him squirm in the seat and struggle for an answer. That his reaction will crush the last five years I spent dreaming of being with him one day. It was those dreams—fantasizing about another life—that got me through some of my roughest days of high school. I always convinced myself that one day I'd change, everyone would see it—Kyler would see it—and my life would get better.

But now I'm sitting here with him, completely changed, yet my life is falling apart.

"I sometimes used to watch you when you were out on your balcony drawing," he confesses. "You always looked so into it. I envied the way you could tune everything out like that. I've always had a really hard time not giving a shit about what people were doing, thinking, saying."

"I wasn't always focused on my drawing," I admit. On the inside, though, I'm like *holy cupids and chocolate hearts, Kyler used to watch me like I did him?* "Sometimes, I just pretended I was when . . . when I was worried you might see me."

A smile breaks out across his face. "So, you watched me too?"

I roll my eyes. "You know I did."

"No, I didn't," he tries to lie. But when I blast him with a skeptical look, he caves. "Okay. Okay. I did know, but I liked knowing you did. It made me feel . . ." He wavers. "Special, I guess."

A laugh bursts from my lips, and I slap my hand

across my mouth. "I'm so sorry. I didn't mean to laugh. You just said special and it sounded so . . ."

"So what?" he presses. When I shake my head, he reaches over and tickles my leg. "Come on. You can't laugh at a guy like that and not explain why."

I do one of my infamous pig snorts. "Kyler, stop!" I cry through my laughter.

"Not until you tell me why you laughed." His fingers lightly trace over my leg until I finally throw my hands in the air, surrendering.

"Fine. I laughed because it sounded like a line from a cheesy romantic movie." I wipe the tears of laughter from my eyes.

"It kind of did, didn't it?" His lips pull into a grin. "You're really cute when you laugh that hard, especially with the whole pig snort thing. That was super attractive."

I playfully swat his arm. "Whatever. I love my pig snort."

"So do I," he says, sounding genuine. "It's so real. A lot of girls do that whole high-pitched fake laugh."

I know what kind of laugh he's talking about because Hannah does it all the time.

An extremely intense look crosses his face. I have no clue what he's about to say, but I hold my breath in anticipation. Before he gets a chance to say anything, though, my phone chirps and ruins the moment.

"It's my grandma," I say then answer it.

"Okay, I've got everything taken care of," she says in a rush. "For now, you'll be staying with me."

"For now?" I ask, panicking. "Does that mean I'll eventually have to go back?"

"No, that means that, for now, your dad's agreed to let you stay with me until things have cooled off," she explains. "I'm going to have to fight him, though, once

Lynn gets involved. I can already tell that. But I will fight it. I'm not letting you go back to that house. I need you to do something for me, though. I need you to be on your best behavior. The last thing we need right now is to give them anything that they can use against us."

I'm worried about what this will do to her health. "Are you sure you want to do this? I don't want to stress you out or anything."

"Stressed out? It'll be a relief to know you're away from all that shit," she replies matter-of-factly. "I've spent so many nights worrying if you're okay."

"What if they call the cops and report me as a runaway or something?" I ask. "I don't want to get you into trouble."

"They're not going to call the cops," she insists. "They may have threatened you with that, but I have a feeling if they did, they'd end up in more trouble than you would."

A weight falls off my shoulders, but I have to wonder . . ."Why would they get into trouble?"

"Lots of reasons, hon'. Like if I reported them as neglectful, abusive parents. And you told me she grabbed you, right?"

"It's not that bad," I say quietly, wrapping my fingers around my wrist.

"I don't care if it's bad. She has no right to grab you like that," she says. "Plus, there's that whole thing with your dad's company."

Huh? "What're you talking about? What's going on with my dad's company?"

"Nothing that you should worry about," she replies hastily. "Look, I have to go. I'm getting ready to go through security. I should be home around eleven or so and then we'll talk more. And I don't want you sitting around and stressing out about stuff. Go out and do something.

Maybe you could ask that Kyler boy to take you to a movie or something. I bet that'd be a *great* distraction."

I resist the urge to cover the phone. Kyler's probably already heard everything she's said anyway.

After I hang up, Kyler confirms my suspicions that he's overheard every embarrassing word my Grandma Stephy said when he turns to me and says, "She wants me to take you to a movie, huh?"

I feel my cheeks warm. "You don't have to. She just doesn't want me sitting around at the house by myself. I'll be fine, though. Sometimes I think she still thinks of me as a little kid who needs to be watched twenty-four seven."

"I'm sure she's just worried about you." He presses on the brakes, stopping at a red light. "I don't blame her. It has to be hard, dealing with parents like that."

"It is, but I'm used to it." I shrug, like what're-you-gonna-do-life's-life-man.

He considers something while studying me. He keeps his eyes on me until the light turns green, and then he flips on his blinker and veers left, breaking about five traffic laws.

"I'm not going to let you sit around by yourself all day." He steers the car down a road that leads toward the center of Sunnyvale. "I'll keep you distracted until your grandma comes home."

I glance at the clock on the dash. "But that's not for like eight hours."

He arches a brow. "You don't think I can distract you for eight hours?"

I keep my mouth shut, refusing to say what runs through my head: *Maybe if you took your shirt off.* Instead, I say, and might I add, awesomely calmly, "What're we going to do?"

His eyes sparkle mischievously. "I have an idea."

"Okay." I'm a little nervous, but curiosity gets the better of me. "What's your idea?"

He stops the car in front of the park right by the court then silences the engine. "A game of Horse."

"That sounds fun." I unbuckle my seatbelt. "But I'm not sure even you can make a game of Horse last eight hours."

"Oh, that's just the start of the distraction." He grins wickedly. "I'm going to make a little game out of it."

I smirk at him. "Um, you do realize Horse is a game, right?"

He counters with a dirty look. "That's not what I meant."

I can't help giggling. "Then what did you mean?"

He slides the keys out of the ignition. "For every game I win, I get to pick something crazy we both have to do. And for every game you win, you get to pick something."

"You do realize I rock at Horse, right? And I've kicked your ass at it before."

"I've gotten a little bit better since I was twelve." He reaches for the door handle, flashing me cocky smile. "But if you're too afraid of getting your butt kicked we can do something else."

I kind of want to hug him right now because I'm smiling and hardly thinking about Lynn, my dad, and how awful it'll be if they end up sending me to Montana.

"Game on, dude." I comb my fingers through my hair as I catch sight of my reflection in the mirror. Ugh. I haven't had a chance to clean myself up since the whole meltdown thing yesterday. Between the smeared eyeliner and the runny mascara, I look like I'm trying to go Goth. "Just one sec."

I retrieve my brush from my bag and pull my hair

into a ponytail as he gets out of the car and grabs a basketball from the trunk. I use one of my shirts to wipe the day old makeup off my face. I consider reapplying it, but don't want to make Kyler wait on me. It's been a while since I've gone this natural and I'll admit, I feel a bit self-conscious. Still, I hold my head high as I get out of the car and hike toward the courts with Kyler. I'm not going to feel bad for being me and looking like me. I've already spent too many days feeling like that.

As we near the edge of the grass, Kyler inches toward me. "You have the cutest freckles." He brushes his fingers across my cheek. "I've always thought that."

I have to remind myself to breathe. The way he touched me, so intimately, I'm not sure how to react. It's strange that the thing he thinks is cute about me is the thing I've been covering up with makeup.

I'm not sure what to make of what's going on between us, but I definitely smile. The smile vanishes, though, when I notice a dark blue car with tinted windows driving by the park at an exceedingly sluggish pace.

At first I don't pay too much attention to it, but as it rounds the park for the third time, almost slowing to stop beside the courts, unease stirs inside me. What if it's someone looking for me? Like maybe my parents? It's not their car but I wouldn't put it past them to borrow one just to surprise attack me? Or could it be an unmarked police vehicle?

"What are you staring at?" Kyler asks as he jogs across the court, going in for a slam-dunk.

"I . . ." I peek back to the where the car was, only to find it speeding off toward the main road. "There was this car driving around but I guess it was nothing."

He dribbles the ball, his brows knitting. "Do you think it was your parents?"

"No, I don't think so . . . It wasn't their car. And I don't think they'd look for me here." They don't know me well enough to.

I shrug the uneasiness off the best that I can, and raise my hands in front of me, focusing on the game. Still, something doesn't quite feel right, like the calm before a storm. I just wish I knew what kind of storm was coming.

Chapter FIVE

KAI

"*A thousand bucks? A thousand* bucks?" Big Doug repeats the same thing over and over again with a look of astonishment on his face. Finally, he sits down in the chair in front of his cluttered desk, his eyes wide as he shakes his head. "Kai, how the fuck did you end up in this mess? I thought you were being more careful."

"I was being careful." I sink down in a foldup chair. "But then I vouched for Bradon even though he has a shitty rep. I figured since he was my friend, he wouldn't screw me over."

Big Doug reaches for a bag of opened chips propped against one of his multiple computers. "Dude, Bradon screws everyone over, friend or not."

I lower my head into my hands. "I'm realizing that

now."

"You're too nice, man."

"Is there such a thing?"

"Um, yeah. When you try to help people you know are going to get you into trouble, that's called being too nice."

"All right, I get it. I made a bad decision. Tell me something I don't know." I raise my head. "But I need to focus on fixing the problem. What's done is done, and now I need to come up with a thousand bucks before I get my ass kicked. T plays dirty. He'll probably get a bunch of his buddies to jump me. He won't give a shit if it isn't a fair fight."

He munches on a handful of chips. "I have a couple of small jobs I need done. It won't get you a thousand, but it's a start."

I wish I had a better solution, but right now, Big Doug's offer is the only thing I've got. "I'll take whatever I can get."

"Okay, let's get you started." He spins the chair around, facing the largest computer screen. "I have to ask, though, why not just ask your parents for the money?"

"They wouldn't give it to me, even if I did ask," I mutter, rubbing the heels of my hands against my eyes. This shit's giving me a headache, but it's going to mild in comparison to what will happen if I don't come up with the cash.

The keys click as he taps his fingers against them. "Even if you explain the situation to them? Maybe you could tell them the truth. I mean, I know it's not ideal, but I'm sure they'd rather help you than see you get hurt."

I refuse to feel the wave of hurt washing over me. "Trust me. My father wouldn't care. He'd probably tell me that I deserved whatever was coming for me."

I can hear him now. *"You got yourself into this mess, so you can get yourself out of it. It's not my problem.* You're *not my problem."* He's right, too. This is all my fault. Every dumbass choice I've made has led me to this point in my life.

I force thoughts of my dad's disappointment out of my head. "What exactly are these jobs?"

"The first one's pretty simple." He clicks the mouse a few times, opening multiple programs. "I just need you to deliver something for me."

"That doesn't sound too bad."

"It doesn't sound bad, but this delivery is super fucking important. You can't mess it up at all, okay man?" he says and I nod. "It pays a hundred bucks, and gas is included."

"Gas?" I rise to my feet as the printer turns on. "How far am I driving?"

He wheels the chair over to the printer. "To Mapleview."

"But that's like a two hour drive each way." I run my hand over my head as I pace the length of his basement.

Normally, I wouldn't give a shit about taking a four-hour drive, but with everything going on with Isa, I want to be close in case she needs me. She hasn't called yet, and she promised me she'd call after she was done talking to her dad.

"If it's too far, I can get someone else to do it." His tone implies I should keep my mouth shut and be grateful he's doing me a favor.

"No, I'm good. I just needed to do something, but it can wait, I guess." I take my phone out of my back pocket and check my messages.

Nothing.

I decide to message her to see if she's okay.

Me: Hey, just wanted to make sure everything is okay. You never called me, but maybe you're still talking to your dad. I'm actually headed out of town for the day, but I'll be back later today.

Isa: Oh my God! Sorry I forgot to call you! All crap hit the fan when I went home and I completely forgot! I'm okay. I'm not even at the house right now. I ran out after Lynn threatened to send me to some reform school in Montana. I'm actually going to be staying with Grandma Stephy for a little bit until we can figure out what to do, but she promised me she wouldn't let them send me away.

Anger simmers inside me. Dammit. Her parents are such assholes.

Me: WTF??? They're trying to send you away to Montana? What the hell is wrong with them?

Isa: Well, Lynn said it was because of my violence problem because apparently pushing her once means I have a violence problem. But honestly, I have a feeling she's been planning this for a while. She had all these papers printed out and she was all ready to ship me off tomorrow morning.

Me: God, I hate that woman . . . What did your dad say?

Isa: The usual. That he agrees with Lynn. I'm not surprised. He always agrees with Lynn when it comes to me. I'm guessing it's because he feels guilty I'm a product of an affair he had.

Me: I don't care if he feels guilty or not. He's your dad and he needs to act like one.

Isa: I wish he did, but I honestly don't think he ever will. I'm starting to make peace with that, though. I'm just lucky I have my Grandma Stephy. She's practically like a mom and dad to me. I don't know what I'd do without her. And Indigo too.

Me: You know I'm here for you if you need anything.

Isa: I know. You've really been awesome to me lately, Kai. I appreciate it. I really do.

I want to be there for her today. After what happened with her parents, I'm betting she could use someone to talk to.

Me: Are you with your grandma now?

Isa: No. She's actually out of town, but she's flying in tonight.

There's no way she should be alone right now.

Me: Want to take a little drive to Mapleview? I could use a driving buddy.

It takes her a minute to answer and I know the moment the message buzzes through, I'm not going to like her answer.

Isa: I'm with Kyler right now. We're supposed to hang out until my grandma gets home. Why are you going to Mapleview? If you need me to go with you, I totally will, especially if you want to talk about whatever's going on with you and that T guy.

I open and flex my fingers. She's with Kyler? What the hell? Did he just wait around the house so he was there to jump in when Isa needed rescuing then cleared his entire schedule? I know for a fact that he had plans later today after he took Isa to breakfast. I heard him talking about it with his friends on the phone after Isa left our house, saying something about needing to get some practice hours in.

Me: Nah. It's okay. I think I'm just going to ask Big Doug to drive with me.

It's a complete lie. Yeah, it hurts like a bitch thinking about her and Kyler hanging out, doing God knows what, but I don't want her to come with me just because she feels sorry for me. I've had too many girls do that—hang out with me because they felt bad for using me to get to Kyler.

Isa: Okay . . . If you change your mind, let me know. I think we should definitely talk about what's going on with you. Can we hang out tomorrow?

Me: Yeah. Maybe. I'll text you later and let you know.

I leave it at that and put my phone away, trying not to think about what her and Kyler could be doing. But it's all I think about. Fuck, I have way too vivid of an imagination. Seriously. I swear my mind's trying to torture me to death with images of Isa and Kyler and what they could be doing.

"So, who is she?" Big Doug's question rips through my thoughts.

"Huh?" I take a manila envelope he's holding out to me.

"The girl who's got you all worked up," he says, swiveling the chair around. "You look like you're about to lose your shit."

"No, I don't." Stamped across the top of the envelope in bright red letters are DO NOT OPEN along with a smiley face sticker. "What's with you and these stickers? You put them on everything."

"They're my mark," he answers simply. "It lets people know where I've been and what work is mine. I don't want other people taking credit for my shit."

I give the envelope a shake, noting it feels really light. "What's in this?"

"Don't worry about that." He waves me off, then continues on with his questioning. "Is it that girl from the party? The one who needed me to find info on her mom?" When I reluctantly nod, he adds, "How'd she take the news about her mom?"

I tuck the envelope under my arm. "I haven't told her yet."

He blinks at me in shock. "Why the hell not?"

"I was planning on it, but then some shit happened with her family . . . I'm worried she might not be able to handle it right now."

"It doesn't matter what you think. She deserves to know and the longer you sit on this, the more pissed she's going to be when you do tell her."

"I know." I crack my knuckles as his words sink in. He's right. Even if Isa is going through a ton of family drama right now, I need to tell her as soon as I can. "Dude, you're starting to sound like Dr. Phil."

Big Doug tucks his arms behind his head. "I watch that show all the time."

I give him a *really* look. "Are you being serious?"

"What? I got nothing better to do between jobs. Besides, I learn a lot from it, like when to tell a girl you're obsessed with that you know something about her family. Something, I might add, that she asked for help with."

"All right. I get it. I'll tell her. Just stop Psych 101-ing me and drop it."

He holds up a finger. "One more thing." He opens a drawer to a filing cabinet, collects a folder with a smiley face sticker on it, and hands it to me. "I felt bad about being the bearer of such fucked up news, so I decided to do some more research on this Bella woman and found out more about her case."

"What'd you find out?" Considering Big Doug rarely does favors for people, I'm shocked he did this.

"Some pretty interesting stuff. I'm actually kind of surprised the woman was found guilty. Then again, some of the stuff I pulled up wasn't used in the case, and isn't accessible to the public. She filed for an appeal a couple of times, and I think her most recent one got approved, but it might take a while for anything to happen. I'm still looking into a few more things, but I thought I'd give this to you for now. It might give Isa a little bit of peace of mind until I can find out more."

"Wait. Did you hack into the case records or something?" I peek into the folder and cringe as I skim over the top page.

Before I can get too far into it, he slams his hand down on top of the folder, closing it. "You can look at that later. Right now, we work."

Then he jumps right in and gives me a list of instructions to follow when I deliver the package. After hearing the list, I realize it is a bigger job than I originally thought and I feel even more uneasy about what the hell's in the envelope.

1. Under no circumstances am I to look into the envelope.
2. Before I pull up to the set location, I'm to drive around the block three times.
3. If I see anyone who looks even a bit suspicious, I'm supposed to drive off and head home without dropping off the envelope.
4. Keep my car door locked at all times. Even when

the guy comes to pick up the envelope, I'm only supposed to crack the window and slip it through.

5. The guy picking it up will be wearing a hoodie and brass knuckles.
6. The second I give the guy the envelope I need to leave Mapleview. But don't drive straight home. I need to cruise on the back roads for about an hour before getting on the highway.
7. I can't take my cell phone with me.

"What?" I say after he rattles off number seven. "Why the heck not?"

"For tracking purposes." He sticks out his hand. "Hand it over man."

I retrieve my phone from my back pocket, but don't hand it over. "Just a second." I hurriedly type a quick text to Isa, deciding it's time to tell her.

> *Me: Yeah, let's definitely get together tomorrow. Just let me know what time to pick you up.*

Before I receive a response, Big Doug snatches the phone from my hand.

"Dude, give me that back," I gripe, reaching to take it back.

He spins the chair around, shoves my phone into a desk drawer, and then locks it away. "I'll give it back to you when the job's done. And the hundred bucks."

When I hear my phone vibrate inside the drawer, I grind my teeth. "Just let me check that."

He shakes his head. "You have the envelope. You're officially on the clock."

I considering telling him to fuck off, but stop myself since he's doing me a huge favor.

"See you in five hours." He starts a timer on a computer.

Sighing, I turn for the door, feeling unsettled about what I'm about to do. Yeah, I've done some shady things over the last year. I've broken into cars, partied, done some illegal stuff like helped hack into security systems, bought weed off T and dealt for him a couple of times. The whole drug thing was a little too intense for me, though. I was nervous and panicky making the drops, and I quickly stopped both buying and selling. When Bradon tracked me down at a party, it'd been months since I had seen T.

"I need a favor," he said, nervously glancing around at the people drinking and smoking around us. He was so twitchy I wondered if he was on something.

At first, I just shook my head. A favor for Bradon usually meant trouble.

But then he begged and pleaded. "Please, Kai. My family's in some serious financial trouble, and I need the money, like really bad or we're gonna lose everything."

He looked upset, and I started to feel sorry for him.

"What'd you need?" I asked.

"For you to vouch to T for me," he said quickly. "Just tell him that he can trust me."

"Can he?" I question because Bradon was never the trustworthy type. He was either stealing from people or stealing and lying about it.

"I won't screw you over," he promised. "I just need to do a couple of jobs for him so I can earn some cash fast. But he needs someone he knows—like you—to vouch for me."

Every one of my instincts screamed at me not to do this, that Bradon was going to end up screwing me over, but then he gave me this whole speech about his family losing their house and car, and I caved liked a sucker.

In the end, Bradon ended up selling the drugs for T and never giving him any of the money. At first, I didn't get too pissed off, because I thought maybe he did it in a panic move to bail his family out of their financial trouble. But a couple of days ago I found out that was all a lie.

Bradon has gotten into some pretty hardcore drugs and needed quick cash to feed his addiction. From what I understand, his parents gave him an intervention yesterday and he took off to rehab. I feel like an idiot for believing his sob story and not seeing his drug problem had gotten that out of hand. But there's nothing I can do about it now. T warned me that, if Bradon screwed him over, his debt would fall on me.

I just hope whatever I'm about to do isn't going to end with me being in even more trouble.

Chapter SIX

ISABELLA

I dribble the ball against the concrete as I calculate where to make my next shot. So far, Kyler and I are both tied at HORS. It's taken us over an hour just to get to that point because we both rock at the game and rarely miss a basket. It's fun spending time with him. What's really cool is that he hasn't brought up my mom and dad. While I know I'm eventually going to have to talk about it, it's nice taking a break from the emotional chaos.

"Quit procrastinating losing," Kyler taunts as he watches me walk the length of the court.

I stop near the half court and smile sweetly at him. "You mean, you losing?"

He chuckles, fishing out his phone from his pocket. "In your dreams. And when I win, you owe me," he says, reading a text.

"You're so not going to win. And you want to know why?" I raise my arms with the ball in my hands.

He leans against the pole of the hoop, folding his arms, amusement dancing in his eyes. "Because you're so awesome?"

"Yep." Grinning, I take the shot. From out of my peripheral vision, I swear I see a flash, like a camera and I wonder if it might be Kyler, but when I look at him again, I don't see his phone in his hand. And why would he take a photo of me?

Shoving the weird paranoia aside, I watch the ball soar through the air, swish through the basket, and I break out in a goofy dance, throwing my hands in the air and tapping my feet.

Kyler laughs as he chases down the ball. "Cute victory dance, but FYI, you haven't won yet." With that, he strolls up to where I'm standing and easily makes the basket.

I stop dancing, gather the ball in my hands, and inch back farther to make a shot. But I try to go too big and end up missing. Now Kyler's the one to dance around, like he's already won.

I can't help giggling at his silly dance moves. "You still haven't won."

"I've got this in the bag now." He appears pretty confident as he strides around behind me and presses his solid chest against my back. My breath gets caught in my throat as my heart dang near explodes out of my chest. My body shakes from the sensation and I quickly step forward before he notices.

But his fingers fold around my arm and draw me back against him. "Nope. You need to stay put for this one." He lets go of my arm and rests his elbows on my shoulder.

After he shoots the basket, I spin around and put my hands on my hips, giving him the death glare. "No fair."

"Why isn't that fair?" he asks innocently.

"Um, hello, because you're, like, five inches taller than me." Sure, I'm not short or anything, but Kyler is tall. For me to be able to even get my elbows onto his shoulders, I'd have to get a stepstool.

"I'll tell you what." He's totally enjoying this. "I'll make it easy on you. Just make the shot from here."

Like hell I'm taking the easy way out.

I square my shoulders. "No way. I'm *going* to win this fair and square." I skip around him. Then, with a jump, I hurry and rest my elbows on his shoulders for a split second, quickly tossing the ball. It arches through the air, and at first I think it's going to make it, but at the last second, it curves left, dings the rim and falls to the ground. "Mother of all zombies."

Kyler whirls around with a ha-ha-I-just-kicked-your-behind look on his face. "You should've taken the easy shot."

"No way." I grimace, partly joking, but partly not because man, I hate losing! "It wouldn't have felt like a real win."

"But now I win." His grin is as shiny as a disco ball.

I want to sulk and be a sore loser, but he looks too adorable standing there shirtless with his hair a tousled mess and his skin lightly damp with sweat. "Fine. What crazy thing are we doing?"

"Aw, don't pout." He lightly prods me with his elbow. "I promise I'll pick something fun."

I frown for two point five more seconds, before the smile wins. "Fine. What're we doing?" I bounce on my toes, bursting with anticipation.

He laughs, his eyes crinkling around the corners. "I think that might be the quickest I've ever seen anyone get over losing."

I rub the light sheen of sweat from my hairline with the back of my hand. "What can I say? I'm a sucker for surprises." I clasp my hands together. "Now please, pretty please, tell me what we're doing."

He shakes his head, scooping up the ball. "No way. It won't be a surprise if I tell you."

I follow after him as he starts across the grass toward the car. "Oh, come on." I grasp his arm. "We never agreed it had to be a surprise, just that the winner got to pick something crazy that we'd both have to do."

He digs his car keys from his pocket. "Yeah, but I think it's more fun this way."

I jut out my bottom lip. "Says who?"

"Says me." His gaze briefly falls to my fingers on his arm.

All of my insecurities overwhelm me and I pull away from him, my cheeks warming.

A beat or two skips by and the silence makes my cheeks heat even more with embarrassment. Trying to chill out, I focus on everything else except Kyler staring at me: the leaves gusting across the dry grass, a horn honking in the distance, the playground swings squeaking against the wind, the tree Kai and I used to hide in when we were younger and just a couple of days ago during lunch when we almost kissed, and a twenty-something-year-old guy with dark brown hair, leaning against a tree, watching us as like a creeper.

What the hell? Maybe he was the one who took a photo of me when I made the shot? But why? That doesn't make any sense.

Stop worrying so much, Isa. No one wants a photo of you.

When the guy notices me observing him, he waves sheepishly before jogging toward the parking lot and across the street, disappearing into a nearby neighborhood.

I'm not sure what to make of it or if I should make anything of it.

Just chill, dude. You seriously watch too many horror movies.

"I think you're adorable." Kyler tucks a strand of my hair behind my ear, drawing my attention back to him. "You get so excited over the simplest things. It's such a nice break from what I'm used to."

"You know that's the second time you've mentioned I'm a nice break from what you're used to." I cringe at the breathlessness in my voice.

"I know." His voice is soft and his eyes are on mine as his tongue slips out of his mouth and wets his lips. Then his gaze drops to my mouth.

Wow, wow, wow in my wildest dreams, is he going to kiss me? is the first thought that races through my mind, but then it's followed by hesitancy. Is this really how I want the kiss to go down? On the day my parents threatened to send me off to reform school? Wouldn't that make the memory of it tainted?

I shove the thought aside, though, when my stomach does a kick flip. No, I want this kiss. Who cares if this morning was crappy? I can erase the crappy and replace it with *fireworks. Fireworks, everywhere.*

I barely breathe as I wait for him to kiss me, my heart shape-shifting into a freakin' hummingbird, fluttering a million miles a minute.

But he suddenly hesitates, raking his fingers through his hair as he stares at the street. "Isa, I want to get to know you more. In the past, I've never taken the time to get to know the girls I've gone out with. But I want things to be different with you. I want to take my time and enjoy every moment."

A couple things cross my mind at the moment: 1). Does he mean get to know me as a friend? 2) He's obviously working on reinventing himself, but why? Where did the sudden change come from? Because there's usually a reason behind someone wanting to change, like me, like Kai, even though I still have no clue why he went from popular, preppy guy, to bad boy in the span of a night.

I want to ask Kyler if something's going on with him, but I chicken out. "Okay."

He looks at me again, smiling as he threads his fingers through mine and pulls me toward the car.

I feel the slightest bit of excitement from his touch but a drop of disappointment at the same time. I don't know why. Is it just lingering sensations of the almost kiss? Or something else?

"Ready for crazy task number one?" he asks, squeezing my hand.

I nod, tearing my thoughts from my worries. Nope, I'm not supposed to be worrying about stuff today, whether it's my parents, my mom, or what's going on with Kyler. Today is supposed to be about being distracted from the craziness in my life and dammit if I'm going to go into worrying-about-a-guy mode. I'm going to focus on whatever Kyler's got in store for me and nothing else.

Chapter SEVEN

ISABELLA

"*Um . . ." I'm unsure what to* say to the scene in front of me.

Kyler said it was a surprise, and while I wasn't sure what to expect, I wasn't expecting this.

"I promise it'll be fun." He reaches over the console, brushes my ponytail off my shoulder, and gently massages my shoulder. "And it's an excellent distraction."

My muscle tense from his touch, mostly because I'm not used to being touched so much. But he doesn't seem to notice, his fingertips delicately kneading my muscles.

I concentrate on the football field we're parked by. A bunch of guys are on the field, throwing and catching the ball, and a group of girls a year or two older than me are watching from the benches. A couple of girls I've seen at the parties Hannah's thrown at our house, and most of the guys are Kyler's friends from high school. Nausea forms in the pit of my stomach when I realize a few of them have made fun of me at one point or another.

"None of the girls are playing." I offer a lame excuse.

A challenge glimmers in his eyes. "I didn't think you were the kind of girl that cared about stuff like that."

"I'm not." It's the truth. I just used the girls not playing as an excuse to avoid telling him the real reason I don't want to play flag football with a bunch of dudes—because I'd rather spend time locked in a dungeon than play football with his friends who can be total douchebags.

I rack my brain for a legit sounding excuse but all that pops into my mind is, *sorry, can't. I'm allergic to football and all balls in general. Yep, sounds super legit, Isa. Face palm.*

"Look, I know you said you thought football was kind of boring, but I really think if you try to play it, you might like it," he says. "Besides, it might get your mind off other stuff."

He has a point, but paintballing or playing video games would do that for me too, and I wouldn't have to hang out with a group of people who spent years bullying me.

"No one's going to say anything to you," he adds, as if reading my mind. "I promise."

I give him a fake smile, wondering if he can tell it's forced. "Okay. Yeah. Sure. Just give me a second. I need to make a call first."

"You want me to wait for you?"

"Nah. It might take a minute."

He nods and hops out of the car. Once he shuts the door, I punch in Indigo's number. She doesn't answer so I text her to call me ASAP, saying I need a ride. I give her exactly one minute to respond before I panic and dial

Kai's number. I know he said he was going to Mapleview but I'm hoping upon hope that he ended up not going. He never did text me back, though, when I replied to his message about hanging out tomorrow. I told him sure and asked where he wanted to meet. Maybe he never replied because he didn't have a signal. The drive to Mapleview is pretty much a deadzone.

After four rings, his phone goes to voicemail.

"Hey, it's me . . . Isa . . ." I'm unsure if I should tell him what's going on. "Look, I'm kind of in a mess and really need a ride. I know you said you were leaving town, but I'm hoping maybe you haven't left yet . . . But anyway, yeah, I'm guessing you have; otherwise, you probably would've answered your phone." I hang up, shaking my head at my rambling message.

I don't get out of the car right away. Instead, I sit in the car and watch Kyler and his friends from out the window. I know I'm being a coward, but I feel like a mouse about to walk into a lion's den. I have no idea why Kyler would bring me here when he knows how much his and Hannah's friends despise me. Could that be the point? Perhaps this is some trap Hannah's set up and when I get out of the car, she'll step out from underneath the bleachers and her and her Ra-ra Space Cadets will break out in a chorus of Isabella Smellera.

After a few minutes tick by, I decide it's time to face the inevitable. I grab the door handle and open the door. Part of me wants to flee in the opposite direction and run down the road. I honestly might have if Kyler didn't spot me. He waves me over with a smile on his face and all of his friends stare at me.

Cringe. Cringe. Double cringe.

Why couldn't I have just taken the easy shot during Horse?

I bump the door shut, zip my jacket up, and keep my

head down as I hike across the field toward them. It feels like the first day of school after I got back from my trip, all made over, a completely different person on the outside. Still, I hardly looked up at anyone as I walked, too afraid they'd still see me as Hannah's dorky younger sister.

But I'm not Hannah's dorky younger sister. I never really was. Hannah and Lynn just made me believe that. But if I look down at the ground right now, then I kind of am, aren't I?

Sucking in a deep breath, I level my gaze on Kyler. I'm not sure what he told his friends about why I'm here but none of them seem that interested in me. The guys go back to warming up and most of the girls go back to chatting with each other. But a couple of them have their gazes locked on me, like they're ready to swoop in and attack.

"So, when you said come play flag football, did you actually mean I had to play?" I ask Kyler, coming to stop in front of him.

He thrums his finger against his lips. "What do you think?"

"I don't know. I'm kind of hoping you just meant you'd teach me how to throw a ball." I give him my best hopeful look.

He chucks the ball in the air, giving me a lopsided grin. "Come on, Isa. I thought we talked about this." He catches the ball and grips it in his hand. "That you were going to be different then them." He nods his chin over at the girls then waggles his brows. "You know you wanna."

If it were any other sport, I'd be all over this. But I know zilch about football. "All right, but you're going to have to show me a couple of things first." I put my hands together and bow to him. "Oh great one, please show me your knowledge."

He chuckles, but I can tell my remark's goes way over

his head. Huh. Guess it only works with Kai. "Okay, first we'll practice catching."

For the next twenty minutes, Kyler does just that. He's passionate about it too. While he looks super cute with his eyes lit up with excitement, I find myself getting kind of bored. Still, I act like a good pupil and pay attention even when my stomach grumbles in hunger. I tell it to shut its trap, that food will come later, but then a guy walks by munching on a cup of ice cream. It looks like strawberry too with cheesecake bits.

Man, I'm so hungry that even vegetables is starting to sound good.

"We'll get something to eat after the game," Kyler tells me, rotating the football in his hands.

Um . . . Did I just say that aloud?

"Okay." I resist the urge to take the damn ball from him, toss it into the tree, and declare the game over. . . . Hmm . . . Kai said I was like a Gremlin when I get hungry. I guess he was right.

Kyler spends another couple of minutes making me catch the ball before he deems me ready to play. He and a guy I'm guessing Kyler knows from college, because he looks older, get voted captains. I quickly find out his name is Wes and that he's kind of a sexist asshole.

"If she's going to play," Wes says to Kyler while pointing a finger at me, "another girl's going to have to too so the teams will be fair."

"Why? Isa's more athletic than Ben and Tim," Kyler replies, tucking a ball under his arm. "In fact, she might be better than you." He winks at me.

Pride swells in my chest as I smile at Wes. *Yeah, dude, just because you have a penis, it doesn't mean you're the shit.*

Wes rolls his eyes. "Whatever man. You're so just trying to get laid right now."

A few of the guys snicker but Kyler shoves Wes, and kind of hard too.

"Shut up," he warns, glaring at Wes. "You're such a prick sometimes."

I look away as I feel my cheeks flame. Oh my God, I'm so uncomfortable right now. Maybe I should just bail out and chase Ice Cream Dude down. I could be all like, "Hand over the ice cream or else a murderous, man-eating monster will sprout from my flesh."

"Whatever. Let's just get the teams picked," Wes mutters, shooting me an annoyed look.

He makes his first pick and then Kyler goes, choosing me. I smile appreciatively at him then wait while Wes makes his choice. Kyler puts an arm around me and starts massaging my shoulder again. A few of his friends are staring at us curiously but Kyler doesn't seem to notice as he makes his next pick. Me, I notice. Like way, way notice. Not just because he's touching me but because he's touching me in front of his friends.

I probably hold my breath the entire time the teams are divided up. When there turns out to be an uneven number of players, Wes starts having a Drama Queen Fit.

"I'll play." A girl with long brown hair pulled into a side braid leaves the bleachers and crosses the field toward us. She looks about my age, but I don't recognize her from school. And unlike the other girls chilling on the sidelines, she's not decked out in heels and a dress, but a pair of skinny jeans and a plaid shirt over a black tank top.

"Lily, go sit your ass down," Wes barks at her. "You can't play football for shit."

She flips him the middle finger. "Neither can you."

Wes glowers at her. "Whatever. If you want to play then play. But you're on Meyer's team."

"Good. That way, when we kick your ass, the win will feel that much sweeter." She grins haughtily at him then strolls up beside me. "Hey, only other girl crazy enough to play, I'm Lillian, but my friends call me Lily. And well, my dumbass brother too." She throws a dirty look in Wes's direction.

"He's your brother." I feel sorry for her. The guy kind of reminds me of male version of Hannah. "He seems . . ."

"Like a jerk," she finishes for me. "Yeah, he is. But he's that way to everyone so don't take it personally."

I wonder why, but don't ask. "I'm Isabella by the way. You can call me Isa."

"Isa. I like it." Her smile is so big it's nearly blinding. "I like your shoes too. Totally killer."

I think she's just trying to be nice, but Lily's cheerfulness remains as we start the game. Either the girl was inhaling laughing gas before she came here or she's one of the most genuinely happy people I've ever met.

For most of the game, Lily and I get put in positions that don't require a lot of moving or participating. While I wasn't too thrilled playing, I do find it irking that the guys are taking over.

"Are you doing anything cool for Halloween?" Lily asks as we stand in the field waiting for something eventful to happen.

"Honestly, I haven't really thought about it." Usually, I'm all about dressing up but this year I've been severely distracted with other stuff.

"You're dressing up, though, right?" She eyes me over from head to toe. "You look like the kind of person who dresses up."

"Is that a good thing?" I wonder, feeling insecure.

She nods, still all smiles and sunshine. "It's definitely a good thing. A lot of people think they're too old to dress up, but I plan on doing it for the rest of my life. It's too much fun getting all dolled up, you know. Why give it up just because society thinks you should stop having fun when you're a little bit older."

"I completely agree. And yes, I dress up, usually in something really over the top," I admit. "This year, I've been really busy, though, and haven't gotten around to deciding."

"You should go steampunk. You have a good look for it."

"You think so?"

"Oh, yeah. I can help you put something together if you want. I know where a lot of killer stores are, and I'm pretty awesome at sewing."

"Um . . . okay." I don't mean to sound hesitant, but considering how many times Hannah has set me up to think I'm making a friend, only to have it thrown in my face later, I can't help it.

For a tiny raindrop of a second, Lily's smile falters. "Or we don't have to. I just thought it might be cool to have a shopping buddy who enjoys Halloween as much as me. Most people can't handle how excited I get."

"No, it's cool. I want to go." I steal a glance at the bleachers. Most of the girls are watching the game, but two of Hannah's friends are staring at me while whispering to each other. I wonder if she's friends with them. Would it matter, though, if she's nice and everything?

"You don't like them, huh?" she says, not as a question but as a fact.

I fix my attention back on her and shrug. "It's more like they don't like me. Well, not all of them. But I don't know all of them."

She nods, as if completely understanding. "The two sitting on the top are pretty cool. They go to UW with Wes and Kyler. The three sitting toward the middle, I have no clue who they are, but they seem really into Kyler." I must pull a funny face or something because she adds, "Don't worry, though. He seems into you."

I hate that I'm so transparent. "Do you know Kyler?"

She glances at the field where Kyler is dodging around guys with the ball cradled in his arms. "Since, like, I was four."

"Really? How?"

"He's been friends with Wes since then."

I don't recognize either one of them. "Do you guys go to Sunnyvale High?"

She snorts a laugh. "No. We're not that lucky."

Lucky? What? That makes no sense since Sunnyvale is a public school. "What do you mean?"

She pulls a *whoops* face. "It's nothing. I just meant that we weren't lucky enough to go to a high school that has such a great sports and art program."

Sunnyvale High may have a decent sports program, but their art program is nonexistent. The only art classes available are basic, beginner classes where you learn how to draw fruit in a bowl and generic nonsense like that. I don't call her out on her lie, though.

"So, do you go to UW too?" I ask, even though she doesn't look old enough to be in college, but clearly the high school topic is a touchy subject for her.

She shakes her head. "I'm actually supposed to be a senior this year, but I graduated early. I wanted to start classes at UW this year but . . . My mom thought it would be a good idea for me to take a year off and save some money."

"Oh." Again, I can tell she's lying, but I don't want to press. "Where do you work?"

"I have two jobs, actually. One at the grocery store."

She pulls a face. "And one at a second-hand store. That one's okay because a lot of old-school, cool stuff comes in and the workers get first dibs. There was this really awesome old typewriter that I got and this 1940s cocktail dress that I bought for, like, ten bucks. I was going to wear it to prom, but . . ." She trails off, growing sober for a moment before she's bouncing off the walls. "You should come work there. The owner is hiring right now. It's a really fun, easy job, and it'd be nice to have someone cool to work with. Right now, the only person working there besides me is Mr. Belforid, who once showed up to work without pants on."

I choke on a laugh. "Really?"

She giggles. "Yeah, he's really old and got confused. He did have swim trunks on, thank God, but it was in the middle of winter and he nearly froze to death."

After our laughter dies down, Lily turns serious again. "But seriously, you should come work there," she says. "I need someone sane to hang out with."

I hadn't thought too much about it, but since I'm going to be living with Grandma Stephy now, I should definitely consider getting a job so I can help out. "You know what? Maybe I will."

A smile expands across her face. I just start to smile too, when I hear my name being shouted.

"Isa, heads up!"

My gaze darts down the field just in time to see Kyler throwing the football in my direction. I start to mad freak out as the ball soars through the sky and a herd of guys come barreling at me. Sure, I know it's flag football and they can't tackle me, but watching them run at full speed is super intimidating. At first, I contemplate just letting the ball hit the ground, but then I see Wes, standing at the end of the field, looking bored, as if he's completely convinced I'm not going to catch it.

Screw this. I'm totally catching it and making a touchdown, just so I can do an awesome victory dance and throw it in his face.

Lily squeals and skitters out of the way as the guys charge toward me. Me, I run backward with my gaze locked on the ball and my hands in front of me. Wait for it. Wait for it. Wait . . . It lands right in my hands.

Hell yeah! I start to celebrate, but then Kyler yells, "Isa, run!" and I realize I still have to make it to the end zone. I reel around and run like a boss, trying to ignore the sounds of heavy footsteps charging toward me. Seconds later, I step over the line. Touchdown, baby!

I throw the ball down and do a dance until Kyler picks me up and spins me around. I'm not even sure if we won, but it's all very exciting. It might have turned out to be a pretty good ending to a crappy starting day if at that very moment I didn't spot the dark blue car again, driving as slowly as possible on the road beside the field.

I try to convince myself it's not the same car, but then I see a Superman sticker on the back window. I'm pretty sure the car circling the park had the same sticker.

Kyler sets me down on the ground and raises his hand for a high-five. "See, pretty fun, right?"

I distractedly tap my palm against his. "Yeah, it kind of was."

"And the game's over, so you can celebrate that too." He's beaming from ear to ear, his bare chest sheen with sweat.

I try not to gawk, but I steal a few glances at his ripped, defined muscles. "It's over?"

He laughs at me. "Yeah, you just scored the winning touchdown."

"Holy crap. I'm awesome," I joke, but my voice

sounds flat. I can't seem to get into celebrating with that car right there.

"You are awesome." He drapes an arm around my shoulders. "And awesome people get rewards."

The scent of his cologne and sweat engulfs my nostrils. I'm not sure if I'm supposed to love the smell or hate it. Maybe a little of both.

"I get a reward?" I ask, and he nods. "What is it?"

He gives me a side hug and my heart flutters. "I'm taking you out for ice cream."

"Yeah!" I fist pump the air. "I'm so hungry."

"Just let me say goodbye to the guys and we'll go." He heads across the field toward his friends with his arm still slung around me, leaving me no other choice than to go with him.

I glance over my shoulder at the car and frown when I see it turning into the parking lot. I half-expect it to slam to a stop and a policeman to jump out of it. But all it does is stop by Kyler's car for a moment before flipping a bitch and speeding off.

So strange and creepy.

Even though it might be nothing, I need to make sure to mention the car to Grandma Stephy, just in case.

Chapter EIGHT

ISABELLA

While scoring the touchdown felt epic, it didn't earn me any mad cool points with Kyler's friends. I learn quickly that I don't fit in with any of them besides Lily. All the guys want to talk about is the big game next week and whose party they're hitting up tonight. The girls talk to each other until the party is mentioned, and then they're all about the conversation, rattling off different ideas. Once plans are finalized, they all part ways for their cars.

Lily pulls me aside so we can exchange numbers, and while I'm sending her a text so she has mine, I notice an extraordinarily beautiful girl hugging Kyler.

"That's Jesmine. They dated before she dumped him for some older dude," Lily explains when she notices me staring at them.

"I don't ever remember them dating." I shove back the jealousy when Kyler doesn't seem in too big of a hurry to stop hugging Jesmine.

"It was over the summer and only lasted about a week." Lily slides her phone into her jacket pocket. "She's a couple of years older too, so they spent a lot of time at college parties and stuff because she thought she was too cool for his friends. At least that's what Wes says. I guess she got over it, though, since she's here. Or maybe it's okay now because most of his friends are in college."

I stab my nails into my palms, once again feeling like the dorky girl next-door, harboring a silly crush on her sexy next-door neighbor.

"Are you two like together, together?" Lily asks. "Because if you are, you might want to go break up the hug."

"Nah, we're just friends." Once I say it, I realize it's the truth. He can hug whomever he wants whenever he wants. It's not like we're a couple. Still, that doesn't mean I don't want to march over there and go all hungry zombie on both of them. Well, either that or go home and eat a gallon of ice cream.

Finally, the two of them pull away, but they don't put very much space between them. They lean in as they talk seriously about something and he tucks a strand of hair behind her ear.

Ugh! I can't take this. It's like I'm back to square one and if I'm being honest with myself, it's kind of a turn off.

"I have to make a call," I say to Lily. "I'll call you tonight to get more deets about the job."

She smiles at me, but there's a hint of pity in her eyes. "All right. Cool. Call me to get the details about the job, okay?"

I nod, wave to her, then powerwalk to the car. I don't

really have anyone to call, but I dial people's numbers anyway, hoping someone will pick up. No one does and I'm left with no other option than to climb into the car and pretend to mess around with my hair. Thankfully, Kyler climbs in only a couple of minutes later.

His cheeks are flushed. "Ready for that ice cream?"

I nod even though I just want to go to my Grandma Stephy's. "Sure."

He pauses as he's slipping the keys into the ignition. "Is something wrong?"

I shake my head, reaching over my shoulder for the seatbelt. "I'm just tired. Playing football is exhausting."

He doesn't appear like he's buying it. "She's just a friend."

"Huh?"

"Jesmine. I mean, we dated for like two seconds, but we both realized we weren't right for each other. Her dad passed away a couple of weeks ago and I wasn't able to go to the funeral. This was the first time I've seen her since then."

"Oh. Okay." I'm so confused. Why is he telling me this? Because he can read the jealousy all over my face? Am I that transparent?

He puts a hand on my thigh. "I like you, Isa. Like a lot. I'm sorry if I haven't made that clear."

"No . . . you have." God, I sound like a spaz. *Think of something else to say! Something awesomely epic!* "Um . . . I like you too."

Not really awesomely epic but it gets him to smile.

"Good. Now that we have that settled, let's get you some ice cream and then go back to the court." He shoves the car in park and backs out of the parking space. "I think there's still enough time for me to kick your butt one more time at Horse."

I roll my eyes, like you wish buddy, but my joking attitude goes right out the window the moment we pull out onto the road, because that damn blue car pulls out right behind us.

Chapter NINE

KAI

The drive to Mapleview is long and boring. I've never been one for driving solo and, I usually have a driving buddy with me. I turn on some music to try to liven things up, but when a Katy Perry song clicks on, all I can think about is that time Isa and I danced to it, how I licked her neck, pretending the move was playful when I really just wanted to get a taste. She shocked the shit out of me when she licked me back, but I think she did it because she was drunk. Sober, I'm not so sure things would've gone down that way.

Even if Isa did like me the way I like her, she's never been the kind of girl to bluntly announce how she feels. I've seen her dismiss a lot of things that probably shouldn't have been dismissed. With a simple shrug or by tucking her head down, she spends a lot of time pretending she's okay, even when she's not.

I've known this about her since we were in seventh grade. It was during the start of our brief friendship. Everyone in the entire school knew she was obsessed with Kyler, mainly because Hannah had blabbered it to anyone who would listen.

"Seriously, you should read her diary," I heard her saying to Kyler and a group of their friends during lunch. "It's all Kyler this, Kyler that. Kyler's so dreamy. I hope we get married some day. She even has some kind of weird chant thing written down on one of the pages that looks like a love spell or something. Seriously, she's such a stalker." Then she giggled in that shrill way that always made me want to jab my eardrums out. And, of course, her friends joined in, like a bunch of wannabe hyenas.

Kyler didn't say anything at first, merely chewing on his burger. His friends all remained quiet, waiting for him to say something. And me . . . While I sat at the same table, I never really joined in on their conversation. I was always just there, Kyler's younger brother, who everyone was nice to because my last name was Meyers.

"What do you mean there was a love spell?" Kyler finally asked, setting his burger down on the lunch tray in front of him. "Does she, like, think she's a witch or something?"

"Yeah, she talks about it all the time," Hannah said, but I could tell she was lying, just like she was probably lying about the love spell and Isa having a diary at all—she didn't really seem like a diary kind of girl. "She thinks she can curse people and stuff." She wiggled her fingers in front of her, giggling. "You better watch out, Kyler. She might put a love spell on you, and the next thing you know, you'll be kissing her."

Kyler visibly shuddered, but I could tell it was more for show than over the fact that he was that creeped out about the idea of kissing Isa. I knew he hung out and played basketball with her sometimes, and there were a couple of times when I caught him staring at her balcony.

While Isa wasn't popular, she wasn't a hideous beast. She had clear skin; long, brown hair; and yeah, she was a bit on the gangly side, but her height made her awesome at shooting hoops. Her biggest problem was that she was super socially awkward and shy. Plus, she dressed really weird sometimes, wearing superhero shirts and even a cape once. And yeah, while I thought superheroes and comics were cool, I knew better than to go advertising it to the entire middle school. Although, I did envy her ability to be who she was, unlike me.

"There's no way in hell I'd ever kiss her." Kyler shot her a horrified look at the table where Isa was sitting by herself, eating lunch, and reading a book. "That'd be worse than kissing my dog."

"And you would know how?" I didn't even mean to say it aloud. It just sort of slipped out.

Kyler gave me his stupid I'm-the-shit-and-you're-not smirk. "You got a thing for weirdoes or something?"

"No." It was one word, but it felt like such a betrayal. I didn't defend her. I didn't do anything at all except sit there and listen to them as they started making fun of her. I was too afraid that, if I spoke up, they'd make fun of me. It made me no better than them, maybe even worse.

I hung out with Isa, and yeah, while I didn't declare to the world that she was my friend, I still sort of thought of her as one. She knew more about me than any of my other friends. She knew the real me. And she made me feel like I mattered, like I wasn't just Kyler's little brother who disappointed his father time and time again.

Things got progressively worse from there when Hannah stood up on her chair and announced to the entire cafeteria what she had just told Kyler. Almost everyone busted up laughing and stared at Isa.

I didn't laugh. All I did was watch as Isa quickly gathered her things and hurried out of the room with her head tucked down.

Later that day, when we were sitting in the hollowed out tree, I asked her if she was okay. She simply shrugged, focusing on the drawing she was working on of a woman in a cape getup. "Yeah, I'm fine."

I stuffed a couple of chips in my mouth, trying to decide if she was really fine or not. She looked like she was unbothered, but how could she be? It would suck to get laughed at by everyone.

"Are you sure?" I slid closer to her. "Because you can tell me if you're not. I'm a great listener."

She paused, and I thought she was going to open up to me, but then she looked up and smiled. "What do you think of this drawing? Does it scream 'I'm a badass mofo about to save the world'? Or is it coming off too 'I'm a beotch'?"

It hurt that she didn't trust me, but then again, what had I done to earn her trust? Nothing at all. I was no better than everyone else.

"I like that she looks pretty badass," I said, hoping to at least get her to feel good about her drawing. "Who is she?"

Isa shrugged and used the pencil to shade in the woman's cape. "I'm not sure. I just see her in my head sometimes." She paused, pressing her lips together. "You really think she looks badass?"

I nodded. "Like she's about to save the world from every jerk out there."

She faintly smiled at that, like my words really meant something to her. It made me feel good about myself because the girl rarely smiled.

But that feeling quickly faded about a week later when one of my so-called friends saw me hanging out with her. I had two choices in that moment: 1.) I could own it and finally just be who I was without hiding. But that would mean getting teased like crazy, and with everything going between my dad and me, I wasn't sure I could handle that. Or 2.) I could lie and cower out of the situation by calling her a stalker like Hannah did all the time.

I stupidly and very cowardly went with option two, and to this day, I still hate myself a little bit for it. Maybe I deserve to be in the position I am now—sitting here, trying to make money to pay a debt that isn't even mine while Isa is back in Sunnyvale with Kyler.

The thought, while probably true, is really effing depressing, so depressing I turn on my Emo playlist just so the music fits my mood.

Forty-five minutes and nine angsty songs later, I'm finally pulling into Mapleview. The town is a tiny blip on a map, even smaller than Sunnyvale, which says a lot.

After I circle the designated block three times without spotting a guy wearing a hoodie and brass knuckles, I grow worried he might be a no show. Still, I drive around the block six more times before pulling over into the parking lot of a nearby gas station.

I'm not sure what to do. I don't have my phone, so I can't call Big Doug. He did say that, if I saw anyone sketchy, I wasn't supposed to drop off the envelope. But it's not like I've seen anyone sketchy; I just haven't seen anyone at all.

I make another few loops around the block, which

basically consists of a few abandoned houses, a boarded up warehouse, and the gas station. Again, I don't see a single damn person, so I return to the gas station parking lot and sit in my car, trying to figure out what to do.

I pick up the envelope, turn it over, and fiddle with the clasp, debating whether to open it or not. I know Big Doug said not to, but dammit, I'm really curious what could be in this thing that's worth all this trouble.

I mess around with the clasp for a minute or two before setting the envelope back down without opening it. *If I want to get paid for this job, then I need to do it right.*

I climb out of my car and head for the gas station to see if the cashier will let me use their phone. But halfway across the parking lot, I realize that Big Doug is speed dial number seven in my phone, and I don't know his number.

"Shit. What the heck am I supposed to do now?" I curse under my breath, turning back around for the car.

That's when I spot a guy near my car, wearing a ski mask and holding a crowbar. When he raises the crowbar to break the window, I run at him.

"Don't you fucking dare!" I shout at him.

The guy is completely unfazed as he bashes the crowbar against the window. Glass shatters as he reaches inside, snatching up the envelope.

I barrel toward him, ready to beat his ass. But the closer I get, the more aware I become that the dude is fucking hella big, like sumo wrestler big. I slow down as I reach the back of my car, deliberating how far I want to take this. Sure, I promised Big Doug I'd guard the envelope with my life when I left, but I didn't mean that literally.

Sumo guy knows he can beat my ass too, because he's just standing there, waiting for me to make a move.

I linger near the rear end of the car, keeping some

space between us. "I'm going to call the cops on your ass if you don't give me that back." Sure, I don't have my phone on me, but he doesn't know that.

I swear I hear him laugh. Then he's suddenly striding toward me. Stepping back, I swing my fist around to punch him at the same time he raises the crowbar at me. My knuckles collide with his jaw as the metal bar slams against the side of my face. I hit the ground hard.

He hovers over me, grasping the crowbar. "Tell Big Doug his three strikes are up," he growls then raises the crowbar and whacks it against the side of my head.

Everything goes black.

Chapter TEN

ISABELLA

After we buy our ice cream, we sit in the car and eat it. I'm trying to be super cheery, but my thoughts are all over the place. I'm exhausted, on edge, and I'm sure I'm coming off as an energy draining downer. Despite the fact that the dark blue car hasn't made a grand appearance since we pulled into the ice cream shop, I can't shake the feeling it's going to materialize at any given moment. Even the cup of ice cream I'm holding doesn't help alleviate my worries.

"I still can't believe what you put in that." Kyler stares at the cup of ice cream in my hand, his face scrunched.

I can't help smiling as I replay the look he gave me when I ordered strawberry ice cream with cheesecake, sprinkles, cookies, gummy worms, and chocolate syrup toppings.

"You have no idea what you're missing out on. It's so yummy." I stuff a spoonful into my mouth to prove my point. "It took me years of trying out different concoctions to get it right, and all of the concoctions were good."

His lips quirk. "It took you that long to put together something that looks that disgusting?"

I stick my tongue out at him. "I've made ones that look way worse, like when I put gumballs and nuts into a cotton candy flavored ice cream. I almost threw that one up."

He makes another repulsed face. "That sounds so gross, but anything with cotton candy in it sounds gross to me."

My eyes widen. "You don't like cotton candy?"

He visibly shudders. "Ever since I was ten and ate an entire bag before I rode the Zipper at the carnival."

"Let me guess." I try not to laugh at how intensely serious he seems over the subject. "You threw up?"

"Yep. And trust me when I say it may taste good going down, but not so much when it comes up."

"I'll have to take your word for it, but I don't think it's going to stop me from eating cotton candy or cotton candy flavored ice cream."

"You're kind of crazy." A sudden, almost thoughtful, expression appears on his face. "A crazy girl who makes touchdowns like a boss and likes the most disgusting looking ice cream I've ever seen."

"Hey, you can't mock the ice cream until you've tried it." I scoop up another spoonful, slowly put it into my mouth, and exaggerate a moan. "Mmm . . . soooo good."

He stirs his cookie dough ice cream, his attention zeroed in on my mouth. "When you put it that way, it does kind of look tasty."

I feel my skin warm like gooey caramel. I try to think of something flirty to say, but my brain flatlines.

He stares at my mouth for a beat or two longer before dragging his gaze to meet mine. He pulls his bottom lip between his teeth. "Can I try it?"

"The ice cream?" My voice sounds unnaturally high.

He bites down harder on his lip, restraining a smile. "Sure."

For some reason, I don't think he meant the ice cream.

I take a subtle inhale, collecting myself before I speak again. "I don't know. It's not really for amateurs." I mentally high-five myself for how light and flirty my voice sounds.

He teasingly glares at me. "Come on, give me a taste. I can handle it."

I tap my finger against my lips, pretending to consider it. "Oh, fine. But if you hate it, don't blame me."

He grins, leans over the console, and opens his mouth.

My mouth goes dry. *Umm . . . He wants me to feed him?* While Indigo taught me a thing or two about flirting, I was never able to do it as easily as she can. I always got nervous, and that was with guys we just met in clubs and stuff. This is Kyler—Kyler Meyers sitting here, waiting for me to feed him ice cream.

Willing my hand not to shake, I shovel up a spoonful of ice cream and move the spoon toward his mouth. His eyes are fixed on me as he waits. My heart is losing it inside my chest, throbbing like a song with a pulsating deep bass. My pulse only quickens when his lips wrap around the spoon and he slowly sucks the ice cream off.

I've heard Indigo use the term erotic before: for the sound of a guy's voice, the way someone dances, the way a guy she likes says her name. But I don't think I ever quite understood the term until now.

Kyler slants back, licking his lips, and his gaze floats upward as he lets the flavor sink into his taste buds.

"So, what do you think?" I must have a fairy godmother or something, because, by some miracle, my voice comes out as smooth as taffy.

"It's not too bad." His lips spread into a grin as he steals a chunk of my ice cream with his spoon. "It's actually really good." He licks the ice cream off the spoon, and again, the word erotic flashes through my mind.

I'm not sure what my expression looks like, but something about it makes Kyler chuckle.

"I think, the next time we come back here, I just might get a cup for myself," he says, licking his spoon clean.

"Oh, yeah?" I ask. *Next time.* "Not brave enough to make up your own concoction?"

His lips part in mock shock. "Are you challenging me?"

"Maybe. I think the only way you could win the challenge is if you put some cotton candy flavored ice cream in it."

"Nope. Never gonna happen."

I shrug. "Then I guess you lose the challenge."

He considers something. "What would I get if I did it? What would you give me if, the next time we came here, I ate a whole bowl of cotton candy ice cream with any toppings you put on it."

"That challenge sounds dangerous. I get really excited about ice cream toppings."

"I didn't ask about the dangerous risks I'd be subjecting my taste buds to. What I asked is what I'd win if I did it. What would you give me?"

"Why would it have to be something I gave you?" I grin. "Wouldn't the reward be getting to eat awesome tasting ice cream?"

His eyes flare with something I can't quite decipher as his lips tug to a grin. "No, I'd definitely want something from you."

It's getting really, *really* hot in here.

I stuff another bite of ice cream into my mouth while I consider a reply. "Fine. What would you want?"

"I'm not sure yet. I definitely have to think about it for a while and make sure it's something really, *really* good."

"Well, when you decide, let me know."

"Oh, I definitely will." He winks at me before resting back in his seat.

I let a slow breath escape my lips. Mother of all hot chocolate syrup, that was one of the most intense flirting moments I've ever had.

Thankfully, for my flushed skin's sake, Kyler changes the conversation to a much lighter topic as his phone buzzes. I think it's a text, but then he opens a calendar.

He sighs disappointedly. "And there goes our awesome moment."

"What is it?"

"A reminder that I need to write a paper for English."

"If you need to drop me off, that's cool," I say, not wanting to be a pain.

He waves me off, reclining back in the seat. "Nah. I can do it tomorrow." His head tips back as he gazes at the ceiling. "God, classes are killer. It makes me wish I appreciated high school more."

"What're you majoring in?" I pick a chunk of cheesecake out of my ice cream and pop it into my mouth.

"Right now, just general. I might change it eventually, but my dad . . . He wants me to focus on sports right now." His jaw clenches, and I get the sense that maybe Kai isn't the only one who has issues with their dad.

"What about you? Do you want to focus on sports?"

"I guess so. I mean, I'm good at it, so I probably should."

"Being good at something doesn't mean you have to do it," I point out. "I'm good at basketball, but I never actually wanted to join a team. It was never my thing."

He turns his head to look at me. "What is your thing? I really want to know because it feels like I know you, yet I don't."

"My thing," I drum my finger against my lip, "is probably awesomeness," I joke then sigh. "I really don't know." I feel self-conscious to tell him about my manga obsession and how I love to draw my own comics.

"You like to draw, right?"

I nod. "It's not artsy stuff, though. It's more . . . comic stuff."

"That's cool." He cracks his knuckles. "Kai was into that stuff for a while. He had all these posters and stuff on his walls."

"Yeah, I know." I conceal a smile with a bite of ice cream. While I knew Kai was into comics, I never knew he had posters all over his walls.

A pucker forms at his brows. "How do you know? I don't think he ever told anyone, not even his friends."

"Back in seventh grade, we hung out for a while, and he told me then."

"You two hung out? I never saw you."

"It was after school."

He seems like he's tripping out over the idea. I don't know why. Is it that weird that Kai would hang out with me? Yeah, we were on two totally different social levels, but we have a lot in common.

"It's not that weird, is it?" I find myself asking.

Kyler straightens in the seat, shaking his head. "No, it's not that. It's just . . . I don't know. It just surprises me. I mean, I know you guys hang out now, but I didn't realize you've been friends since then."

"We haven't been friends since then," I correct him. "We had a falling out that lasted pretty much until the beginning of this school year."

"What was the falling out over?" he wonders.

Um, yeah, there's no way I want to tell Kyler the story about how Kai called me a stalker when one of his friends caught us hanging out. It's too embarrassing, and with how much the two of them fight, I'm not sure how Kyler will react to the story.

"I don't know." I shrug. "Just middle school drama, and now we're over it."

He studies me intently, as if trying to unravel my thoughts. "But you two are just friends, right?"

For a microsecond, I'm thrown off by his question. The slight pause lasts just long enough that the air between us shifts into awkward land.

"Yeah, we're just friends."

He assesses me for an uncomfortable amount of time before speaking again. "I still don't think you should hang out with him, not until he gets his shit together. You're too good for that."

"I'm not that good."

"Yeah, you are."

I want to argue, but he seems pretty adamant about it.

"So, you're into art and comics, huh?" He muses over the idea. "I've always wondered what you were drawing whenever I saw you sitting out on balcony with your notebook."

I don't bother mentioning that I also spent time drawing him . . . shirtless.

"I've been doing it since I was, like, six. It's really

relaxing."

His lips pull into a lopsided grin. "You should show me some of your stuff sometime."

"Okay," I say, even though I'm not sure he'd get my stuff.

"And teach me a thing or two about this whole comic world," he adds.

That gets me to smile. "I might consider it if you're lucky."

"Personally, I think I'm pretty lucky. I mean, I'm sitting here with you, aren't I?" he asks with a charming grin.

I cover my mouth as laughter bubbles in my throat. He laughs, though, so I let it out.

He chuckles. "I know. I'm the worst. I don't know why I say shit like that. It just pops into my head."

"Maybe you should stop watching so many rom-coms," I tease, twisting the end of my ponytail around my finger.

He points a finger at me. "I never watch rom-coms."

"Yeah, right. I bet you do all the time," I tease. "I bet you watch them and memorize the lines."

He wiggles his fingers at me. "Don't make me tickle you again. Take it back or else."

I make a big show of zipping my lips together, and he dives for me, tickling me until I can barely breathe.

"Fine! I surrender," I gasp through my laughter. "You don't watch rom-coms."

He leans back, seeming satisfied. "Now say you'll show me your art."

I nod, catching my breath. "I'll show you whatever you want just as long as you stop tickling me."

He misses a beat, a strange look crossing his face. It takes me a second to process what I just said, but before I can get too mortified, he starts talking again.

"Okay, no more tickling," he says right as his phone vibrates again. He sighs, glancing at the screen. "And now it's reminding me to do my pre-Cal paper."

I draw a heart with an arrow going through it on the fogged up window. "Are you sure you don't need to take me home?"

"I said you were fine, and I meant it." He watches me add a thorny pattern around the heart like it's the most fascinating thing on the planet. "So, is that what you're going to college for? Art?"

My fingers fall from the window as a realization crashes down on me.

"I haven't thought much about it." Mostly because my family never really talked about it. College questions were always for Hannah. Me, I was just supposed to sit and listen. Listen and not be heard; those were the rules.

"I'm sure you'll figure it out," he says. "You still have time."

"Yeah, I know." On the inside, I'm freaking out. Art school sounds awesome, but isn't stuff like that expensive? Where would I get the money?

Suddenly, that job Lily suggested I apply for sounds like a good idea.

I remain stuck in my own head as Kyler starts the car and drives out onto the street.

"So, what's next on the distraction to-do list? We could go to the theater and watch a movie," he says as he cruises down Main Street. "One more game before we go hang out at your grandma's house? Whatever you want, name it, and it's done."

"Isn't it too dark to play basketball?" I stir the melted ice cream as I peer up at the dusty grey sky. A handful of stars are sprinkled across it, and the moon is shining brightly.

"Yeah, it might be." He flips on the brights. "I could always leave these bad boys on. I think the park has lights, too."

As awesome as Kyler has been, the events of today are gradually sinking in. I'm tired and worried, not just about what Lynn and my dad will do to me, but my future. I desperately need to talk to Indigo and Grandma Stephy, the two people who have pretty much been the only family I ever had. Besides, Kyler has other places to be. I heard him make plans to meet up with his friends at some party later tonight after hanging out with me.

"Kyler, I really appreciate everything you've done for me, but it's been such an intense day." I set down my empty cup of ice cream, crossing my fingers that I don't sound rude. "I kind of just want to go to my grandma's if that's okay."

He dims the car lights for a vehicle driving in the opposite direction. "Yeah, no. I totally understand. It's been a really hard day for you. You should probably relax." He pulls off to the side of the road and flips a U-turn, heading toward Sunnyvale Bay Community. "You want to stop somewhere and grab something to eat first? I was thinking maybe we could watch a movie or something when we get to your grandma's."

"What about that party your friends were talking about? I don't want to make you miss it. And you have those papers for school you need to work on. I feel like I'm stealing all your time."

"The party and homework can wait. I honestly don't feel like going out and partying tonight, anyway. I have to get up early for training and then spend the evening writing that paper."

"Are you sure you're okay with staying? Because I'll

be fine at my grandma's if you want to just drop me off."

"Isa, I'm sure, so stop arguing." His voice is firm, but his eyes sparkle. "Besides, I was thinking maybe we could watch one of those zombie movies you love."

I perk up, lean back, and prop my feet up on the dash. "You like zombie movies?"

Shame crosses his face. "I actually haven't ever watched one."

"*Ever?*" What the hell of all apocalypses is happening right now?

He shrugs, looking like a kid who just got told he wasn't cool. "It's just never really been my thing. I'm more into sports movies and stuff. Is there, like, a sports zombie movie?"

"I don't think so. But I promise that, after tonight, you'll no longer be a zombie movie virgin." Oh, my God, I can't believe I just said something unintentionally dirty like that. *Again*.

My cheeks flame like the goddamn sun. Fortunately, it's dark enough in the cab of the car, so I don't think he can see it. But I do notice his lips twitching, as if he's struggling not to laugh.

When he speaks, his voice sounds gruffer than normal. "That sounds really interesting."

I laugh to breeze over the situation, but I sound breathless. To stop myself from saying something else embarrassing, I focus on deciding what movie to ease him into his soon-to-be developing zombie obsession.

As I'm mentally going through my favorite list of zombie movies, his phone vibrates again. He collects it from out of the console, glances at the screen, and then grimaces before pressing talk.

"What's up?" he says into the phone. He momentarily remains quiet then says a lot of yeah and no several times and one maybe before glancing in my direction. "I'm actually kind of busy right now. Can it wait until a little bit later?" He frowns, seeming tense and kind of irritated. "Fine. I'll do it." He hangs up and tosses the phone into the console. "Isa, I hate to do this to you, but I need to bail out a little early. That was one of my friends on the phone. They did something pretty stupid and need my help fixing the mess."

"It's fine." I lower my feet to the floor and sit up. "I'm kind of tired, anyway. I'll probably end up falling asleep the second I sit down."

"Still, I feel like a jerk for leaving you alone . . . I'll make this up to you. I promise." He pauses. "How about a zombie movie marathon and dinner next weekend?"

"You don't have to do that. I understand. Really—"

He places two fingers over my lips. "I know I don't have to, but I want to."

My breath falters as his touch sends the strangest tingling sensations throughout my body. His gaze briefly flicks to my lips then to the road again.

I will my voice to come out even. "How about we compromise? One zombie movie and one sports movie. That way, I don't scare you off. Zombie movie virgins need to be eased into the blood and gore."

He smiles, moving his fingers away from my mouth. He lets his fingertip trail downward to my chin, neck, and collarbone before returning his hand to the steering wheel. "Just as long as you let me pay for dinner."

My pulse throbs as I nod. "Sounds like you've got yourself a date." I instantly want to take back my bold comment, wondering if I'm being too forward. But Kyler smiles, seeming pretty content, so I decide to just own it.

We don't say much for the rest of the drive, and before I know it, we're turning into the apartment complex.

He's parking the car in front of my Grandma Stephy's building when I receive a text message.

As I'm rummaging for my phone inside my jacket pocket, Kyler warily eyeballs the building in front of us. "I really hate the idea of leaving you here by yourself."

Most of the lights are off in all the apartments except for a few porch lights. It's only seven o'clock on a Saturday, but it's like everyone's in bed already. I'd chalk it up to old people time, but after meeting some of my Grandma Stephy's crazy friends while we were in Europe, I wouldn't be surprised if some of them were out clubbing or something.

"I'll be fine. I promise. But I do have pretty good fighting skills, just in case." I make fists and laugh before swiping my finger across the screen of my phone.

"Mad fighting skills or not, I'd still feel a little bit better if I weren't leaving you here completely alone." He keeps his eyes fixed on the building, as if waiting for something terrible to do down.

Indigo: I got yours and Grandma Stephy's messages! I'm home right now! Where the heck r u?

"I actually won't be here alone. My cousin's here." I stuff the phone into my pocket and open the door. "Thanks for everything, Kyler. I had a lot of fun. If it weren't for you, I probably would've spent all day stressing out and eating my weight in cookies."

A soft laugh escapes his lips. "While I think you could probably handle eating your weight in cookies and then some, I'm glad you had fun." He reaches forward and his palm molds around my cheek. "And thanks for playing football with me. I know it bored you to death, but you actually kicked some ass at the end."

"It didn't bore me to death. It just . . ." I trail off as he leans forward and places the gentlest kiss on the corner of my mouth, causing me to nearly choke on my nerves.

But I force myself to remain composed and focus on the kiss, the way he tastes, like cookie dough and strawberry ice cream, and his breath smells like gummy worms. So yummy.

My stomach briefly goes kerplunk, like on a rollercoaster but the feeling fades into a soft lull, leaving me wanting more.

"Sorry, I couldn't resist." He shifts back in his seat with a slightly confused yet somewhat pleased look on his face. "I'll call you tomorrow, okay?"

I nod then grab my bags and climb out of the car. He waits for me to get inside the apartment before he backs out of the parking space, which I greatly appreciate considering the whole thing with the blue car.

Through the window, I watch him drive away, only turning away when he disappears down the road.

"Holy crap, I can't believe that just happened," I say to myself, slumping against the wall. I try to sort thoughts. While the kiss was amazing, it wasn't the firework show I'd been expecting. But then again, it only lasted like a half a second.

"What just happened?" Indigo asks as she walks out of the hallway, wearing a pair of plaid pajama bottom shorts and an oversized T-shirt, running a brush through her damp, auburn hair.

I let my arms go limp, my bags sliding off and dropping to the floor. "Kyler just kissed me. Well, kind of kissed me. It was on the corner of the mouth, so I'm not sure if it counts." I expect her to get all giddy, but she simply stands there, combing her hair. "That's a good thing," I feel the need to tell her. I flop down on the sofa, slip the elastic out of my hair, and run my fingers through my tangled hair, feeling as though I'm floating on clouds of marshmallows. "I've been dreaming for it to happen forever."

"I know you have." She sets the brush down on the kitchen counter then sits down in the chair across from me, tucking her legs underneath her. "It's kind of bad timing, though."

"There's no such thing as bad timing when it comes to getting kissed by Kyler Meyers."

"Isa . . . You basically just got kicked out of your house, found out your mom is . . . Grandma Stephy told me what happened today. I hate to say it, because I'm all for kissing, but considering your emotional state, I don't think any guy should be kissing you right now."

"I'm not that emotionally unstable." Even when I say it, though, I feel a tremor inside me, bottled up pain trying to explode. I swallow it down, knowing once I let it out, it'll be yesterday all over again. "Really, I'm not."

She gives me a look. "No, you're just trying to live in the land of denial."

"I'm not living in the land of denial. If anything, I'm living in the land of who-the-hell-am-I?" I bite down on my lip until I taste blood. "Look, I'm just afraid that, once I let it all out, I won't be able to turn it off. Yesterday . . . When Lynn said my mom was dead . . . I nearly lost it." Hot tears pool in my eyes, and I attempt to blink them away. "If Kai didn't find me before I took off . . . I don't know what would've happened."

"Kai found you?" Her head angles to the side as her brows dip. "Where? When? And how the heck did you end up with Kyler, instead?"

Sighing, I sit up and give her a brief rundown of everything that happened over the last twenty-four hours, including the creepy car that kept showing up everywhere

I went.

"You think it was your parents?" she asks after I finish. "Or Lynn and your dad, anyway . . . I'm sorry. I'm not sure what to call them anymore."

I pick at my nail polish. "Me, either."

She drums her fingers against her knee. "How about those douchey assholes we used to know?" The small smile that touches my lips encourages her to go on. "Or we could just refer to your dad as the sperm donor, 'cause that's kind of what he is. And Lynn can be the Botox Bitch, and Hannah—"

"How about The Half-Sister from Hell."

"More like the She-Devil from Hell. She doesn't even deserve the title of half-sister. She may be related to you by blood, but that bitch has never acted like an older sister. None of your family has ever really acted like your family."

"I know." But, God, do I wish I didn't know.

I coil a strand of my hair around my finger, thinking about Big Doug and how I haven't heard anything from him yet. "I wish I could find out more about my mom . . . even if she's . . ." I suck back the tears. "Even if she's dead like Lynn says, I still want to find out more about her. I mean, what about her parents? Maybe they're still alive. And what if she has kids? What if I have, like, a half-brother or sister somewhere I don't even know about? And what if they're, like, nice or something? What if there's people out there I can call family?" By the time I'm finished rambling, I'm out of breath, and Indigo's eyes are wide.

She blinks a few times, shaking her head. "Okay, first of all, you do have a family: me and Grandma Stephy. We're always here for you. You're not alone in any of this." I open my mouth to tell her I know that, but she talks over me. "And second, we're going to get to the bottom of this whole mystery of your mom. We just need to come up with a plan."

I pick at my thumbnail. "Actually, I have a guy looking into it already."

She looks taken aback. "Who?"

I shrug. "Just some guy Kai knows."

Suspicion fills her eyes. "And how does Kai know this guy?"

"It's just a friend of his."

"A friend who does what exactly?"

"I don't know. Looks stuff up on the computer, maybe. I'm not really sure. I didn't really ask too many questions when I met him." I scratch at my arms, squirming under her unwavering gaze. "Why are you acting so weird? It's not that big of a deal."

"Did you pay this guy?"

"No."

"So, let me get this straight. Kai introduced you to some random guy with a computer, who supposedly is going to look up stuff about your mom and do it all for free? Because, let me tell you that sounds sketchy and like, eventually, you're going to have to pay for it."

"It's not sketchy," I argue, not bothering to mention I met Big Doug in a pool house with some really expensive-looking computer equipment. "He's Kai's friend. I'm sure that's why he's doing it for free."

"Hmmm." She doesn't seem too convinced. "I think I want to talk to Kai about this."

I'm about to tell her that's not necessary—after everything Kai's done for me, the last thing I want is for Indigo give him the third degree—when my phone goes crazy, an unknown number flashing across the screen, and I hesitate. I'm not sure why. It's not that weird or anything, but considering all the stuff that happened today, I find myself nervous about the unknown.

"Who is it?" Indigo wonders, braiding her hair.

My finger hovers over the talk button. "I don't recognize the number."

We sit there in silence as the phone rings three more times before it switches to voicemail.

"I don't know why I'm so nervous." I balance the phone on my knee. "I'm just so afraid the cops are going to show up and drag me outta here. Every noise and out of place thing has me jumping out of my skin."

"Grandma Stephy took care of the whole police thing, and she wouldn't have told you she did unless she really has the situation handled."

"I know . . . but I can't shake the feeling that Lynn has something else up her sleeve and she's just waiting for the right moment."

Silence stretches between us as we both sit on my declaration. Then my stomach lets out a loud grumble, breaking the tension.

We both erupt in giggles.

"Have you eaten at all today?" she asks after our laughter dies down.

I drape my arm across my starving belly. "I had some ice cream. That's about it, though."

"I'll find us something to eat." Instead of heading for the kitchen, she walks over and gives me a hug. "I'm so sorry this is happening to you. And I'm so sorry I haven't really been there for you over the last couple of weeks. I've been a really shitty friend."

"You don't have to apologize." I hug her back. Sometimes, it still feels so strange getting hugs. Growing up in a household where no one really liked me, I rarely—if ever—got them. "You've been busy with work and stuff."

"I know, but still . . . I should've made time for us to hang out more, especially with everything you've been going through." She steps back. "You know what? Tomorrow, I'm going to blow off work, and you and I are going to drive into the city and go shopping."

"You don't have to do that. I promise, I'm f—"

"Don't you dare say you're fine. You have a bad habit of doing that sometimes."

"Doing what?"

"Acting like you're fine, even when you're not."

"I don't do that," I protest. "I mean, look what I did yesterday. I totally lost it. Like, crying until I had no tears kind of lost it."

"Probably because you held it in all those years in that house," she says. "You dealt with all that shit and hardly ever complained about it once. If I were you, I would've lost it a long time ago."

"Maybe I did lose it a long time ago," I suggest. "Maybe that's why I'm so weird. Maybe my sanity button snapped a long time ago."

"Maybe." She pats my head. "But we're still going shopping."

"Fine." I pick up my phone as it notifies me I have a voicemail. "Well, whoever it was left a message." I dial to my voicemail and chew on my thumbnail as I wait anxiously to see who called while Indigo wanders into the kitchen, eyeing me worriedly.

"Hey, Isa, it's Kai . . . I'm guessing you're either busy with Kyler still or not answering because some weird-ass number showed up on your screen, but I really need to talk to you." He pauses, and when he speaks again, tension pours from his voice. *"Okay . . . I guess I'll call back in a few minutes. Hopefully, you'll answer."*

When the message ends, I hang up. "That was Kai."

"What'd he want?" She grabs a box of macaroni and cheese from the cupboard and then closes the door.

"I don't know." I stare at my phone, willing him to call back. "He sounded funny, like he was nervous or something."

My stomach winds into knots. What if this has something to do with T? What if he's in trouble somewhere? Or worse, what if he's hurt?

"Did he say he'd call back?" She flips over the box to read the instructions on the back.

"Yeah." I keep my eyes glued to the phone. *Come on, Kai. Just call back.*

A few minutes trickle by, and my phone remains silent. I'm just talking myself into dialing the number, seeing if Kai will answer, when my phone rings again. The unknown number crosses the screen, and I quickly answer it.

"Kai." For some reason, I sound like I just ran a marathon.

"Hey, you answered." A relieved exhale floats through the line. "I was worried maybe you didn't have your phone on you."

"Sorry I didn't answer the first time you called. I didn't recognize the number, and after the weird day I had . . ." No. Now's definitely not time to get into that conversation with him. "Where are you? And whose phone are you calling from? Is everything all right? You sounded nervous on the message."

He chuckles, the sound like calming music to my ears. "Which one of those do you want me to answer first?"

"Umm . . . How about, where are you?"

"In Mapleview."

"Still?"

He heaves a weighted sigh. "Look, it's a long story, but before I even attempt to get into it, I need to ask you for a favor."

"Whatever you need, I'm there." After how much Kai has done for me, I owe him like a gazillion favors.

It takes him a second to answer. "I need you to drive over to Big Doug's house and tell him something happened, that I'm stuck in Mapleview, and he needs to come pick me up. I'd call him, but I don't have my phone, and I can't remember his number."

"If you need a ride, I can come and pick you up," I find myself saying without even putting a lot of forethought into the decision.

"You mean you and Kyler can come pick me up, right? Because I don't want him knowing about this." A drop of jealousy lands in his tone, leaving me feeling guilty and sort of confused.

Is it because he despises Kyler that much, or is it something else? One thing I do know for certain is that the whole being friends with Kai while kind of dating Kyler thing is going to be pretty complicated since the two of them don't get along at all.

"I'm not with Kyler anymore," I tell Kai. "He dropped me off at my Grandma Stephy's house a while ago. I'm with Indigo right now. And I'm sure she'll let me borrow the car."

"Oh, I will, will I?" Indigo says from over by the stove. She's only kidding, her expression laced with curiosity.

"It's okay," he says. "Big Doug can do it. I need to talk to him, anyway."

"Are you sure? Because I really don't mind." I don't, either. Yeah, I'm tired and in desperate need of a shower, but he sounds like he might be in trouble, and I want to help him like he's helped me. When he hesitates, I add,

"If you don't let me, then I'm just going to sit around and worry all night. I probably won't get any sleep, and then I'll be cranky when Indigo takes me shopping tomorrow. She'll end up never taking me shopping again, and I'll be forced to wear the same clothes forever because I suck at shopping by myself, and honestly, being in a store alone kind of freaks me out."

"It does, does it?" He sounds amused.

"Um, yeah. It's like the worst place to be if an apocalypse happens," I continue on with my awesome story. "But, anyway, all my clothes will eventually get holes in them, and I'll end up having to go everywhere naked. I'll get kicked out of school because of their whole no being naked on school grounds policy, and I'll have no choice but to join a nunnery and wear their robes because it'll be the only way I'll ever be able to get clothes again."

His laughter fills the line. "A nun, huh? Because I can't picture you being a nun."

"Exactly. That's why you have to let me come and pick you up." I love that he sounds more relaxed and that I've played a part in it. It makes me feel like I did something right.

"Are you sure you don't mind?" He double-checks. "Because, honestly, I'd rather you come get me. I'm a little pissed at Big Doug right now."

I wonder why. I wonder what happened. I wonder a lot of things, but I can ask him all that when I pick him up.

"Yep. I'm already heading for door," I say, dragging my ass off the couch. "Just tell me where you are."

He gives me the address, and I punch it into my notepad app. Then I tell him I'll be there in two hours tops, and he thanks me at least ten times.

After we hang up, I go into the kitchen to get the car

keys from Indigo. "You're cool with me borrowing the car, right?"

She's turned off the stove and is dumping the water out of the pan and into the sink. "Grandma Stephy would chew my ass off if I let you drive by yourself to Mapleview this late."

"I doubt it. I mean, she's not strict. She let us run around all the time by ourselves on the trip." I zip my jacket up, cringing at the giant mud stain on it. I haven't changed or showered since yesterday morning. I can only imagine how I look and smell right now. "Besides, I'm almost eighteen."

"That doesn't matter." She puts the unopened box of macaroni and cheese into the cupboard. "You've had a rough day, and she won't want you being by yourself."

True. She told me that on the phone when I talked to her earlier.

"So, here's what we're going to do." She dries her hands on a dishrag. "I'm going to change into some clothes while you change yours, because that mud stain is going to drive me nuts. If I have to look at it the entire drive, I might just pull it off you and burn it." She smiles at me, so I know she's kidding. Well, kind of kidding, at least about the burning part.

While she goes back to her room, I change into a pair of clean jeans, a long-sleeved black shirt, and slip on my favorite pair of red velvet boots. Then I hurry to the bathroom to wash my face, brush my teeth, and put on some deodorant. I don't bother looking in the mirror. I know it will only make me want to clean up more, and there's no time for that.

"Ready?" Indigo asks as she pokes her head into the bathroom.

Her hair is curled, and she's put on a touch of lip-gloss

and mascara. She has on a skirt, knee highs, and a leather jacket, along with gladiator sandals. How the hell she managed to get all dressed up like that in five minutes is beyond me.

"You know we're just picking him up at some gas station, right?" I give a pressing glance at her outfit.

"Yeah, but I need to be prepared. You never know when you're going to run into the love of your life." She heads down the hallway. "For all I know, I could get a flat tire on the way there, and when I flag down someone for help, it could be the guy I'm supposed to fall in love with."

"Or the guy who's going to murder us and bury us in the woods," I say, following her. "Do you know how many scary movies start that way?"

She rolls her eyes as she collects her keys, purse, and phone from the kitchen counter. "Jesus, Isa. Why do you have to ruin my fun?"

"Just promise me you'll call a tow truck if we get a flat tire." I open the front door. "No flagging down cars . . ." I suddenly get the feeling I'm being watched. My hair stands on end, and my heart rate accelerates as I get a bad case of the heebie-jeebies.

"What's wrong?" Indigo asks as she steps out onto the porch and locks the front door.

My gaze skims the parking lot, the buildings, the trees, the street. "It's nothing . . . I just got the strangest feeling I was being watched."

She tosses the keys into her purse and zips it up. "Okay, I think I'm banning you from scary movies for a while. You're seriously getting paranoid."

"It's not that." I scratch at the back of my head, trying to figure out why I feel this way. No one's around. Even the parking lot is almost completely bare. "Sorry. I think

I'm just really tired, and this blue car thing has me on edge."

"Totally understandable. And, like I said before, when Grandma Stephy gets home, we'll tell her about the car, but honestly, I think it might've been either Hannah messing with you or just some freakish coincidence. This town is too small. I see the same cars all the time and the same annoying people."

Huh. I hadn't even thought about it being Hannah, but after how mad she was about Kyler and me hanging out, I wouldn't put it past her. Now, what she could be up to is another story.

"Hannah doesn't have a blue car, though, with a Superman sticker on it," I point out.

"So, she could've borrowed a car from one of her friends."

"Yeah. I guess so." Still, I can't see Hannah being friends with someone who would drive a car with a Superman sticker on it.

"Stop over-thinking everything." Indigo links arms with me and hauls me toward the car. "Come on. Let's go get your man candy."

I don't correct her about Kai being my man candy. I just follow her to the car and cross my fingers that we don't get a flat tire.

Chapter ELEVEN

ISABELLA

By the time we make it to Mapleview, it's almost ten o'clock. Indigo tells me I should probably text Grandma Stephy so she doesn't freak out when she gets home and we aren't there. I send her a text, but she doesn't reply.

"She's probably still on the plane," Indigo says, ashing her cigarette out the window. "When was her flight supposed to land?"

"I'm not sure. She said she'd be home by eleven, though."

"I hope her flight doesn't get delayed. She'll come home all cranky if it does." She slows down the car as the speed limit drops. "What road was this gas station on?"

I open the notepad app and tell her the address. "I think it's on the east side of town."

She flicks her cigarette out the window and focuses on the road. "This town is dead. Not a single store is open, and it's only ten o'clock on a Saturday night."

"Mapleview's like that," I tell her. "It's lower key than Sunnyvale."

She frowns at the stores bordering the street. All of them are closed up, the only lights coming from the lampposts. "It looks like a ghost town."

"It kind of is." I type the address into a map app so we can get directions. "I mean, people live here and everything, but it's the kind of place people live when they've done something shady or do stuff that's shady and don't want to be found."

"Then why's Kai here?"

"He probably was just visiting someone or something." But I know that's not true. He mentioned something about Big Doug getting him into this mess. I just wish I knew what kind of mess he was in. "Make a right off here." I point at a street sign.

Indigo does what I say and turns down the side road. The longer we drive, the sketchier the area gets: fewer lampposts line the streets; the stores turn into boarded up warehouses; and people have gathered in parking lots and street corners, doing God knows what. By the time I spot the gas station, I'm ready to grab Kai and say "peace out" to the town.

"There's his car." I point at it while unbuckling my seatbelt.

She pulls into the parking lot and parks next to Kai's car. That's when I notice the passenger side window is shattered, the hood is dented, and the headlights look cracked.

Indigo's eyes practically bulge out of her head as she takes in the condition of Kai's car. "Did he get in a wreck?"

"I have no idea." Panic sets in. What if he's hurt?

I jump out of the car and don't stop, even when Indigo shouts at me to wait a minute. By the time I fling the door open and stumble inside the gas station, I'm a nervous wreck, all wild-eyed and trying to catch my breath.

My gaze skims the gas station. I spot Kai sitting behind the counter at a table, playing poker with an older man, who's wearing a button-down shirt with the gas station logo on it.

"I think you might be cheating," Kai says to the man, glancing down at the cards he's holding.

"Quit whining and make your bet," the old man grumbles, "before I make you wait outside."

Kai adds a few red poker chips to a small pile in the middle of the table. "Yeah, yeah, you've said that, like, twenty times."

"Well, this time, I mean it," he growls. "Whatcha got? I bet nothing."

"Ha!" Kai lays down his cards. "A full—" He catches sight of me. "Hey, you made it."

"Of course I made it." I smile back, but my smile falters when I see the bruises and cuts on his face. One of his eyes is so swollen I wonder if he can see out of it. A cut runs along his hairline, dry blood dots his cheek, and his lip is puffy. "Holy crap, Kai! What happened to your face?"

"What? It doesn't always look like that?" the old man asks, smirking at Kai. "Is this that girl you were yammering about being in love with?"

Ummm . . . What?

Kai seems unbothered by what the man said, grinning as he scoots the chair away from the table and stands up. "Quit trying to get me in trouble," he tells the man then turns to me. "I'll explain the face thing in the car."

"Okay." I keep my eyes on him as he rounds the counter, trying to tell if he's injured anywhere else.

Blood stains dot his long-sleeved grey shirt and jeans, and his face looks horrible, but other than that, I can't see anything else.

"Are you okay? Did you get hurt anywhere else?"

"You and your questions." He tsks at me, seeming in an oddly good mood considering how beaten up he looks. "You're always so full of them."

I cross my arms. "You call me from an unknown number, ask me to drive out to Mapleview to a random gas station in the middle of nowhere, and your car is all messed up, not to mention so is your face, so questions are totally justifiable right now."

Humor dances in his eyes. "Am I in trouble?"

I have to work really hard to appear angry. "Yes. At least until you start explaining."

He starts to suck his lip between his teeth, but there's a small gash on it, and he winces. "Are you going to punish me if I don't?"

I feel a flush heating my cheeks. "How can you joke right now when it looks like your face got into a fight with a rock and lost big time?"

"Actually, it was a sumo-sized dude and a crowbar." His shoulders sag. "Look, I know I messed up, but joking is the only thing keeping me from losing it."

His honesty throws me off. Usually, Kai jokes about everything and hardly ever admits his true feelings.

"Do we need to get anything before we go?" I glance around the store. "Maybe some band-aids and an icepack?"

He cups his cheek with his hand, as if he's in pain. "An ice pack sounds nice."

"All right, let me grab some stuff, and I'll meet you in

the car." I start for the back of the store.

He trails behind me down an aisle. "I just got my ass mugged right outside, and that was in broad daylight, so I'm not about to let you wander around by yourself when it's dark."

I open the freezer door and grab a bottle of water. "Mugged by a sumo wrestler?"

"I know it sounds crazy, but it really happened." He dazes off, looking like he doesn't quite believe it himself. "I walked away from my car for, like, five seconds, and this guy shows up, breaks my window, steals . . . something out of my car, then hits me over the head with a crowbar. I blacked out, and when I woke up, my car was all jacked up. He even destroyed the battery and slashed the tires. Stupid crazy bastard."

A few things run through my mind at once, but the biggest thing that stands out is, "He hit you over the head with a *crowbar*?" I reach for his head. "Do you have a concussion?"

"I'm not sure." He squints his eyes as my fingers brush across his hairline. "What does a concussion feel like?"

"I don't know. I've never had one before." Okay. Now I'm really starting to get worried. "I think we should take you to the hospital."

"No," he says firmly. "No hospitals. No doctors. My parents can't know about this."

"They're going to find out when you show up, looking like that." I gesture at his face.

He touches the corner of his eye and winces. "I know it's bad, but I can't tell them. They already . . . my dad . . . I'm not going home. I'll just crash at Big Doug's house or something until my face heals." He doesn't seem too thrilled about that idea, though.

"That could take at least a week. Won't your mom and dad get mad when you don't come home for that long?" Isn't that what normal parents do?

"They won't care," he says. "They'll be glad I'm not there."

I remember the night I saw Kai's dad yell at him and smack him on the back of the head. While it wasn't very hard, it still didn't sit right with me. It makes me wonder if that's why he doesn't want to go home. Perhaps he's worried his dad will hit him or something. And then there's that thing Kyler said in the car about how his dad wants him to play sports. Clearly their dad's a demanding guy, the complete opposite of my barely-there father.

I think about how scared I was to go home last night, how Kai stayed up and watched movies with me, and how we ended up falling asleep on the couch together when I thought I wasn't even going to be able to sleep at all.

"You can stay with me if you need to."

"At your grandma's house?"

"She won't care. She's nice. She'll probably make you sleep on the couch, but it's pretty comfortable. And she makes breakfast in the morning."

As he considers my offer, a series of emotions flash across his face: hesitancy, confusion, gratitude, and ultimately, hilarity. "Are you going to sleep on the couch with me?"

I roll my eyes. "No. You have to be a big boy and sleep all by yourself."

He juts out his lip, sulking. "But I slept on the couch with you. Doesn't that mean you have to return the favor?"

I smash my lips together to keep from smiling and encouraging him more. "I'll return the favor another time.

My grandma's cool and everything, but not that cool."

Grinning, he reaches forward and traces his finger down the brim of my nose. "I'm going to make sure you follow through with that."

His touch makes me feel like a swallowed a jaw full of very alive, very excited butterflies. All from a freakin' touch.

Afraid my voice will come out all wobbly, I say nothing and search the store for an icepack. I end up settling on a cup full of ice and grab a couple of napkins to clean up the blood with. The band-aids are a no go, so I pick up a couple of candy bars and a soda, hoping a little sugar rush might help him feel better.

After we pay, he waves good-bye to the cashier, and then we head out to the car. Kai grabs a thin folder and his jacket out of his car before sliding into the backseat of my Grandma Stephy's car.

Indigo rotates around in the seat, takes in the sight of his face, and her jaw drops. "Whoa. You look like shit."

"Gee, thanks," he says dryly then sighs. "But seriously, thanks for coming and picking my sorry ass up. It was really cool of you."

"No worries." Indigo starts the engine. "You're okay, right?"

"I am now." He wiggles around, knocking his back against the seat. "I think this seat is busted." He reaches over and fiddles with a latch, folding the back of the seat forward and peering into the trunk. "Your grandma really needs to get this fixed."

"She won't," I say, sliding into the seat beside him. "She'll say it's old and has character and that fixing it would be ruining it."

Kai shoves the seat back, his eyes landing on me. "You don't have to sit back here with me. I promise I can handle sitting by myself for a couple of hours without getting into trouble."

"I don't know about that. You're kind of a handful." I set the bag of stuff I bought onto the floor and pull the door shut. "I'm going to try and clean up your face, okay?"

"Aw, my very own naughty nurse." He presses a hand against his chest. "I've always wanted one of those."

Indigo giggles as she drives out of the parking lot. "I forgot how adorable he is."

"Don't encourage him," I warn her. To Kai, I say, "I'm not your naughty nurse. I'm just trying to get you bandaged up, and then I'll try to see if I can find info about concussions."

He rubs his lips together, suppressing a smile. "Don't ruin my fun. Right now, I'm totally picturing you in a tight, short, white dress." His gaze drags up my legs. "With knee-highs that go all the way up those long legs of yours. It looks really good on you, by the way."

Tingles spill across my skin, but I quickly shrug them off. I'm not sure whether to be happy he's in a good mood despite everything going on or worried that maybe it's a concussion making him act like this.

"Lean back in the seat," I instruct as I dig out the napkins and water. "I'm going to clean the blood off your face. Then you can press one of the soda bottles to your cheek while I do an internet search on concussions. Whatever you do, don't go to sleep, though. I think I remember reading something in health class about needing to stay awake after a concussion or something."

He pouts. "What if I'm tired, though?"

I wag a finger at him. "I don't care if you're tired. Keep your eyes open. If I even so much as see them starting to shut, I'll pinch you."

He lifts his hand to cover his mouth and hide his smile. "You're cute when you're bossy."

I suck a discreet inhale through my nose, trying to remain nonchalant. But I can't help thinking about Kyler and how, earlier today, he called my freckles cute. While I know Kai's just messing around with me, it still feels uncomfortable to have both of them call me cute in the same day.

After I settle my breathing down, I twist the lid off the bottle of water and pour a couple of drops onto a few napkins. "So, are you going to tell me what you were doing out in Mapleview?" I gently press the napkin to a dried spot of blood on his cheek.

He flinches but doesn't move his head, keeping his eyes trained on me. "I was doing something for Big Doug."

"What kind of something?" I delicately run the napkin against his cheek, slowly moving it toward his jawline.

"Just something."

"Something sketchy? Because Mapleview doesn't have the best rep for being a good place for people to go to do good things."

"Are you judging me?" He hugs the folder to his chest like a teddy bear, looking hurt.

"What? God, no . . . I'm just worried about you." I inch closer to him, press a couple of fingers to his other cheek, and tilt his head so I can clean off the blood on the other side of his face. "This morning, when we were in the hallway, you started to tell me something bad was going on with you and that T guy, but you never got a chance to finish."

"Because Kyler interrupted," he grumbles, scowling.

"I know. I wish he wouldn't have. I wanted to—want to make sure you're okay."

"I'm okay." His gaze is so intense, so fixed solely on me, that my fingers tremble. "You guys hung out all day?"

I reluctantly nod. "Well, until about seven."

"What did you guys do?" he asks, not really sounding like he's sure he wants to know.

I shrug, turning on the ceiling light to get a better look at the cut on his forehead. "Played basketball for a little bit. Then we went to the football field and played flag football with his friends."

"Ew," Indigo says, and I realize she's been listening to our entire conversation. "Football? That's what you guys did all day?"

It makes me a tiny bit uneasy that she's paying so much attention to Kai and me. Indigo is too observant for her own good, and she's got a soft spot for Kai. She's determined Kai and I belong together, even though she's never met Kyler, and is very blunt about her opinion.

"It wasn't that bad. I even scored the winning touchdown." I examine Kai's face to make sure I got all the blood off.

As I'm leaning over him, he starts combing his fingers through my hair. The movement, while subtle, centers all of my attention there. I become hyperaware that his face is two inches from my neck, the warmth of his breath tickling my skin.

"Touchdown or not, it still had to suck balls playing with his friends. They're such dicks, and I know they've been mean to you in the past." He makes a face. "I bet they were super nice to you now, though, just like Kyler, because you're hot. They don't even know you, not like I know you," he murmurs, fixated on playing with my hair. "Your hair's so soft. It reminds me of velvet."

I sit back to get a good look at him. "I think I need to look up symptoms of a concussion."

"I'm fine," he insists, resting his head back against the seat and lowering his eyelids. "Totally . . . fine . . ."

Panicking, I pinch his arm.

His eyelids pop open, and he glares at me. "Ow. That hurt."

"I warned you I'd do it." I take out my phone. "Now keep your eyes open while I look this up."

"Yes, boss," he mumbles, resting his head on my shoulder.

Indigo catches my eye in the rearview mirror, and even though I can't see her mouth, I know she's smiling. Me, not so much. I'm starting to get worried. Kai's acting like he's drunk or something. Maybe he is. But he doesn't have alcohol breath or anything.

It takes me fifteen minutes of fighting with an in and out signal before I can pull up a useful webpage. I have to pinch Kai three times to keep him awake, and each time he responds, he makes less sense. Confusion is a symptom, and he's definitely confused. When I ask him questions about the last couple of hours, he can't even remember how he started playing poker with the cashier at the gas station.

"What about right after you were hit by that guy?" I ask him. "Can you remember what happened then?"

"Yeah, I blacked out for a minute, woke up, called you because I have your number memorized." He presses two fingers to his temple. "It's all up here. Every single number engrained into my mind . . . And I knew, if I called you, you'd help me without judging me." He strokes my cheek with his fingers. "You're so nice like that. Too nice, honestly. Too nice to be with me or my brother or anyone. No one's worthy."

At this point, his touches and rambling doesn't faze me. He clearly has a head injury, and while he doesn't want to go to the hospital, I'm not sure I feel okay with not taking him. Not knowing what else to do, I call Grandma Stephy.

"Where are you?" she asks the moment she picks up.

"Didn't you get my message?" I ask. "I left you one."

"Yeah, but it doesn't mean I'm just going to be okay coming home to an empty house after everything that happened today." She sounds mad. "And I tried to call you a ton of times, but your phone kept going to voicemail."

"Sorry." I feel bad for making her worry. "We were in Mapleview, picking up one of my friends who needed a ride. It was kind of a last minute thing. His car . . . broke down, and he was stuck there.

"Are you heading home now?" she asks, calming down.

"Yeah, we're about fifteen minutes . . ." I stammer over my words as Kai lies down and puts his head in my lap. "Um, yeah, we're about fifteen minutes out."

"Good," she says. "I don't like you being out this late, especially with everything going on."

I think about all the crazy stuff she let Indigo and me do while we were overseas. It doesn't make sense that she'd be worried about us being out late now.

"Is there something going on that I don't know about? Are my parents really not okay with me staying there?"

"What? No," she says. "I may omit the truth sometimes, but I'd never flat out lie to you."

I want to believe her—I really do—but considering she let me believe Lynn was my mom for all those years, I'm not completely convinced she's being one hundred percent truthful. I also know she would lie to me if she thought she was protecting me from something. But trying to get into it with her over the phone won't do any good, and I need to focus on the problem lying on my lap right now.

I give Kai's arm a soft pinch since he starts to drift to sleep again.

"Grandma, do you know anything about concussions?"

"Why?" she asks warily.

I explain to her how Kai was mugged and hit over the head with a crowbar, and now he refuses to go to the hospital because he's worried his parents will get mad at him. When she questions why he's so worried his parents will get angry with him, I don't know what to tell her.

"Was he not supposed to be in Mapleview?" she asks. "Did his parents not know he was out there?"

"I don't know." I look down at Kai lying on his side, his face nuzzled in my lap. I have the craziest urge to run my fingers through his hair, do the same thing he did to me just minutes ago. I restrain the urge, though, telling myself I don't have a concussion, so I don't have an excuse to touch him like that. "I think he just doesn't get along very well with his parents. I think he's just worried his dad will get mad at him for the car getting ruined and stuff."

"His dad sounds like an asshole," she says matter-of-factly. "If he got mugged, then it wasn't his fault."

"His dad is kind of an asshole. He kind of reminds me of Lynn, only not so out to get you. He's just kind of a mean, angry guy." Poor Kai. I absentmindedly slip a few fingers through his hair, but then quickly pull away. Whoa. What am I doing?

"Don't stop," he mumbles, reaching for my hand and moving it back on his head. "That feels so good."

I stare down at my hand with uncertainty. Should I do it? Isn't it weird?

"Just do it," Indigo urges. "He probably won't

remember it in the morning, so you won't have to worry about things being awkward, but he'll be grateful for it tonight."

Maybe not awkward for him, but I just spent the day with his brother and let him kiss me on the corner of my mouth. And now what? I'm going to sit back here with Kai and play with his hair? Isn't that crossing a line? But since he's hurt, I somehow rationalize that it's okay and lightly run my fingers through his hair.

It's so soft . . .

"Isa, what's going on?" Grandma Stephy says through the phone, startling me.

I completely forgot I was talking to her.

"Nothing." No, it's definitely something. "What should I do about the concussion? Do you think he'll be okay if I don't take him to a doctor?"

"I'm not sure. I don't know much about concussions." She pauses. "I have a friend who's a retired doctor. He lives a few buildings down. Let me give him a call and see if he's still awake. Maybe he can help us out."

I recline back in the seat with my fingers still in Kai's hair. "Thanks, Grandma."

"You can thank me by getting your ass home. I'll feel better when you're here."

Yeah, me, too, but mostly because I just want to make sure Kai's okay.

By the time I hang up, we're almost to the apartment complex. Kai still has his head on my lap when we turn into the parking lot, and I'm still combing my fingers through his hair. I don't know why, but I'm starting to find the movement almost as soothing as he does.

"Kai," I whisper as Indigo shuts off the engine. "We're here." When he doesn't respond, I talk more loudly, leaning closer. "Kai, we're at my grandma's house. You have to get up so we can go inside."

The only answer I get is the soft sound of his breathing.

"Kai." I pinch him. Nothing. Panic. Panic. Panic. "Kai, you have to wake up."

"I am awake," he groans. "So quit yelling."

Relief waves over me at the sound of his voice. "Come on. I'll help you walk in, but I can't carry you."

He rolls to his back, and his eyelids flutter as he opens his eyes. He blinks up at me, dazed and confused. "Where are we?"

"At my grandma's," I tell him. "Remember, I said you could stay here."

He doesn't seem to have a clue what I'm talking about but sits up, anyway. He remains quiet as he opens the door and stumbles outside into the cool night air. I hurry and hop out, chasing after him as he wanders across the grass, heading in the wrong direction.

"Nope, this way." I catch his arm and haul him in the opposite direction.

He follows me, blinking around at the surroundings, being strangely quiet for Kai. I don't relax when I get him inside. If anything, I freak out even more. In the light, he looks so much worse. His eyes are bloodshot, his expression dazed. Thankfully, my grandma's doctor friend is already there.

He's an older guy, probably in his seventies, with salt and pepper hair. He seems nice enough as he tells Kai to sit down on the sofa then pulls a chair up and asks him a series of questions. Kai answers the best he can. Then the doctor checks his reflexes. I decide to mention to the doctor that I think Kai also hurt his ribs so he'll check them out, too. I don't bother mentioning that it was from yesterday, because I don't even want to try explaining why Kai's getting beaten up so much. I couldn't even if I tried since Kai hasn't explained what happened yet.

"I'm sure he's fine," Indigo tries to reassure me.

"Yeah, I know." But I don't know for sure. I don't know much of anything anymore. I'm becoming the most clueless girl in the world. Isabella Anders, the clueless girl who doesn't know who her mother is, who plays with a guys' hair after she kind of, sort of kissed another guy, who's so worried sick right now she feels like she's going to puke.

Indigo offers me some cookies. "You need to eat."

I grab a handful and stuff them into my mouth, but I barely taste them. "I'll feel better when I know he's okay."

"I wonder why that is." Her accusing gaze bores a hole into the side of my head, but I refuse to look at her.

After the doctor finishes, he gets up from the chair and addresses Grandma Stephy. "He has a mild concussion, and that cut on his head might need a couple of stitches." He looks at me. "I tried to tell him he might need to get it taken care of, but he says he's fine. I don't have anything to stitch him up here, so I suggest trying to get him to go in the morning. As for the ribs, he may have broken one, but there's not much I can do for that. He'll just need to take it easy. He could go in and get an x-ray to confirm it, but that's about it."

I nod, but considering how adamant Kai was about not going to the hospital, I don't think I will be able to persuade him.

The doctor makes a list of symptoms to watch out for and says that, if he shows any signs of them, take him to the hospital right away. Then he gathers his stuff, and my Grandma Stephy walks him out.

Kai's gaze collides with mine from across the room and he pats the cushion beside him. "Come and sit with me and play with my hair some more." He seems more alert than he did in the car, but the wounds on his face are more prominent under the light.

When I dither, Indigo nudges me in the back with her elbow, shoving me forward. "Go and take care of your man candy."

I shoot her a dirty look, but she only laughs at me.

Shaking my head, I pad across the room and sit down on the chair beside Kai. "Do you need anything? The doctor said you could take a couple of painkillers, and I think my grandma might have an ice pack in the freezer."

He lies down and puts his head on my lap again. "I just want to rest like this."

"Is my lap that comfortable?" I joke, smiling down at him.

He bobs his head up and down, looking up at me, all serious and intense, like he gets sometimes. "It's better than a pillow."

"I highly doubt that."

"Ha. Then you clearly haven't rested in your lap before."

"That's kind of impossible."

"Maybe." He drapes his arm across his forehead, shielding his eyes from the light as he stares up at me. "You should try my lap, then. It might be as comfortable."

"How would we ever know for sure, though? It's not like we can compare."

"True. But I think we should at least try." He starts to sit up; I guess so I can lie on his lap.

I place my hand on his chest and guide him back down. "We can try that tomorrow. Tonight, you rest."

"You promise?"

"Promise what?"

"That tomorrow you'll put your head in my lap."

I think about how Indigo and the doctor said Kai

might not remember much about tonight. "Sure."

He smiles up at me. "You're so pretty, like seriously, gorgeous. I've thought that for a while."

Indigo chokes on a laugh, spitting pieces of cookie all over the carpet. "He's even charming when he's completely out of it."

He's more charming if you ask me, but even though he's kind of a flirt normally, he's never flat-out told me I'm gorgeous.

Unsure what else to say, I trace a line with my fingertip around the cut on his forehead. "You should listen to the doctor and go to get stitches. He said you could end up with a noticeable scar if you don't, and it'll take more time to heal."

He waves me off. "Scars are cool."

"Not on your face."

"Uh-huh. It shows you're tough, that you've done crazy stuff. And it helps you remember when you did that crazy stuff."

"Do you really want to remember the crazy stuff that happened tonight?"

His expression sinks. "Isa, I think I messed up." He reaches up, circles his finger around my wrists, and lifts my hand away from his face. At first, I think it's because I'm hurting him, but then he positions it on his scruffy, swollen cheek and sighs. "With this T guy . . . with what happened tonight . . . with the stuff I haven't told you yet . . ."

My forehead furrows. "What stuff haven't you told me?"

His lips part, his eyes flooding with worry, but before he can say anything, my grandma walks in. She takes one look at me and Kai on the sofa then shakes her head.

"All right, the boy sleeps on the couch," she

announces, pointing at the hallway. "Isa, you're sleeping in the back guestroom. You can set an alarm to come and check on him in a couple of hours." She snatches ahold of the handle of a suitcase propped against a wall near the door. "I'm going to go and take a shower. Isa, before you get into bed, you and I need to talk." With that, she walks out of the room, dragging her suitcase with her. Indigo starts to open her mouth, but before she can say anything, grandma calls out, "Indigo, give Isa a moment to kiss her cute boyfriend goodnight."

Indigo chokes on another mouthful of cookie while mortification sweeps across my face. Oh, my God, did she seriously just say that?

My embarrassment only amplifies when Kai chuckles. "She thinks we're dating," he singsongs with his eyes closed, sounding completely entertained by the idea. "And that I'm cute."

"She thinks everyone's cute," I tell him, wanting to crawl into a hole and die.

His eyelids slowly open, and he squints against the light as he focuses on my face. "Yeah, but does she think every guy's your boyfriend?"

I almost say, "Yeah, she does. She's said similar things about Kyler." Thank God, I manage to stop myself; otherwise, I would've made the situation even more awkward.

"You should let me up so you can get some rest," I tell Kai. "I'll come and check on you in a bit."

He grunts a protest but sits up and lets me off the sofa. I go to the linen closet and get him a blanket and a pillow. By the time I return, he's fast asleep on his side. I slip the pillow under his head and then cover him with a blanket before heading for the hallway.

Indigo is in the kitchen, getting a soda from the fridge. She looks up at me as I pass by. "That was sweet of you.

It kind of seems like something a girlfriend would do for her boyfriend."

I scowl at her but smile so she knows I'm not really mad. "I'm not going to just leave him there without a blanket. Grandma lets her house get super cold at night."

"That's because she has hot flashes." She pops the tab on the can of soda. "It gets really bad when Harry sleeps over. The two of them go at it like rabbits all night and then crank down the heater when they're done because they get too hot."

I cover my ears with my hands. "TMI."

She laughs, takes a sip of her soda, and then motions for me to follow her as she heads for her bedroom. "We better get to sleep. We're still going shopping tomorrow, even if you gripe that you're too tired."

"Maybe we should go next weekend when stuff's calmed down."

"Nope. I've got my heart set on a new pair of shoes, and my heart always gets what it wants." She slips an elastic off her wrist and twists her hair up in a messy bun. "Besides, the last thing you need to do is sit around in this house, thinking about stuff. You need to get out, and get some fresh air—breathe some Sunnyvale-free air."

"Fine, I'll go." I sigh. "But Kai's probably going to have to go with us since I told him he could stay here for a while."

"I'm completely fine with that. He seems nice and fun. Honestly, if he wasn't so in love with you, I'd probably try to date him."

I feel the slightest ping of jealousy at the idea of Indigo and Kai dating. "He's not in love with me." Although, according to the cranky, old man in the gas station, he is. But Kai probably had a concussion the whole time he talked to him and probably wasn't making a lot of sense.

"Are you being serious right now?" She stops in front of her bedroom door. "Because, if you are, then I've clearly taught you nothing." She points a finger toward the end of the hallway. "Take it from me, that boy's in love with you. All that stuff he said in the car . . ." She gets this swoony, goofy smile on her face. "Oh, my God, what I'd give for a guy to say something like that to me."

"He has a concussion. He didn't even know what he was saying."

"He might not remember what he said, but everything he did say tells me he's thought about you before: about knowing your number, about no one being good enough for you, about how gorgeous and amazing you are."

I squirm self-consciously. "I really don't think you're right." But deep down, a tiny part of me wishes she is. I don't know what to do with the feeling. Or if I should do anything with the feeling at all.

"Of course you don't because you're stupid fucking family stripped every ounce of confidence away from you." Her expression softens. "Sorry, I didn't mean for that to come out so rude."

"You weren't being rude. They've messed me up. I know that." I swallow the lump in my throat and turn toward the guest bedroom across from Indigo's. "I should probably get ready for bed then go and talk to Grandma, or else I'm going to get no sleep."

She sighs but lets me leave. When I get into the room, I close the door and recline against it. All I want to do is lie down in the bed and go to sleep, forget this day and yesterday ever happened. But I have a feeling these last twenty-four hours of revelations and stress are just the beginning.

After I pull on a tank top and a pair of red, plaid

pajama bottoms, I pad down the hallway and rap on Grandma Stephy's door.

"What're you knocking for?" she calls out. "Open the door and get your butt in here."

I twist the doorknob and enter. She's sitting on the foot of her bed, dressed in a matching shirt and bottom pajama set. A lamp is on and the door to the attached bathroom is open, allowing lingering steam to dampen the air.

"What did you want to talk to me about?" I ask. "Is it about Kai sleeping here? Because I didn't think it'd be that big of a deal."

She waves me off, patting the spot beside her. "I don't care about that. Although, I am curious how you ended up with him when you told me you were with Kyler this afternoon."

"It's a long story," I say through a yawn. "I'm glad you're cool with Kai staying here, though, because I kind of told him he could crash on the sofa for a week."

"Am I running a motel now?"

"I'm sorry. I know it's a lot—taking me in and letting Indigo live here—but he doesn't want to go home until his face heals, and I didn't want him to be homeless."

"He has nowhere else he can stay?"

I shrug, not wanting to lie to her but not wanting to tell her yes, either. For some reason, and I can't really explain why, I don't like the idea of Kai crashing at Big Doug's place. Maybe it's because whatever he was in Mapleview for had something to do with Big Doug. Or maybe it's because I'm not even sure where Big Doug lives. The only time I ever met him was in that rundown pool house, and the thought of Kai sleeping there wigs me out.

"I don't care if he stays here, just as long as he sleeps

on the couch and you sleep in the bedroom." She gives me a stern look.

Just what does she think is going to happen?

"You know he's just a friend, right?"

"Friend or not, I still don't want you two canoodling. He looks like the kind of guy who would do that."

"He's not as bad as he looks. He's just had a rough night. We all have those. I had one last night, and he was there for me."

She puts her interrogation face on, crossing her arms and staring me down. "What do you mean he was there for you? Did you sleep at his house last night?"

"No." The lie shows through my voice. "Okay, fine. I did, but nothing happened. We just watched movies until we fell asleep. It's not like I could go home."

"You could've called Indigo to come and get you," she says. "You can always call us, Isa, no matter what."

"I know that, but . . ." I shrug, unsure what else to say. "Kai helped calm me down, and I don't know . . . I didn't really think much about calling anyone else."

"Hmmm . . ." She presses her lips together, studying me closely.

Her scrutiny makes me all squirrely. What the hell is she looking for?

"Well, I'm glad you had someone there for you," she finally says. "But from now on, no more spending the night with boys, got it?"

I salute her. "Yes, ma'am. And thanks for letting me stay here. And Kai. And for calling your doctor friend and my parents. Really, just thanks for everything. I promise I'm going to make this up to you."

"Don't worry about that." She draws me in for a hug. "Right now, all I want you to do is worry about graduating high school and deciding which boy you want to date. I know it seems fun to date more than one, but trust me when I say it can get pretty complicated."

Great. Now she's got it in her head that I'm dating Kyler and Kai. I could argue with her, but I don't see the point. She'll just keep saying the same things until I agree with her, and I have bigger problems to worry about.

"About my dad." I lean back to look at her. "On the phone, you said his company was in trouble. What'd you mean by that?"

"I don't know the whole story, but I know they've been doing some iffy stuff, and now the company is under investigation. I threw it in his face on the phone because I knew it'd scare him enough to back off. The last thing he needs is police digging around in his personal life on top of his business." She smoothes her hand over my head. "I don't want you worrying about that stuff. Like I said, I just want you to focus on being a teenager."

"What about my mom? Lynn said she was dead, but I still want to find out more about her."

"We will. I have a friend who's a retired cop. He might know where we can start."

"Man, you have all sorts of awesome friends, don't you?"

"I'm telling you. These retirement communities are where all the cool kids go."

We trade a smile and a hug, and then she shoos me out of the room, telling me to get my butt to bed.

But I pause in the doorway and quickly tell her about the car I saw everywhere.

"What do you think about it?" I ask when I've finished telling her.

Her forehead creases as she shakes her head. "I'm really not sure, hon. It might just be Hannah trying to mess with you like Indigo said, but I think we should keep our eyes open and be extra careful. Don't go wandering off anywhere alone. If you do see it again, try to get the plate number."

"Why? Are you going to have your cop friend run the plates?" I'm partially joking, so it surprises me when she nods.

"Yep. I sure as hell am," she says. "If someone's harassing you, I'll track the bastard or bitch down."

I smile at that. "Love you, Grandma."

She fluffs a pillow, getting ready to climb into bed. "Love you, too, sweetie. I'm really glad you're here."

Her words warm my soul.

I head out of her room, feeling better than I did earlier today. Before I go to the guestroom, I check on Kai. He's fast asleep with the blanket kicked off, murmuring something about ninja kicking someone's ass. I giggle under my breath at how cute he looks then head to the guestroom and climb into bed.

As I lie there, trying to fall asleep, I tell myself everything will be okay, that I just need to do what my grandma says and focus on being a teenager. But in reality, I know there's no way I can do that, not with everything going on.

I'm afraid I won't ever find out who my mom really was. I'm afraid I will find out Lynn was right, that she was a terrible person who did terrible things and gave me up to my dad because she didn't want me anymore. I realize right then and there what might just be one of my greatest fears.

That my mother might have never wanted me.

Chapter TWELVE

KAI

I wake up to the smell of eggs and bacon. At first, I can't figure out where the hell I am. My mom used to cook breakfast, but she stopped when Kyler graduated because he was hardly ever there anymore.

"It's pointless to cook breakfast for just you and me," she told me when I griped about it. "And you know how much your father hates the smell of bacon."

So when the scent of bacon hits my nostrils, I'm like, *wait, where the fuck am I?* As I lay still with my eyes shut, I manage to figure out that I'm on a sofa in a house that doesn't seem to have a working heater and that the person in the kitchen is an older woman who likes to sing 90s rap songs while she cooks.

"What's up with the 90s flashback?" a girl asks. Her

voice is familiar, but I can't place a face with it.

"Hey, don't mock my music," the older woman retorts. "We all have our guilty pleasures, like you and those silly, little riddles you think are so funny but are really stupid."

Shit. Did I do something stupid last night, like go to a party and pass out on someone's couch? It kind of sounds like something I'd do, but I don't think it's what I did, especially when I was so worried about Isa . . .

Bits and pieces rush back to me. Mapleview. The hit over the head. My car getting messed up. Calling Isa. After that, things become blurry, but I remember being looked at by a doctor in Isa's grandma's house and playing with Isa's hair . . .

I open my eyes, slowly realizing where I am and why my head feels like it's been run over by a truck.

"Aw, good morning sunshine," Indigo, Isa's cousin, greets me from across the living room. "Feeling better?"

I sit up, wincing as my body groans in protest. "Kind of." I press my finger to my temple as my head pulsates in pain and dizziness overcomes me. "Where's Isa?"

Just behind her, an older woman I haven't met before stands near a stove. Her eyes shift from the pans to me. "My lovely granddaughter is in bed, sleeping, and we're going to let her sleep because she deserves it." Her tone is firm, her eyes hard, but I detect the slightest bit of amusement in her expression.

"I completely agree." I rub my eyes, planting my feet on the floor. "What time is it?"

Indigo leans back and checks the time on something in the kitchen. "It's after ten. Why?" Her gaze lands on me. "You got somewhere else to be?"

Umm . . . I'm not sure what to say. While I need to go and have a little chat with Big Doug and get my phone back, I don't have much else to do. But I'm not sure if they want me to leave or what.

"No. Not really." I put on my best charming grin. "Well, except for spend the day paying back Isa. I owe her big time." And I need to tell her about her mom. I just hope I can do it the right way, without her getting mad at me. Is there even a right way to break it to someone that their mom's in jail for murder?

"Good boy," Isa's grandma says to me, looking pleased. "That girl needs to be doted over. She's special, even if she doesn't realize it. She should be treated like a princess."

"Grandma Stephy," Indigo hisses under her breath. "Don't say shit like that. Isa would be so embarrassed right now if she heard you."

"I'm just saying what needs to be said." Her grandma flips over the bacon in the pan with a fork. "Besides, Isa can't get embarrassed over something she doesn't know about." She looks at me, waiting for me to agree with her.

I raise my hands up in front of me. "I won't utter a word."

"Good boy," she says again, making me feel like an obedient dog. "That's exactly what Isa needs."

Indigo wavers between being irritated and amused. "What's with you and trying to play matchmaker lately?" she asks her grandma. "Or should I say playing matchmaker for Isa? With me, you're always so anti-boyfriend."

Her grandma points the fork she's holding at Indigo. "You don't need any more boys in your life. You have enough."

"There's no such thing as enough boys." Indigo props her elbows on the countertop of the kitchen island. "That's like saying there's enough air."

"Or enough cheese in your eggs," her grandma says

as she sprinkles cheese to the eggs.

"No, there's definitely such a thing as enough cheese." Indigo glares at her. "So stop putting so much in."

"There's no such thing as enough cheese in eggs," her grandma quips. "You could put a whole damn block in there, and there'd still be room for more."

"Don't you ever put a block of cheese in any eggs I'm eating," Indigo warns, sinking onto a barstool.

"Why? Afraid your pipes are going to get backed up?" Her grandma sneers as the pans hiss.

I clear my throat, trying to cover up a laugh.

"No, that's *your* problem, not mine," Indigo says. "That's probably why you have to eat so much damn yogurt and bran flakes. To clear out all that cheese."

"Would you guys quit arguing? You're worse than an old, married couple," Isa mumbles as she trudges out of the hallway.

She's wearing her pajamas, and her hair's braided to the side. She doesn't have a drop of makeup on, so I get a clear view of those cute, little freckles she has on her cheeks and nose.

"Hey, I take that offensively, miss," her grandma scolds Isa but then grins. "Your grandfather and I rarely fought unless it was over the remote or who got to drive or who had to shovel the snow from the driveway . . ." Her grin broadens. "Okay, maybe you're right."

"I'm always right." Isa yawns, stretching her arms above her head. The tank top she's wearing rides up, revealing her stomach. "It's about time you learned that."

I subtly check her out, but apparently, I'm being obvious because Indigo gives me a you're-so-busted-buddy look.

I shrug and smile, giving her my best innocent look, and she laughs.

Isa's arms fall to the side, and she quickly turns around to see what Indigo's laughing at.

"Oh, you're awake." She chews on her thumbnail, seeming nervous for some reason. "When I came and checked on you a half an hour ago, you were so passed out that I thought you were gonna sleep all day."

"The bacon woke me up."

God, there's so much I want to say to her. I want to thank her a thousand times, hug her for taking care of me last night, kiss her just because. But with her grandma and cousin standing there, watching us, I feel too on the spot. I mean, I'm not shy or anything, but it's a conversation that I kind of want to have without an audience.

"Will you guys quit being so weird?" Isa begs her grandma and cousin. "He's not used to your sparkling personalities."

"Yeah, I'm not buying that." Her grandma throws a glance in my direction. "After some of the stuff he said last night, I'm guessing he's just as big a weirdo as us."

Okay, I can handle being called weird, but what the hell did I say last night?

"They're cool, Isa." I motion for her to come over to me. "Come and sit down by me. There's some stuff I need to talk to you about."

"He said that a lot last night, too," Indigo says, smirking at me. When Isa gives her a pleading look, she elevates her hands in front of her. "Fine. I'll shut my mouth." She wanders over to the fridge and starts digging around in it, disregarding her grandma's lecture about staying out of stuff.

"Hey." Isa winds around the coffee table and stops in front of me. "Sorry if they woke you up."

"They're fine. It's their house." When she doesn't sit down by me, I reach for her hand and pull her toward me. "Come here. You're too far away."

She's hesitant as she sits down, leaning away from me and keeping her eyes on the floor.

Shit. How bad did I mess up last night?

"Okay, I just want to apologize for whatever I did or said last night." I clear my throat. "I can't remember much, but I'm getting the feeling I might have been an ass."

"You weren't an ass." She nudges her shoulder into mine, giving me a small smile. "And even if you were, you had a concussion, so anything you did totally didn't count."

I frown, touching my head. "Fuck. I almost forgot about the concussion." I let my hand fall to my lap. "How bad do I look right now on a scale of one to ten?"

"I don't know . . ." She bites her bottom lip, mulling it over. "I mean, you always look good. Everyone knows it. You know it." She grows flustered. "Why are you asking me this?"

She's seriously so adorable right now I almost can't stand it. It takes all of my willpower not to reach out and brush my finger across her flushed cheek.

"Technically, I meant how bad does my face look, but it's good to know I always look good." I wink at her. "And that you think so."

"Oh, my God." Her cheeks turn bright red as she lowers her head, letting her hair fall forward and hide her face. "I'm tired, okay? Can you just forget I said that?"

"No way. You can't take it back." My mouth turns upward into a smug smile. "Once you say something like that, it'll always be there for me to replay over and over again. And trust me; I will replay it over and over again."

"I'm sure you will." She grimaces, tucking a strand of hair behind her ear. The movement sparks a memory of last night—me . . . lying on her lap . . . playing with her hair . . . telling her she's gorgeous.

Okay, maybe that's why she's acting uncomfortable.

It seems like maybe I should feel bad for making her feel that way, but I don't. The only thing I regret is that I wasn't very coherent when I put my head on her lap and ran my fingers through her hair. I can't even remember what it felt like.

I almost reach over and sweep her hair away from her face, but out of the corner of my eye, I catch her grandma watching us like a hawk.

"So, are you going to tell me what you were doing out in Mapleview?" Isa asks, changing the subject. "You weren't really clear about that last night. I mean, you said a couple of things about Big Doug, but nothing specific."

I scratch my chin. "It's kind of a long story."

"Well, we've got all day." She bites back a smirk. "Because you and I are going to the city to go shopping with Indigo."

I arch a brow. "Oh, we are, are we?"

She nods, grinning. "Which means we'll have plenty of time in the car for you to tell me *everything*."

By everything, I'm pretty sure she means the thing with T, too. I hate the idea of telling *everything*. Knowing Isa, she's going to want to help me, and I don't want her getting involved. I probably shouldn't have even called her last night. But her number was the only contact in my phone I have memorized.

"You're not thinking about lying to me, are you?" Isa suddenly asks, eyeing me over suspiciously. "Because you have this look on your face like you're trying to think of some bull crap story to tell me."

"No . . . It's not that."

"Good. Because I want you to trust me."

"I do trust you." And I really fucking do, more than anyone.

What Isa did for me last night—offering to pick me up then getting a doctor to come here and look at me because I was being a pain in the ass and refusing to go to the hospital—was one of the most kind, caring things someone has done for me. She's so damn amazing, more than I think she realizes.

"Good, because I trust you, too." The smile that lights up her face makes me feel like an asshole.

I think about the talk Big Doug and I had yesterday and how I still haven't told Isa about her mom. I don't know when the right time is or if there's a right time. What I do know is that the longer I wait, the worse it's going to be. It might be time to just tell her while she's here with her grandma and cousin—a whole support system. Although, I sort of want to see what's in the folder Big Doug gave to me. He said it might be helpful. It might be able to soften the blow.

"Did I by chance bring a folder with me?" I ask. God, I hope I didn't leave it in my car that doesn't have a window. My car that I have no clue what to do with. *I'm in such a mess.*

Isa nods. "Yeah, you had it in the car with you last night. I think you left it in there. Do you need to go and get it?"

Nodding, I stand up. The room spins around me as the blood rushes from my head, and I sway sideways.

It must scare Isa or something, because she jumps to her feet, and her fingers fold around my arm.

"Kai, the doctor said to take it easy. You have to move slowly and don't overexert yourself." Taking ahold of my hand, she positions herself in front of me and looks me in the eye. "I'll go and get your folder. You stay here and get something to eat."

"No, I need to get it."

"Why?"

"Because . . ." I struggle for words, knowing once I say them, it's going to break her. I'm going to have to be the one to break her. "Walk with me out there, okay?"

I can tell she senses something is wrong, because she doesn't press.

Gripping onto her hand, I head for the door. She walks beside me as we step outside. When the cool morning air makes her shiver, I untangle my fingers from hers to take off my jacket and offer it to her.

"Aw, look at you and your gentlemen skills," she jokes, putting on my jacket. "If my grandma saw this, she'd probably try to marry us on the spot. She loves guys who act like a gentleman."

"I could live with that. In fact, it might be a dream come true." I wink at her, drape an arm around her shoulders, and guide her toward the parking lot.

"Ha! You're such a liar," she says, pointing a finger at me. "That's more like your worst nightmare."

"Quit being a little weirdo. You're not worst nightmare material. That's on the level of marrying someone like, say, Hannah." I purposely drag my gaze up and down her body. "You'd make a pretty hot wife."

She rolls her eyes then looks away, either to hide a smile or a blush.

"Speaking of Hannah." She returns her attention to me. "What happened two summers ago? Because I've been dying to ask you. She looked so worried when you said that to her yesterday, so I know it has to be something bad."

Two summers ago . . . It was such a shitty summer for the most part. My dad spent a lot of time pissed off at me because I wasn't spending enough time working out for the upcoming season, at least not as much as Kyler was.

"I don't get it," he said to me. "I don't get how one of my son's can be so lazy, while the other one is so motivated."

Lazy meant working out five days instead of seven, and the only reason I wasn't doing seven is because I got a part-time job to save up some money for a car. That didn't matter in his eyes. In his eyes, I should've still been able to work out seven days and keep the job.

Toward the end, though, when Hannah accidentally revealed a secret, things weren't so bad, mostly because I knew the secret could become useful one day.

I smile at the memory. "I'll tell you." But then my smile vanishes. "But I have to tell you something else first, something important."

"Is it about T?"

I move my arm from her shoulder to hold her hand. "It's actually something about you . . . or, well, your mom."

Her hand trembles in mine. "It's bad, isn't it?"

Worried what she might do when I break the news to her, I grasp her hand for dear life. "Maybe."

Confusion swirls in her eyes. "What do you mean maybe? Either it's bad or it's not."

She's starting to panic, which makes me want to take it all back, tell her I was joking, that I found out nothing. I want to lie to avoid breaking her heart, but I hate lying, and I know she would hate me if she ever found out.

"At first, it seemed bad." I pull her closer to me. "But then Big Doug gave me another file yesterday and said it might not be as bad as he originally thought."

Her confusion deepens. "Wait, how long have you known about this?"

"For two days. I was actually heading to tell you when I found you crying on the sidewalk. I wanted to tell you then, but you were so upset and I . . . I just didn't want to hurt you more."

I'm uncertain how she's going to take it. I'm sure some people would get angry for not telling them the second they found out. Isa doesn't seem angry, though, just worried.

"Are you okay?" I ask, tucking a strand of her hair behind her ear with my free hand.

"I don't know." Her bottom lip quivers. "You haven't told me what it is yet."

God, I wish I weren't the one who had to do this to her. No, I wish what Big Doug found out weren't true. I wish she had a normal life with a great family who knew how amazing she is.

I summon a deep breath. "Your mom's in jail, Isa."

Her eyes snap wide as she instinctively jerks back, but I tighten my hold on her hand.

"For what!" she shouts, flinching at the loudness of her voice.

I swallow hard. "For murder charges."

I expect her to yell some more. Freak out. Panic. Instead, she does nothing except stand there, staring at the road. It might be even worse than yelling. At least with yelling, I know how she's feeling. But this . . . I have no clue what she's thinking.

"I know it sounds bad," I say when the silence becomes maddening. "But the folder Big Doug gave me . . . He said it might not sound as bad as it seems and that she's getting an appeal. I don't know all the details, but I think we should go and look at what's in the folder."

She shakes her head, tears pooling in her eyes. "No wonder my dad hates me. He probably thinks I'm going to turn out like her."

"Don't ever fucking say that!" I snap, instantly feeling bad for losing my cool with her. I gently pull on her arm, tugging her closer to me. It's so unexpected she stumbles forward. I seize the opportunity to circle my arms around her and trap her against me. She's stiff in my arms, but I don't let her go. "Whether your mom did it or not, your dad doesn't have any right to treat you like shit. Your mom made the mistake, not you." I cup her chin and tilt her head up, forcing her to look at me. "And you are the most kind, caring person I've ever met. You've put up with so much crap, and yet you're still so amazing. Don't let this change that, okay?" My voice is firm and demanding.

She shakily nods her head. "I just don't know how to feel . . . this is . . . I didn't expect this."

"I know. But I think we should go and look at what's in that folder before we do anything else, okay?"

An uneven breath slips from her lips. "Okay."

I relax a little. At least she's being cooperative.

I move back, take her hand, and hike across the grass toward the parking lot. She grasps on to me the entire way to the car, like I'm the only thing keeping her from falling.

Still holding her hand, I maneuver the door open, and then panic immediately sets in.

"There's nothing in there. Are you sure I brought it with me?"

"Yeah. I remember you took it out of the car before we left the gas station." She unlaces her fingers from mine and nudges me aside so she can climb in the backseat. She searches the car before hopping out with a puzzled look on her face. "I know you had it. You were hugging it like a teddy bear for most of the drive."

"Then where'd it go?"

"I don't know . . . Maybe Indigo took it in the house." Her voice wobbles with anxiety.

"Let's go find out." I grab ahold of her hand again, hoping it might help calm her down as we head back inside the apartment.

The moment we step foot in the door, Isa asks Indigo and her grandma if they took the folder. Both of them shake their heads.

"I remember Kai having it in the car," Indigo says, setting a plate of eggs and bacon down on the table. "But I'm pretty sure he never brought it in with him."

"Why? What was in it?" their grandma asks, pulling out a chair at the table.

"Something important." Panic fills Isa's eyes as she helplessly looks at me. "You don't think someone took it, do you?"

"I don't know who'd take it." I yank my fingers through my hair. "Maybe the car was broken into and someone took it, thinking it was something else."

"What?" their grandma drops her fork and scowls at Indigo. "How many times have I told you to lock up my car? I have CDs and shit in there that are irreplaceable."

"Irreplaceable because they no longer make CDs," Indigo retorts. "And would you chill? I do lock up the car. And I know for a fact I locked it last night."

"It was unlocked just barely," Isa utters quietly. "Don't worry, Grandma Stephy; nothing else is missing. Your CDs are still in the console."

"So, the only thing missing was the folder?" I ask.

That's weird. Like, really weird. First the envelope yesterday and now this? Why do I have an unsettling feeling it's not a coincidence?

Isa fidgets with the bottom of her shirt. "That's weird,

right? That someone would take that?"

"Yeah, very weird." What the hell was inside the folder? I need to get ahold of Big Doug and find out.

"I think you guys are forgetting the most important part," Indigo says, rising from her chair. "How did someone unlock the car when we're the only ones with a set of keys?"

Isa bites on her fingernails, staring off into space.

I remove her fingers from her mouth and lace them through mine to keep her from chewing off her fingernails. "I have an idea."

I just hope they don't judge me over how I know.

Chapter THIRTEEN

ISABELLA

I feel so lost as Kai leads me outside and toward the car with Grandma Stephy and Indigo trailing at our heels.

Lost.

It's all I feel.

Not angry. Not sad. Not hurt.

Just lost.

Nothing makes sense. And I mean, nothing: myself, my life, everything around me. I feel like I'm floating, like my body has somehow remained on the ground, and my feet are moving, but my mind has soared away to the sky where it can sit and try to process what Kai just told me. But there's too much to process, too many questions running through my mind at once.

My mom is in jail for murder.

My mom is a murderer?

My mom's alive, but I probably won't ever see her again.

Lynn was right; my mom is a bad person.

Does that make me a bad person?

"I wish someone would explain to me what's going on," Grandma Stephy says when we reach her car. She puts on a pair of sunglasses and crosses her arms as she inspects the outside of the car. "Why is this folder so important?"

Kai gives me a sidelong glance, his eyes conveying a silent question: *are you going to tell her?*

I will eventually. I just need a few minutes to sort through my thoughts.

Kai's fingers leave mine as he circles the car. Indigo moves a few feet away to light up. I want to clutch Kai's hand because it was making me feel a tiny drop better, but I don't know how to go about it without getting insinuating looks from my grandma and Indigo. Plus, the clinginess might weird out Kai.

After Kai checks around the outside of the car, he stops near the trunk. With his arms folded, he leans forward and squints at the lock. His eyes light up as he reaches forward and pops open the trunk.

"What the hell?" Grandma Stephy walks over beside him. "How'd you do that without the key?"

"The lock was busted." Kai dusts off his hands. "Trunks are actually a little bit easier to break into than doors."

She purses her lips. "And how would you know that?"

Kai shifts his weight, scratching at the back of his neck. "Um . . . A lucky guess?"

"Don't play dumb with me, young man." But she drops the reprimand and points at the trunk. "But how'd they get from the trunk to the backseat."

Kai leans forward to examine the inside of the trunk. "I'm guessing the seat wasn't latched. It wasn't last night if I'm remembering right."

Through the back window of the car, I see the top of the backseat fold forward.

"The latch has been broken for a while," Grandma Stephy admits when Kai stands upright. "I've been meaning to get it fixed, but honestly, I think it ruins the car's character."

Kai glances at me, and I shoot him an I-told-you-so look.

I move between the two of them. "Why would anyone think to break into a trunk and climb through the back when you could just break the window, though?"

"It's more inconspicuous." Kai's gaze drifts to the ceiling of the carport. "Especially if there's people or cameras around. You can make it look like you're getting something out of the trunk or like you locked your keys in the car."

Again, my grandma shoots him a harsh look, but Kai ignores it, his attention locked on a camera mounted on the corner of the ceiling of the carport.

"Those are all over the community," my Grandma Stephy says. "They put them up only a couple of months ago after we had a couple of break-ins.

"The person who broke in probably saw them." Kai's gaze travels from the cameras to the trunk. "With the trunk open, they could easily hide what they were doing from the cameras."

"But why would anyone go through that much trouble just to get a folder?" I fan my face as a cloud of Indigo's cigarette smoke laces the air around me.

She's been so quiet the last couple of minutes, relieving her stress by feeding her nicotine addiction. I wish I had something that would help me, something that would calm me down. I think about putting my hand in Kai's again, but I can't find the courage to do so.

"Well, that all depends." Grandma Stephy faces me and crosses her arms, staring me down. "What was in the folder?"

I don't know why, but I glance at Kai, like somehow he's going to help me get out of telling her. I'm not ready to tell yet, not ready to say it aloud.

Kai's not on the same page as me, though. He looks at me sympathetically as he mouths, *I think you should tell her.*

I scowl at him and mouth back, *traitor.*

The corners of his lips quirk.

"Isabella Anders." Grandma Stephy's voice rings with a warning. "Stop looking at your gentleman friend and just tell me what's going on." Her tone softens a smidgeon. "I know you've been going through a tough time the last month or so, but I promise you that, whatever it is, even if you've gotten yourself into some kind of trouble, I'm here for you. But I can't help you unless you tell me what it is you need help with."

I massage my temples with my fingertips, feeling a headache coming on. I know she's right. She can't help me if I don't tell her. Still, it's hard to get the words past my lips, because once they do, they become very real.

Knowing I'm stronger than this, I suck in a deep breath and rip off the band-aid. I tell her what Kai found out about my mom and how the folder contained some sort of information about why she was in jail. By the time I'm finished explaining, my chest feels like it's being crushed. It's hard to get any oxygen into my lungs.

"Isa, you need to calm down," my Grandma Stephy says as I gasp for air. She places a hand on my shoulder. Her fingers are shaking. She's scared. Of me? "I think you might be having a panic attack, hon."

I hunch over, bracing my hands on my knees. "I'm fine . . . I just need a moment."

Air in. Air out. Air in. Air out. Your mom's. A murderer. She killed. Someone. No wonder. No one. Wants you.

"Isa."

I feel another hand on my back and fingers delicately sketch up and down my spine.

"Take a few breaths," Kai says as he wraps an arm around my back. He says something quietly to my Grandma Stephy then urges me to walk with him.

Sucking in an inhale, I stand upright and walk with him. "I don't know what's wrong with me . . . My chest just hurts so bad."

"I think your grandma's right. You're having a panic attack." His voice is quiet, cautious, like he's afraid loudness might cause me to break.

"Where are we going?" I whisper as he guides me away from the apartments and toward the road.

"For a walk."

"For a walk?" That's it?

He looks at me curiously. "What? You act like that's weird or something. We used to do it all the time, remember? Just go for walks to the park. Sometimes, we'd even walk around the park. It always made me feel better."

I wet my dry lips with my tongue. "Really?"

"Yeah. It was the only time I ever felt calm in life. I always tuned out everything and just focused on being me."

"That's kind of sad. I mean, that it only happened for

you when we walked."

"I know, but it was my own damn fault. I let things get that way."

We reach the edge of the apartment complex, and I think we're going to turn around, but instead, he looks left then right before threading his fingers through mine and jogging across the road.

Just across from us is a bare field at least a mile long and surround by a short, wooden fence. When we get to the fence, he releases my hand to hoist himself over. Then he offers me his hand.

I point to a sign hanging on the fence. "It says no trespassing."

"Since when do you care about the rules?" He waggles his brows at me. "Come on, Isa, you know you want to be a rule breaker."

"No, I don't," I say but take his hand anyway.

After he takes my hand, I swing my leg over the fence. Then he helps me down even though we both know I'm not the kind of girl who needs help getting over a fence. Once I get my feet planted on the ground, we start across the grassy field toward a line of trees at the back of the property. Neither of us say anything for a while. The only sounds surrounding us are the soft lull of a gentle breeze and the crunching of the dry grass beneath our shoes.

"Feeling better?" he asks me after a minute or two goes by.

I nod. "A little bit."

"Good." He slings an arm around me and winces. He wraps his free arm around his midsection and cradles the side with the possible broken rib. "I've had a couple of panic attacks before. Fresh air and moving usually helps."

"You've had panic attacks?" I ask, stunned. Kai? Joking, finds-humor-in-everything Kai?

"Not really anymore, but when I was younger, I did."

"What caused them?" The wind kicks up and blows strands of my hair into my face.

His jaw clenches. "It's a long story, one I don't want to get into right now."

I pick a few strands of hair out of my mouth. "You say that a lot."

"I know."

"Kai, you know you can tell me things, right? We spend all this time talking about me, and I feel like we never talk about you."

He flashes me a grin. "That's because I'm not nearly as exciting as you."

"Ha. You are, too. I know you have this really exciting life that you never talk about with me."

"It's not really that exciting."

"You got a concussion from a guy last night that was the size of a sumo wrestler." I count down on my fingers. "There's this thing going on with T that I haven't quite figured out yet, but I know he's the reason you probably have a broken rib. And don't even get me started on Big Doug."

His brow arches. "What's wrong with Big Doug?"

"Nothing, other than the fact that he somehow knows how to look up records on people. Plus, he had all those computers . . . I'm guessing he does some sketchy, probably illegal stuff." When he doesn't argue, I add, "How did you meet him, anyway?"

He shrugs, staring down at the ground.

I sigh. "Let me guess. Another long story."

He halts in the middle of the field, pulling me to a stop with him. "I know you think I'm keeping stuff from you, and I am, but only because I don't want to drag you into my mess."

"But you almost told me about what's going on with you and T."

"Yeah, but only because I was feeling vulnerable."

"About what?"

He gives me a meaningful look that I can't quite decipher. "Just stuff."

I pout my lips. "You have to give me something. Please. Anything to distract me."

He stares at my jutted lip, seeming torn over something. "Want to hear what happened between Hannah and me two summers ago?" He forces his attention away from my lips and his gaze settles on my eyes.

I still prefer he tell me what's going on with T, but I nod. "I guess if that's all you'll give me, I'll take it."

He starts walking toward the trees again, keeping his arm around my shoulder. "So, we were at this party, and Hannah was really drunk, like seriously, one step away from puking all over the place."

I almost smile. "I like this story already."

"Oh, it gets even better." He hops over a large rock in his way and bumps into me in the process. "Sorry," he says, steadying himself by putting his hands on my hips.

When his fingertips slip just under the hem of the jacket and lightly brush against my skin, a shudder rolls through me. I can tell he feels it, too, by the way he stares at me in confusion yet curiously. It's crazy that my body can still react like this when my mind's lost in a living nightmare.

Thankfully, Kai gives me another free pass and doesn't remark about the moment. Instead, he threads his fingers through mine, turns us around, and begins hiking toward the fence.

He's been holding my hand a lot this morning, and I'm confused over whether I should let him or not. I mean, we used to hold hands back in seventh grade when we were friends, but this feels different. Could it be because we aren't kids anymore?

"So, Hannah is super trashed and hitting on everyone," he continues. "And when I say everyone, I mean, *everyone*. She even hit on the mom of the guy who was throwing the party."

My eyes widen. "Holy freakin' unicorns."

He chuckles, swinging our interlaced hands as we walk. "In her defense, though, she thought the mom was the dad."

"Did she look manly or something?"

"No, Hannah was just that trashed."

"Does she always get that trashed at parties?"

"She drinks a lot, but I've never seen her that trashed before," he says. "That night, something was bothering her."

"Really?" I'm not completely buying it. "Because Hannah usually never gets bothered by stuff."

"She doesn't, huh?" He cocks an eyebrow at me. "Like yesterday morning when she had a shit fit because Kyler blew her off for you?"

"He didn't blow her off for me," I reply. "She asked him to do something a couple of days before Kyler and I even made plans."

"Um, no, she didn't," he says. "Didn't you listen to what Hannah said?"

"Honestly, I tune her out a lot." The wind kisses my cheeks, and I rub my hand across them, trying to warm them up. "It's kind of a habit."

"And it's a good habit to have." He traces his thumb across the knuckles of the hand he's holding. "But I'm telling you, I know my brother, and he blew her off because he was hoping your date would go great. And by great, I mean into-the-next-day kind of great."

It takes a second to process his full meaning. "No, he didn't." My voice sounds like a mouse. "He wouldn't do that."

He gapes at me like I'm a mad woman. "Yes, he would. It's what he does, Isa. He's a player. You've watched him for, like, forever. You should know that."

"He's not a player. He's just . . ." But I'm not sure what word fits Kyler. Yes, he flirts. Yes, he's had girlfriends. Yes, he talked to me yesterday about how he's hooked up with girls he didn't really know. "He might've in the past, but I know for a fact that he wants to take things slow."

His gaze bores into mine. "Did he tell you that?"

I nod. "He said he wanted to take things slow, and I know he was telling the truth because he wouldn't even kiss me on the lips."

He grinds his teeth. "But he kissed you somewhere else?"

Crap. "Um . . . Kinda of . . . I mean, he kissed me beside my lips . . ." God, this is so awkward. I should've just lied and said no.

Kai grows quiet. I can't tell if he's irritated, upset, mad, confused, or what.

"You want me to finish the story?" he asks quietly.

I nod, more than relieved to get away from the subject of Kyler almost kissing me. "Yes, I'm dying to hear if she ended up kissing the mom."

"She tried, but the mom wasn't having any part of it, so she moved on to the dad and the guy holding the party, his friends, their friends, pretty much everyone."

"Did anyone kiss her back?"

"A couple of people," he says. "But a lot of them blew her off because she was too drunk."

"I know this kind of makes me a bad person," I say,

"but I like the idea of her getting rejected."

"It doesn't make you a bad person. In fact, I'm pretty sure you could never be a bad person." He squeezes my hand. "You don't have a bad bone in your body."

A couple of days ago, I may have agreed with him, but right now, I can't quite convince myself that I am.

"So, what happened?" I refuse to let myself think about my mom too much; otherwise, I'll drown in the thoughts. "Did she go home alone?"

He stops in front of the fence but doesn't climb over. "No, she actually went home with me."

A sudden, crazy, irrational possessiveness overcomes me. Hannah went home with Kai? Hannah's been with Kai? Kai? My friend Kai? No! The idea makes me maddeningly jealous. I don't know why. He's just my friend. But him being with her . . . like that . . . Ugh. My stomach aches just thinking about it.

"Not like that," he says, as if reading my mind. "Kyler made me take her home after the guy throwing the party said she was too drunk and being annoying."

My jealousy simmers down. "Why did he make you take her home?"

"Because his friends told him to make me," he replies with a shrug. "Because I was the youngest. They did shit like that all the time, and if I argued, they'd make my life a living hell."

What he says makes me wonder if that's why he went from popular athlete to bad boy stoner. But before I can ask, he leans against the fence and continues on with the story.

"But, anyway, I took her home like I was supposed to. Only, when I parked the car in the driveway, she wouldn't go inside. I asked her if she needed help and she said yes. Then she tried to kiss me," he says. "When I leaned out of the way, she started to cry then threw up on the floor. She started babbling about what a shitty day she had, how your dad missed one of her cheerleader competitions. Apparently, he said it was because of work, but she found out it was because he secretly went to some art fair you were part of. And that made her so jealous of you."

"Hannah jealous of me?" I question in doubt. "That doesn't sound like something she'd say or feel."

"Um, yeah, it does. I mean, think about it. You're talented, sweet, and you're so much stronger than she is. Deep down, I think she always knew you'd turn into the pretty, little butterfly you are now." He dazzles me with a charming grin.

I roll my eyes, but my heart's doing all sorts of weird things in my chest. "But she has the perfect life. Why be jealous of someone like me?"

"She doesn't have the perfect life, Isa. She's a fake person who's lived a fake life and feels fake. She admitted that to me, too."

What he says is making me question everything. All those years of living with Hannah, watching her become popular and get whatever she wanted, and now Kai's trying to say she's jealous of me. It doesn't make any sense. None of what he's telling me makes any sense.

"The art fair she mentioned," I say. "I remember it, but my dad wasn't there. No one in my family ever went to any of them."

"She said something about him peeking in on you or something, because Lynn would have freaked out if she knew," he explains, "just like Hannah did."

I'm not sure what to say. The idea that my dad would go to one of my art fairs seems insane. Even if he did, I'm not sure I care since he did it in secret, still putting me second over Lynn. And like Lynn said earlier, he hates me. If he hated me, why would he secretly go to the art fair, though?

I shield my eyes from the sun as it peeks through the clouds. "How did you end up getting Hannah into the house?"

"It was actually really complicated because she kept trying to hit on me again," he says. "No matter what I said, she wouldn't stop. Finally, I had to tell her something that pissed her off enough."

"What'd you say?"

For a fleeting second, panic flashes in his eyes. "I'm not even sure . . . I can't really remember." He's lying, but before I can say something, he hurries on with the story. "Whatever it was got her to go into the house." He picks at a crack in the fence. "But not until she threatened me first. She said, if I ever told anyone, she'd ruin my reputation. But since my reputation is long gone, I figure her threat is pretty useless now."

"It's kind of silly that she got so upset," I say. "I've been embarrassed way worse than that."

"But you're a lot stronger than Hannah," he presses, glancing up at me with those crazy-intense eyes of his. "And Hannah can't handle the idea of people knowing she was rejected. She wants everyone to believe she's perfect, even when she's not."

"Yeah, I know." I look down at mine and Kai's fingers still interlocked. The touch brings me so much comfort. I just wish I could hold onto the comfort forever. "Thank you, Kai."

"For what?"

"For distracting me and getting me to calm down."

"Anytime." He shifts his weight, straightening his stance. "And now that you're calmed down, I'm going to tell you our solution to this whole stolen folder dilemma."

I perk up a tiny bit. "You have a solution already?"

"Of course I have a solution. I'm a badass."

"Ego Man to the rescue, huh?"

"Da-da-da-daaaaa," he singsongs, and I snort a laugh. The sound makes him grin with pride. "See? There's my strong girl."

I smile again, but inside I'm like, *whoa, whoa, whoa, back the freak up*. Did he just refer to me as *his* girl?

"So, what's the plan? How do we get the folder back?"

"The plan's pretty simple, but don't let that take away from my awesomeness." He winks at me. "I'm just going to go to Big Doug's and get him to give me a second copy of the info. I have to talk to him, anyway, and get my phone back."

"Are you sure you should be doing that, though? After what happened last night . . . Maybe you should keep some distance from Big Doug. Plus, you're supposed to be taking it easy today." I hate to say it, but it needs to be said. While I want to know everything there is to know about my mom, I don't want Kai doing questionable, perhaps risky stuff just to make that happen.

"I'll be fine, and I can take it easy and still get this done," he reassures me. When I continue to show my concern, he adds, "I won't do anything crazy. I'll just get my phone and the papers and get out."

"Can I go with you, so I won't just sit around, worrying?"

His muscles wind tight. "I'm not sure if that's a great idea."

"But you let me talk to Big Doug before."

"Yeah, but that was before . . ." He blows out a breath, raking his fingers through his hair. "I just don't want to risk getting you into any trouble."

"What if me and Indigo go with you and sit in the

car?" I suggest. I don't think I could stand sitting around, waiting for him to return, worrying if he's okay while worrying about what kind of information is going to be in the papers. "You need a ride, anyway, right?"

His mouth sinks into a frown, as if just realizing this. "I guess I do. Fuck. I forgot about that. I need to figure out what to do about my car." He scratches his head. "All right, you can come. But you have to sit in the car."

"Thanks for everything." Without even thinking, I circle my arms around him and hug him. "You're, like, the best friend ever."

"I know," he says, slipping his arms around my waist.

We hug for a second or two before I start to pull away, but his arms tighten and hold me against him.

"Just one more second," he murmurs, nuzzling his face against the crook of my neck.

I'm not sure why he needs more time, but I let him have it.

After he finally lets me go, he hoists himself over the fence and then helps me over.

As we head back toward the apartment, my thoughts instantly drift back to my mom. I try to picture her sitting in jail, locked away, a terrible person who's done terrible things. It's hard to picture, though, maybe because I don't even know what she looks like. I know nothing about her other than her name is Bella and that she might be a murderer. The idea of that being it—that's all she'll ever be to me—makes me feel sick to my stomach.

Please, please, let there be something good inside those papers.

Chapter
FOURTEEN

KAI

I was getting worried about Isa. She looked so pale, so out of breath, like she was about to faint. It made me feel like maybe I screwed up by telling her about her mom. After I took her for a walk and distracted her with the story about Hannah, though, she managed to calm herself down a bit. I shouldn't be that surprised. She's always been tough like that. She's been through so much in her life and has managed not to let it drag her down.

I'm glad I could help her. Still, when she asked me what I said to Hannah to get her into the house, I almost had a panic attack myself. For a second, I damn near lost my mind and almost actually told her. Thank God I managed to mentally smack some sense into myself and keep my mouth shut. Maybe I'll tell her one day, but definitely not today. She's already had enough piled on her plate for one day and doesn't need me dumping my feelings onto her.

"I'm not sure I'm a fan of this idea," Isa's grandma says after we return to the parking lot and Isa tells her our plan to drive over to Big Doug's and get another copy of the papers. "After the morning you've had . . . I'd rather you stay home, at least for the day."

Isa shuffles up onto the curb beside her. "Grandma, this is really important. What if there's something in those papers that could," she bites at her thumbnail, "like, prove she's innocent."

Her grandma sighs and places a hand on Isa's shoulder. "Hon, I highly doubt that's what's going to be in those papers. If there were something like that lying around, I'm sure she wouldn't be in jail."

"So, you think she's guilty?" Isa asks, her voice cracking.

"No, that's not what I'm saying." She gives Isa's shoulder a squeeze. "Why don't we avoid jumping to any conclusions until we have the facts?"

"That's what she's trying to do," Indigo chimes in then cups her hands around her mouth to light another cigarette.

"I understand that," their grandma replies through gritted teeth. "But I don't think wandering off to some guy's house to get a few papers about the case is the best idea right now, especially when I know nothing about this young man or how he managed to get this information about Isa's mom." Her eyes land on me as if waiting for an explanation.

"He's a friend of mine," I say, knowing I need to be vague. Big Doug has made it clear from the day I met him that he doesn't want a lot of people knowing very much about him. "And he's really good with computers."

"Is he a hacker?" their grandma asks with distrust written all over her face.

"You know what a hacker is?" I ask, shocked.

Indigo starts hacking on cigarette smoke. "Holy shit, Kai. Now you've gone and done it. You just pissed her off."

Their grandma's eyes narrow, first at Indigo then at me. "Yes, I know what a hacker is. I may be old, but I'm not stupid."

I make an apologetic face. "Sorry. I just thought—"

"You thought, because I'm old, I don't know stuff." Their grandma faces me with her arms crossed, her expression firm. "But I know a lot, like if your friend did somehow get ahold of records about the case, he probably obtained them illegally."

"I'm not sure if they were records about the case." I'm uncertain what else to say because, honestly, knowing Big Doug, they could've been records about the case. "The stuff he found before wasn't illegal. They were public records."

Their grandma's forehead furrows. "The stuff he found before?"

"A couple of days ago, when he broke the news to me that Isa's mom was . . ." I trail off, glancing at Isa. Her arms are wrapped around herself, her head tucked down. "All the information he gave me then was all information you can find on the internet."

"But how did he even find out her last name?" Isa peers up at me, the sadness in her eyes nearly swallowing me whole.

"That might've not been done legally," I admit. "I honestly don't know his exact process. I'm just sort of the messenger."

Isa stuffs her hands into the pocket of my jacket she's wearing. "What is it?" she asks so softly I barely hear her. "Her last name, I mean."

"Bella Larose." I curl my fingers inward to stop myself from touching her again, knowing right now might not be the best time for that.

Isa stares off into the distance. "It's pretty . . . too pretty, I guess."

I'm unsure what she means exactly, but something about what she says triggers a nerve with her grandma.

"All right, you can go, but on one condition. Indigo goes with you, and you two sit in the car while he," she aims a finger at me while looking at Isa, "runs in. I don't want you getting into trouble at all. It's too risky right now with this stuff going on with your parents. They're still your legal guardians, and the last thing we need is for you to get arrested or something. We need to be on our best behavior." She flicks a glance in Indigo's direction and mine. "All of us."

I'm not sure why I'm included in their family decisions, but I find myself nodding in agreement. The last thing I want to do is get Isa in trouble because of something I did. I just wish I wasn't in so much trouble already.

"Maybe Kai should just borrow the car and drive himself." Their grandma grows wary again.

Isa shakes her head. "He can't drive. Doctor's orders, remember?"

"Shit, I forgot about that." Their grandma's narrowed gaze lands on me. "You'll make sure she stays in the car?"

I draw an X across my chest. "I swear she won't go anywhere else."

"I'm not a child," Isa tells her grandma. "If I said I won't go in, then I won't."

"Just like the time when you and Indigo promised

me a thousand times that you could handle getting back to the hotel before midnight," she replies with an arch of her brows.

Isa pulls a guilty face. "Um, I think that was the night my watch broke, maybe."

"Hey, it's not our fault you didn't know five o'clock was the new midnight," Indigo interrupts, a circle of smoke surrounding her face.

Their grandma heaves a sigh. "Please just hurry. The quicker we get this done, the faster I can relax. While you're gone, I'll talk to my police friend and see if he can tell us anything. I'm also going to ask him about the break-in to see if he thinks I should report it." She tosses a set of keys to Indigo. "Take my other car, just in case he needs to look at this one for some reason."

"You could also find out if he has access to the security cameras," I say, bending down to tie my shoelace. "It might be nice to find out who broke into your car."

Their grandma opens her mouth to say something to me but then decides against it and turns to Isa. "Be careful," she warns before walking away.

"I hate that she's stressed," Isa mutters when her grandma is out of earshot. "It's too unhealthy for her."

"It's unhealthy for you, too." I stand up straight and step up on the curb beside her. "You need to try to relax."

She only seems to stiffen more. "I can try, but I don't think it's going to happen, not until I know for sure . . . And even then, I might not be able to . . . depending on how this all turns out."

Indigo flicks her cigarette onto the ground and stomps her boot on top of it. "You want to know what I think?"

Isa glances at her. "I guess so."

She links arms with Isa. "I think that, no matter what happens, you'll eventually be okay again."

"I don't know about that," Isa says. "It doesn't feel like things will ever be the same again."

"They won't ever be the same," Indigo replies. "But that out-of-control, nothing-makes-sense-anymore feeling you have right now will fade."

"How do you know that's how I'm feeling?" Isa asks. "It's, like, dead-on."

"We've all had it at one time or another."

"There's more to it than that. You have a story." Isa eyeballs her cousin. "I can tell."

"Now's not the time for my stories." Indigo jumps off the curb and marches for a car parked in the space across from us. "Right now, we're going to focus on finding out what the hell was in that folder."

I follow them, crossing my fingers Big Doug won't make it a pain in the ass to get another copy. I don't think there should be a problem, but sometimes, he gets weird about stuff for no reason.

Once we get into the car, Indigo backs up out of the parking spaces and drives toward the exit of the apartment complex. When we're about to pull out onto the street, Indigo asks me where to go. I tell her to turn right and keep driving for a while. I'll let her know when to make the next turn. Then I sit back and attempt to relax, but with my head pounding and my worry for Isa increasing, it's pretty much impossible.

I want to comfort Isa or at least try to distract her, but I'm sitting in the backseat, and she's in the passenger seat. She hasn't looked at me or Indigo since we got into the car. I know what that quiet means. It means she's silently drowning in her own worries. I've done it enough times that I get it. The only way to stop it is a distraction.

I slide forward in the seat. "I have this idea."

Indigo meets my gaze in the rearview mirror. "Do I

even dare ask?"

I rest my arms on the console. "My ideas are always awesome."

"I don't know about that," she says. "Last night, you tried to convince us to hike up a mountain. You said it would be so awesome doing it in the dark because we wouldn't know where we were, which didn't really make any sense. But when Isa asked you why that'd be fun, you said 'because dangerous stuff is fun.' "

I smile innocently at her. "That doesn't sound like something I'd say."

"You were pretty out of it." She slows the car down for a stop sign. "But still, I don't know. I could kinda see you saying something like that when you're completely coherent."

My brow teases upward. "Are you making assumptions about my character?"

She fiddles with the heater, twisting the knob. "From everything I've seen, you seem like the kind of guy who likes to joke around a lot."

"Not all the time," I argue, feigning hurt. "Sometimes, I can be serious."

"I haven't seen you act serious, so I'll have to take your word for it." She casts a sidelong glance at Isa, who's still staring out the window, then returns her gaze to the rearview mirror. "So, what's your idea? Something distracting, I hope."

"It's very distracting." I lean forward and rotate the knob of the stereo. "Nope, nope, and nope," I say as I flip through the stations, searching for the perfect song.

After I find one, I settle back in the seat as a song by Icona Pop comes on. As the rhythm thumps, I start to dance, swaying in the seat and bobbing my head. Indigo joins in, tapping her fingers against the steering wheel.

We've done this before, the night she picked Isa and me up from a party. It took Isa a moment to get into it, but she eventually started rocking out with us. Today, though, she doesn't budge. Her hands are in her lap, her gaze focused on that window, her body stiff as a board.

All right, drastic times call for drastic measures.

Unfastening my seatbelt, I scoot forward and swing a leg over the console.

"What the hell, Kai!" Indigo snaps, her fingers clasping the wheel. "You're going to make me wreck."

"Not if you keep your eyes on the road," I say, clumsily diving into the seat beside Isa.

As my hip bumps into hers, her head whips in my directions, her eyes huge.

"What're you doing?" she sputters through a gasp.

"Apparently, causing everyone to panic." I slip a hand between myself and the console to unbuckle the seatbelt. "I can't believe how you two are acting. It's like you've never seen a guy try to be attentive."

"Attentive?" Indigo flashes me an accusing smirk. "That's an odd word choice."

I'm not positive what she's accusing me of, but I smooth over the subject.

"Well, I'm a strange guy." I toss a smile her way while weaving an arm around Isa's back. "Strange guys use odd words."

"Is that all it is?" she questions. "Because it seems like you're trying to impress a certain *someone*."

"I never have to *try* to impress," I quip as I grab Isa's hips and lift her onto my lap. "It just comes naturally."

Isa starts to scoot forward, as if about to climb onto the floor.

"No way. You're not going anywhere." I hurry and loop my arms around her waist, dragging her backward until she's settled between my legs with her back pressed against my chest. Then I reach back, draw the seatbelt over us, and fasten us into the seat. "You promised me you'd rest your head in my lap, remember?"

"Yeah, my *head*," she stresses. "This is way more than my head."

"Oh, I know that." I gently squeeze her hip, causing her muscles to constrict. "But isn't this so much better?" I pull her closer and put my chin on her shoulder. God, she smells so good, like cookies. "It's so cozy and relaxing."

She doesn't respond right away. I think maybe she's thinking of a comeback, but then her body begins to tremble. I realize she's crying at the same time Indigo does.

"Isa." Indigo reaches over and rubs Isa's shoulder. "It's going to be okay."

Shaking her head, Isa rotates her body around and buries her face against my chest. Her hands find the bottom of my shirt, and she clutches fistfuls of the fabric as her shoulders shake.

"I'm trying to be strong," she croaks. "But I feel like I'm losing my mind. I can't stop thinking about her and my life and how everything's connected. How, if she's bad, that means I could be, right?"

I smooth my hand over the back of my head, trying to think of something to say, but my mind is blank. Indigo looks at me, silently pleading for me to do something. I feel as helpless as her.

Not knowing what else to do, I just start talking.

"Do you remember that day in seventh grade when we walked home, but I didn't speak to you the entire time?" I ask, rocking Isa back and forth. "It was raining, and I was in a really bad mood because Kyler's friends locked me in a locker as a prank. You probably thought I was being a jerk because I wouldn't tell you what was bugging me. At least, that's what I figured until we were almost to my house."

"I remember that day. You seemed really sad," Isa whispers. "I hated when you looked sad. You always seemed too pretty to look so sad."

Indigo covers her mouth with her hand, and her shoulders heave as she tries to laugh silently.

Me, I chuckle. "Pretty, huh? I'm not sure whether to take that as an insult or a compliment."

"It's a compliment," she assures me, her voice barely audible.

"I'll have to take your word for it." I draw hearts on her back with my fingertip. "But, that wasn't really my point. My point is what you said right before I went into my house."

She ducks out of my arms and sits up straight to look me in the eye. "I don't remember saying anything to you."

Probably because her words didn't mean as much to her as they did to me. That day sucked balls big time. Kyler's friends treated me like shit, my dad screamed at me that morning because I spilled juice on the floor, and I got lunch detention for being late to class, only because I was locked in the locker.

"You said that, no matter what happened to me, tomorrow was another day, that no two days are the same." I wipe a few stray tears from her cheeks with my thumb. "Then you said probably one of the most adorable things I've ever heard you say. You said not all days can be crappy; otherwise, happiness wouldn't exist. And it had to exist; otherwise, fairytales, dreams, and comedies couldn't."

"Comedies?" Indigo looks at me, puzzled. "That seems random."

"No, it isn't," Isa argues, wiping her eyes with the back of her hand. "Comedies are funny and make people laugh, so they're connected to happiness just as much as fairytales and dreams."

"I don't really connect fairytales or dreams to happiness," Indigo says, setting her hand on the shifter. "My preference is sex and chocolate. One day, you'll see what I'm talking about."

Isa's cheeks redden as her gaze glides to me.

"It's beside the point." Normally, I'd be all over teasing her, but considering she was just sobbing into my shirt, I let her off the hook. "The point is what you said. That not all days are bad. And I know it's crazy to think about right now, because this whole thing with your mom is still really raw, but eventually, that pain will fade."

"But it might not go away completely," Isa whispers, rubbing her hands up and down her arms.

"No, it might not," I answer truthfully. "But it'll get easier."

She studies me for so long I feel myself getting uneasy. "You're kind of wise when you want to be," she finally says.

I shrug. "I was just repeating your words."

"You did more than that." She looks like she might say something else, but instead, she faces forward and settles against me.

She doesn't say much more during the car ride but she's not nearly as distant. I start tracing my fingers up and down her arm, trying to soothe her as much as possible. Then I notice red marks on her wrist.

"How'd you get these?" I ask, rolling up the sleeve of the jacket to get a better look.

She frowns at the marks. "They're probably from when Lynn grabbed me yesterday."

A ripple of anger waves through my body. "She did this to you?"

"Yeah, we were arguing, and she grabbed me. I'm not sure if she meant to do it or not." Isa shrugs. "It doesn't really matter, though, does it? I mean, I'm not living with her anymore, so she can't do it again."

"Don't do that," I say, fighting to stay calm. "Don't brush it off as nothing. Don't lower your self-worth."

"I'm not lowering my self-worth," she whispers, her big eyes all wide, revealing the pain she's feeling inside. "I just . . . I don't want to make a big deal of it. There's already too much going on."

I clench my hands into fists. "If she does it again, we're not blowing it off."

"That's fine, but she won't do it again, because I won't be around her anymore." She lowers her voice. "And I should probably be saying the same thing to you."

Maybe she's right. My dad has never full-on beaten me or anything, but he has crossed a line a couple of times and left some marks and bruises. I never really talked about it with anyone, mostly because his anger seemed justified a lot of the time. I'm a screw up. I get that. I've never been like Kyler and just did whatever our dad said. I always have to question everything he wants from us. I mess up. I defend myself. I'm the disappointment, while Kyler is his perfect son.

"Does Grandma Stephy know about the marks?" Indigo asks Isa.

"I told her she grabbed me," she tells Indigo. "It's part of the reason Lynn and my dad didn't fight her more over letting me move out."

Indigo briefly grows quiet. "I really hate that woman," she finally says. "I'm just glad you don't have to be around her anymore."

"Me, too," Isa mumbles, resting back against me.

We make the rest of the drive in silence. After Indigo

parks in front of Big Doug's house, I unfasten the seatbelt, and Isa climbs out of the car so I can get out.

She observes the simple, ranch-style house from over the roof of the car. "So, this is what a hacker's house looks like, huh? I pictured something more . . . I don't know, big and flashy."

"I never said he was a hacker," I remind her, stretching my arms above my head.

My shirt inches up with my raised arms, and I notice she steals a glance at my stomach before her gaze collides with mine.

She rubs her bloodshot eyes and blinks a few times, as if adjusting them to the sunlight. "You never said he wasn't, though."

Suppressing a smile, I nudge her toward the car. "Get your cute ass back inside the car. I'll be back in a minute."

She sucks her bottom lip between her teeth. "Are you sure you don't want me to go in with you?"

For a split second, all of my attention centers on her mouth. But then I remember how she told me Kyler kissed her. Fucking kissed her. Fuck. I know I have no right to be upset, but I am. I hate that he kissed her first. I hate that he kissed her ever.

"Kai." Isa waves her hand in front of my face. "Are you okay? Is your head hurting? Are you getting a dizzy spell?"

"I'm fine." I shove the thought of her and Kyler kissing out of my head, set my hands on her shoulders, and gently push her toward the car. "And there's no way I'm letting you go in with me. Your grandma would kick my ass."

"You're seriously scared of my grandma?"

"Heck, yeah, I am. The woman has hawk eyes."

Isa giggles, but the sound deflates into a sigh. "Well,

she doesn't have to know. It could be our little secret." She winks at me like we're making a silent agreement.

"Look at you, trying to be all cute and sneaky," I say then push her toward the car again. "But the answer is no. I'm not taking you in there. And not just because I'm terrified of your grandma. It's too dangerous."

"But you let me talk to Big Doug at the party."

"But that was in the pool house at Bradon's. Here . . . Well, he does more business here."

I can tell questions are biting at the tip of her tongue, but she holds them back and gets into the car. I wait until she has the door closed before I head up the driveway. Following Big Doug's rules, I round the side of the house to stay out of sight from his neighbors. When I knock on the door, it creaks open on its own, and I immediately sense something's wrong. Big Doug never keeps his door unlocked, let alone open. If he did, the alarm would be going off.

I think about what the guy said to me in the parking lot before he knocked me out: *tell Big Doug his three strikes are up.*

I push the door open and step inside. The house is quiet, the lights are off, and the curtains are pulled shut. So much dust floats in the air that I start to cough. Covering my hand over my mouth, I leave the foyer and make for the stairway that leads to the basement.

As I pass by the living room, I notice all the furniture has been tipped over, and the bookshelves look like a chainsaw was taken to them. With how much dust is floating in the air, I wonder when it happened. Probably not that long ago.

Shit, what if whoever did it is still here?

I grind to a halt in the doorway of the kitchen when I notice the alarm has been disarmed. I have never seen it off before. He always turns it off to answer the door then immediately resets it. I contemplate what to do. Pussy out and run back to the car? Then what? Call the police? If Big Doug is here, he could easily get arrested if the police showed up. I've heard him mention a couple of times about being off the grid. Honestly, I'm not even sure what his real name is.

I decide to man up and hurry for the stairs. I keep my footsteps light, trying to be as quiet as I can. When I reach the basement, I know right away that some heavy shit is going down. The room that was once filled with computers, printers, and filing cabinets is completely empty. Only a couple of filing cabinets and the desk remain, and they have been emptied out. If I hadn't hung out here with Big Doug a ton of times, I'd guess the house had been abandoned for a while.

I approach the desk and peer inside the open drawers. Empty. I glance in the filing cabinet. Again, nothing.

"Fucking, shit, fuck." I sink down into the computer chair, roughly yanking my fingers through my hair. How the hell am I supposed to go out there and tell Isa that whatever was on those papers might be gone? I know the promise of it is the only thing that's keeping her from crumbling apart completely.

"God, this is such a mess." I slump back in the chair and let my head fall back.

Something on the ceiling catches my eyes. One of the ceiling tiles has a silver, star-shaped sticker on it—Big Doug's mark, as he put it. He told me once that he hid stuff all over the house in case of an emergency. I didn't really know what he meant at the time or what he would even hide, but still, I have to look.

I lift myself from the chair and drag it over to the corner of the room. I climb on top of it, reach up, and push the tile all the way to the side. Then I stick my hand up in the hole and feel around until my fingers brush against something plastic. Jackpot.

I jump off the chair then open a storage-sized bag with a smiley face sticker on it. Inside, is my phone, a flash drive, and a note, all of which have stickers on them. I fish the note out first.

Kai,

Sorry I got you into this mess and sorry for bailing out without explaining, but I need to lay low for a while. I wiped your phone clean in case it was bugged. And I'm sure you were hoping I'd find more about Isa's mom. I found some pretty interesting stuff. This flash drive explains it all. I'll get ahold of you when I can. Until then, peace out, man.

-Big Doug

I don't know who's after him, but if Big Doug ran, it's gotta be bad.

I glance around the room as I tuck the flash drive and note into my boot. Then I head up the stairs, swiping my finger across the screen of my phone to check my messages. Not surprisingly, there aren't any calls from my parents. I do have one voicemail, so I type in my passcode to listen to it.

It's a message Isa left yesterday, asking for a ride. It was during the time she was with Kyler, and she sounds upset. It was probably when he took her to the football field. I still can't believe he did that to her—took her around his and Hannah's friends. He knows how bitchy those girls can be, but he was probably trying to impress her with his football skills, which is just fucking stupid. If he knew Isa, he'd know she doesn't like football, never really has.

That doesn't matter right now. What matters is getting to a computer and opening up whatever is on this flash drive. I just cross my fingers it'll be some kind of good news, maybe even a silver lining. Isa could really use one of those right now, and I'll do anything to make sure she gets it.

Chapter FIFTEEN

ISABELLA

"*Would you quit biting your* nails?" Indigo pleads as she flips down the visor in front of her. "You're going to get ugly, uneven nails if you keep it up."

"I can't help it." I tuck my hands under my legs so I'll stop. "I'm nervous. Kai's been in there for a while. What if something happened? What if Big Doug won't give him another copy of the papers? Or what if he did, and whatever was on there was bad, and Kai just doesn't want to come out and break the news to me?"

She rummages around in her purse for a tube of lipstick. "Stop worrying about the what ifs and just wait to see what happens." She applies a layer of lipstick to her lips and pops her lips together. "It doesn't do any good to worry about stuff that may not happen."

"Yeah, I know." I slump back in the seat, slip my sneakers off, and pull my legs to my chest. I think about what Kai said to me, how tomorrow will be another day, and focus on that. It's the only thing I can do other than start crying again, and my eyes really want to. "Can I ask you a question?"

She drops the lipstick back into her purse. "You know you can ask me anything."

"Yeah, but this is a weird question about life and stuff."

"Isa, almost every question you ask is weird, like that time you asked me if I ever wondered if maybe gnomes come alive at night and dance around the yard."

"Hey, I still wonder about that." I rest my chin on my knees. "You never know . . . about anything."

"Exactly. So stop worrying about what Kai's doing. I'm sure he'll be coming out soon . . ." Her head turns toward the house. "Look, there he is."

I sit up and watch Kai head down the driveway. The sight of him causes my nerves to bubble. I try to get a read on how he's feeling, but his expression is stoic as he rounds the front of the car and opens the passenger door.

"Hop out so I can climb in," he says, glimpsing around at the houses lining the street.

"You really want to sit that way again?" I ask, lowering my feet to the floor.

It's not like I hated sitting on his lap, but now that I'm not a blubbering mess, it kind of seems . . . I don't know, inappropriate. Well, that and now that I'm not shattering into pieces, I'm too aware I haven't showered in a couple of days. I probably smell pretty ripe at this point.

He makes a scooch motion, and sighing, I climb out of the car. I step back and let him slide into the passenger seat. Once he gets settled, he reaches out, snags the hem of my shirt, and drags me toward him. Being my suave self, I end up tripping over my feet and falling into his lap. He grunts as my butt hits his lap, probably squishing his guy parts.

I quickly twist around. "Oh, my God. Are you okay?"

"Yep, just peachy." His face is bunched up in pain as he closes the door.

He doesn't look very peachy. In fact, he kind of looks pale. I wonder how he's feeling, if it's the concussion, if it has to do with what he just found out.

"I think you need to get some rest," I say first, because his wellbeing is the most important.

"I will in a bit." He shifts his weight, bringing my back against his chest. Then he buckles us in and slips his arms around me. "I have some good news and some bad news. Which do you want first?"

When I start to chew on my fingernails, Indigo barks, "Isa, stop biting your nails."

I remove my fingers from my mouth. "Let's go with the bad news first," I say to Kai.

He hesitates. "Big Doug is . . . Well, he's gone."

"What do you mean gone?" I ask. "Like he went to the store kind of gone? Or like he packed up his crap and said peace out, Sunnyvale?"

"Like he was running-for-his-life kind of gone," Kai says solemnly. "Half his furniture is still there, but his house is trashed. And he took all of his computers."

"What would he be running from?" I try not to panic, but I can hear my heart thudding in my chest. Thump. Thump. Thump. Thump. You're. Never. Gonna. Know. If. She. Could. Be. Innocent.

"Lots of things," Kai says, rubbing his eye with the heel of his hand. "When I first met Big Doug, he warned me that, one day, he might just up and leave."

I move around until my back is pressed against the console and I can look at Kai more easily. "How did you even meet him?"

He stares ahead as Indigo pulls out onto the road. "At this party. It was kind of an accident we became friends. We didn't really have anything in common, but we both got high . . ." His gaze glides to Indigo then lands back on me. "*Drunk*. And he let it slip about what he did and told me that, if I wanted in on some jobs, he could hook me up. I was going through some stuff, and his offer to make some fast cash by doing practically nothing sounded perfect, not just because of the money, but because of the change . . . the risk . . . Well, it was different. And I wanted different. I wanted to be a guy who wasn't just Kyler's younger brother."

"You've never just been Kyler's younger brother." I completely understand where he's coming from. Even now, people refer to me as Hannah's sister. "People know you around school, Kai. You have friends."

"Now I do," he says. "But a year ago . . . All of my friends were through association with Kyler, and I hated that. I hate how he's always been better than me at everything, and I wanted to have something that he wasn't good at."

I give him a look. "So, you thought that something should be working for a hacker?"

"I never said he was a hacker," he reminds me, absentmindedly playing with the bottom of my shirt. "And, yeah, I realize how stupid it sounds—getting into trouble so you can break out of living in your brother's shadow—but at the time, it seemed like an awesome idea."

"Maybe it was the weed that made you think that," I suggest, fighting back a shiver when his knuckles graze my skin.

"I already told you I don't do that anymore." His gaze flicks to Indigo again.

"She's not going to judge you," I tell him. "She does it sometimes, too."

"I'm not worried she'll judge me." When he looks back at me, his lips curl into a teasing grin. "I'm worried she'll tell your grandma and then she won't let me play with you anymore."

"She won't tell," I promise then glance over my shoulder. "Right, Indigo?"

"Of course I won't tell," Indigo replies with an eye roll. "You two need to spend time together. You're too perfect together."

Kai grins, but then it fades. "Are you ready to hear the good news?" he asks.

For a split second, I don't even know what he's talking about. His ability to make me forget stuff is amazing.

"Um, yes?" It sounds more like a question, mostly because he doesn't seem too thrilled about the good news. "But if it's good news, why do you seem so depressed about it?"

"Because I'm thinking of all the problems that might come with this good news," he says then sighs. "So, Big Doug left me this flash drive and a note that said the flash drive had information on it about your mom. And I was really excited about it up until about a minute ago when I realized that, more than likely, the damn thing's going to have security and passwords and shit to keep anyone from being able to access it."

"Sounds kind of extreme," I say, frowning.

"That's just how he is," he explains. "He's careful about everything he does."

"Do you know anyone who can crack those passwords and security and shit?" I ask, crossing my fingers and toes that he does.

He bobs his head from side to side, thinking about it. "I might be able to do it, but it'll take some time."

My jaw nearly smacks my knees. "You know how to hack into stuff?"

"It's not really hacking." He shrugs like it's no big deal. "More like solving a puzzle."

I study him carefully. "What else do you know how to do that I don't know about?"

"There's a lot of things I know how to do that you don't know about." His lips threaten to turn upward. "*Yet.*"

I feel my cheeks flush. *Get it together. Stop being weird. He didn't mean it like* that.

"Oh, my God," Indigo abruptly shouts, slapping her hand against the steering wheel. "Would you two just kiss already? I can't take much more of this sexual tension."

I whip my head in her direction and blast her with my best death glare. She smiles sweetly at me and shrugs oh-so-innocently. Collecting myself, I turn my attention back to Kai, wondering what the hell he's going to say about Indigo's remark.

He stares at me with curiosity in his eyes, and then his gaze drops to my mouth. My heart literally skips a beat in anticipation. But then I become hyper aware of my surroundings. *Wait. He's not going to kiss me, right here, in front of Indigo, is he?*

But as he leans in, my worries go right out the window. I remember the night he kissed me in the driveway. His lips were so soft and gentle, and the contact of our lips sent showers of fireworks exploding through my body.

But Kai stops mid lean-in and suddenly leans back. "What kind of a computer do you have?"

What the heck did he just say? "Huh?"

"You brought yours to your grandma's right?" he asks, putting even more room between us.

I have to work really hard not to jut my lip out in a pout. That's the second time he almost kissed me. How many times is this going to happen between us? And shouldn't I put a stop to it? I mean, there's the thing with Kyler . . .

Holy shit, I just kissed Kyler yesterday! What's the matter with me? I've got to stop this!

God, I really am a bad person.

"Or did you leave it at your house?" Kai asks when I don't say anything.

"I, um . . . What? No, I brought my computer with me." I force myself to focus on the conversation. "But it's really old."

"What about your grandma?" he asks. "Does she have a newer one?"

Indigo cackles. "Oh, Kai, you silly guy. Old people don't have computers. You should know that."

"I do know that," Kai says. "But I did meet this guy once who was, like, seventy and knew how to break into the DMV records."

Indigo looks at him like what the hell dude? And Kai counters with a whoops-I-didn't-mean-to-say-that face.

"But, anyway." Kai glazes over the subject, focusing back on me as he puts a hand on top of my thigh. "Maybe we should stop by my house and pick up mine. I've got this really killer program that might come in handy."

I gape at him. "Seriously, who are you?"

"Don't get too excited," he says. "Like I said, I'm not that great, definitely nowhere near as good as Big Doug. And it'll take some time."

"Like how much time?" I ask, too aware that his fingers have started to lightly trace a path up and down my thigh.

Yeah, I'm wearing pajama bottoms but somehow it feels almost as intense as if he were touching my skin.

He shrugs. "A few days, a few weeks. It's hard to know for sure."

"A few weeks." My chest aches again, a near blinding pain. How can I wait that long? I need to know what happened. What she did. Who she was. Was I living with her when she . . . ? "Maybe I should just search the internet for information about her."

Kai promptly shakes his head as his fingers circle my wrist, pressing against my pulse. "Promise me you won't do that."

My pulse hammers against his fingertips. "Why?"

"Because the stuff that's going to show up in that . . . I don't want you to see it."

"Have you seen it?"

He gulps and nods once. "The first set of documents Big Doug gave me had a lot of articles and stuff about what happened."

"And it was really bad?" I shake my head at myself. "Of course it was bad . . . she . . . killed someone." I sound strangled.

"Hey," he warns, softly tugging on my wrist. "I want you to promise not only you won't look on the internet for anything, but you'll stop stressing over this until I can access the files on this damn flash drive." When I start to open my mouth in protest, he cuts me off. "And I don't want to hear any buts. Just stop stressing out and let me fix this."

While it's sweet that he thinks he can fix this, I'm not so sure my mom being in jail for murder is a fixable thing. Still, I nod and bottle up my worries into the little box I keep hidden inside me. It's the same box that contains the pain of when my dad stopped doing stuff with me, the first time Lynn told me I was ugly, and the time Hannah convinced her friends to pin me against the locker and draw freak on my forehead with a permanent marker.

"You want us to take you to your house, then?" I ask and he nods. "What about your parents, though? Won't they ask you where your car is and about these?" I trace my fingertips over the bruises on his scruffy cheek, making sure not to put any pressure on them.

"I'll just run in and out," he says, his voice tight. "They might not even be there, anyway. They sometimes visit my grandma on Sundays."

"Maybe we could just borrow a computer from someone," I suggest, not wanting him to get yelled at by his dad.

He leans into my hand. "I'm a big boy, Isa. I'll be fine."

"That's not what you told me last night when you tried to get me to sleep on the couch with you," I tease in an attempt to lighten the mood.

"I think I should get a free pass on anything I said last night," he counters. "It's like when you're drunk and do something stupid; it doesn't count."

"Yeah, try telling that to my friend Jenna," Indigo says, cracking her window to light up. "She got trashed one night, slept with some random dude, and ended up with herpes."

Kai and I mirror each other's disgusted faces.

"And FYI, I'm making this choice for you guys." She cranes the wheel and turns the car down the street that leads to mine and Kai's subdivision. "We're going to go get this computer so Kai can get into this flash drive and hopefully give you some sort of peace of mind."

"But what if what's on it doesn't give me peace of mind?" I inch over until I'm off Kai's lap and sitting between his legs with my back against his chest.

She reaches for her pack of cigarettes on the dashboard. "Then we'll deal with that when we reach that point." She pops a cigarette between her lips. "You should get in the backseat and lie down. The last thing we need is Lynn, Hannah, or your dad seeing you here and causing more drama."

I unbuckle the seatbelt and move to hop into the backseat. Kai holds onto me for a second or two before reluctantly releasing me from his grasp. Then I lie down on the seat and remain quiet for the next couple of minutes.

When the car comes to a stop, Kai mutters, "Fuck, they're home."

I open my mouth to tell him not to go, but he's already getting out of the car.

Indigo starts fiddling with the radio, not really saying too much. The longer the silence lingers in the air, the more restless I get. In an attempt to distract myself, I text my Grandma Stephy.

> *Me: Hey, how's it going there? Any luck with those surveillance cameras?*
>
> *Grandma Stephy: Sorry, hon, but whoever broke into the car knew what they were doing.*
>
> *Me: What do you mean?*
>
> *Grandma Stephy: I mean, they were wearing a mask.*

I sigh.

> *Me: Well, that sucks. What did your policeman friend say about it? And the blue car? Did you tell him about that?*
>
> *Grandma Stephy: He said the break-in was really*

odd, especially since they didn't really steal anything besides some papers. But he said there's not much we can do about it besides report it. He said the same thing about the blue car, and unless we can get a license plate number, reporting it won't do much. I think, for now, we just need to keep our eyes open. And I don't want you going off by yourself anywhere . . . Where are you now? Are you headed home?

Me: Yeah. We just made a stop by Kai's house so he could get some stuff.

Grandma Stephy: What happened at his friend's house? Did you get what he needed?

Me: Sort of.

Grandma Stephy: ???

Me: The guy was gone. He left a flash drive, but Kai has to break into it.

Grandma Stephy: Isa, I trust your judgment and everything, but are you sure you want to be messing around with this stuff? I don't want you getting into trouble.

"Is that Grandma Stephy?" Indigo asks, and I nod. "What's she saying?"

I roll onto my side to look at her. "She thinks I shouldn't be messing around with suspicious flash drives."

"Text her back and tell her you won't," Indigo says, surprising me.

"You want me to lie to her?"

"It's not lying. You won't be messing around with it. Kai will."

My fingers hover over the buttons. "But Kai's doing

it for me."

She rotates around in her seat so she's turned around and looking at me. She moves her cigarette out of her mouth. "Look, Isa. Sometimes, it's better not to be completely honest when it comes to Grandma. She's older, and when she gets stressed out, it starts to show, you know."

"Maybe I shouldn't mess around with the flash drive, then, if it's going to cause this many problems."

"No, you need to; otherwise, you're going to stay stressed out." When I still seem not entirely convinced, she releases a frustrated exhale. "Look, you can do whatever you want, but I really think you should just let her think we're letting this go. Ask her to have her cop friend look into it. It might be nice to have a backup plan, anyway, just in case Kai can't pull out these badass cracking code skills he says he has." She scratches at her brow with the back of her hand. "Okay, total subject change here, but wasn't it so hot when Kai said he could break into this flash drive?"

"You think computer skills are hot? Because you're usually into guys who are kind of . . . How do I put this nicely? Not very smart."

"Yeah, but they're hot. And besides, it's not like I'm going to marry any of them. I'm young and having fun." Smoke circles her face as she takes a drag off her cigarette. "Does it bother you that I find Kai hot?"

"No." But my lip instinctively twitches, and she totally notices.

"It so does and I love it. I'm going to keep doing it until you admit you're in love with him." She extends her arm to the side to ash her cigarette out the window and grins at me as I scowl at her. "You know he almost kissed you, right? He was like," she holds her finger and thumb and inch apart, "this close."

I want to deny, deny, deny like I usually do, but it's kind of pointless since she witnessed it happen.

"I don't know what to do," I admit, propping up on my elbow. "I mean, I was with Kyler yesterday, and he was really sweet and spent the day trying to distract me from all the family drama. We were flirting, and I liked it . . . And then there was that almost kiss . . . That was . . ." I try to find a word to describe it but the first thing that comes to my mind is nice. And saying that aloud to Indigo, I know she'll just overanalyze it. "But then, today, I'm with Kai, and he's so amazing . . . Like, seriously, who climbs over a seat just to hold a person because they're about to cry? And then he took me on a walk and told me this story about Hannah . . . It's not even just that. It's everything. Like, when he holds my hand, it calms me down." I rub my forehead with the heel of my hand. "But I still think I might like Kyler." I blow out another breath. "I'm the worst person ever. What's wrong with me? Who thinks like this?"

"Um, a lot of people. Your confusion is totally normal. Trust me. I've dated a lot of guys at once, and you haven't crossed a line yet."

"Haven't I? Because I might have let Kai kiss me if he didn't back off."

"Isa, Kyler and you haven't made any sort of commitment. You've hung out a couple of times for a little bit, and he's asked you out. That's it. Until you've had the exclusive conversation, you can do whatever your little heart desires. Besides, it's not like you lie to them. You told Kai about the almost kiss with Kyler, yet he still almost kissed you. And Kyler knows you hang out with Kai. If he's seen you two together, he knows there's chemistry there." Bits of ash float through the air as she returns the cigarette to her lips. "And I hate to say this, but with everything you've told me about Kyler, he kind of sounds like a player and is probably still dating other girls."

I think of Jesmine and the endless hug. Maybe she's right, but that doesn't mean I feel comfortable being involved on a dating level with both of them. It's weird and strange and . . .

"But they're brothers, and they don't really like each other." I flick a piece of ash off my arm. "It seems super messed up to be thinking about kissing both of them."

"Look, you can do whatever you want. Kiss Kai. Don't kiss Kai. Date Kyler. See where that goes." She rolls her eyes. "You haven't dated, like, at all. You need to do that. It's a rite of passage." When I start to nod, she tacks on a, "But . . ."

I grimace. The dreaded "but."

"This thing with Kai, I don't think you should ignore it." She takes another drag off her cigarette and exhales a cloud of smoke. "The way he looks at you . . ." She gets that dreamy look in her eyes. "I'm pretty sure he's in love with you."

"Um, no, he's not," I protest, my voice high, like I just sucked helium out of a balloon.

"He might not be there yet, but he almost is," she says. "Guys don't just do favors like this for girls they're sorta friends with."

Unsure what to say, I keep my lips zipped. I don't believe for one second Kai's in love with me. Sure, we're friends, and yeah, we flirt. But that's just Kai. He's a flirt.

"And eventually, you're going to fall in love with him, too." She flicks her cigarette butt out the window. "Maybe not right now, but definitely this year."

"What? Are your psychic abilities kicking in again or something?" I joke in an attempt to divert the whole love conversation.

She takes my hand and leans over, pretending to read my palm. "Yep, you're definitely going to fall in love this year."

Love. Really? I've never been in love before. I've never been loved. The only love I've ever been shown is from my grandma and grandpa and sometimes Indigo, and those instances were smack dab in the middle of hate that filled my life.

Lynn, Hannah, and my dad worked so hard to prove how little I was worth. They made it a point to show me I meant nothing to them. And now I find out my mom might have killed someone . . . So, yeah, call me a pessimist or whatever, but I just don't see myself falling in love very soon or anyone falling in love with me.

"Speaking of falling in love, here comes mister soon-to-be-the-love-of-your-life." She faces forward in her seat.

Seconds later, Kai opens the back door of the car. He nudges my feet out of the way, sets a bag on the floor, and then slides into the seat beside me. He's changed into a different hoodie and jeans and is sporting a grey, knitted beanie. I don't know why, but I find myself searching his face for fresh wounds. The only injuries I can see are the ones from yesterday, though.

"Everything okay?" I sit up as Indigo pulls out onto the road.

"Yeah, everything's good," he says without looking at me. "I grabbed some stuff . . . clothes and shit. I hope that's okay."

"It's fine." I steal a glance at my house before we drive away. My dad's car is gone, and the house looks so peaceful and quiet. I wonder where they are, if they went to one of their shopping/lunch things they do on Sundays sometimes. I don't know why I care. It's not like they ever took me with them. Yet, part of me does care.

"Did you talk to your parents at all?"

"My dad was there."

I want to ask him more, but before I can, he scoots forward in the seat. "Hey, turn this up," he tells Indigo. "It's my jam."

When Indigo cranks up the song, Kai reaches out, catches my arm, and pulls me across the seat until I'm sitting right beside him. Then he starts singing and dancing and tickling me, and for a crazy, wild second, everything seems normal. But then the song ends and another one turns on that no one knows. All we're left with to distract us is the silence.

And the silence says too much, whispers my worst fears to me, tells me Kai's not okay.

It tells me I'm not okay.

Chapter SIXTEEN

ISABELLA

When we're parking the car in front of Grandma Stephy's apartment complex, I inform Indigo and Kai that I decided to be liar, liar, pants on fire and text my grandma, telling her that I'm not going to do anything with the flash drive. She responds with a smiley face and tells me she was glad I made that decision and that she'll have her retired policeman friend look into it to see what he can find. I hope for the sake of having to lie some more that he does find out something.

"But you still want me to open it, right?" Kai asks as he opens the car door to get out.

I nod, sliding to the edge of the seat. "I just think it might be easier on her if she doesn't know you're doing it."

He nods understandingly, collecting his bag off the floor. I haven't asked him yet how long he's staying or what his parents said to him about the condition of his face, but I plan on getting to the bottom of it as soon as it's just the two of us.

Without saying anything else, the three of us walk into the apartment. The moment we step inside, my nostrils are engulfed with the fresh scent of . . .

"Cookies!" I squeal at the sight of Grandma Stephy in the kitchen, wearing an apron and using a spatula to transfer cookies off a pan and onto a plate.

"I thought you could probably use some sugar," she says to me.

I bounce into the kitchen. "I could use a butt load of sugar."

"Don't eat too much." She slides the plate of cookies across the counter toward me. They are my favorite kind—sugar with buttercream frosting. "For dinner, I'm making those chicken wraps you love."

Great. Now I feel even guiltier about telling her I'm not going to have Kai mess around with the flash drive.

I pluck a cookie on the plate and nibble on it. It's still warm and melts on my tongue. I let out a groan as I turn around to offer Indigo and Kai a cookie. When I find Kai watching me with a curious, intense look on his face, I can't help thinking of what Indigo said in the car about Kai maybe being in love with me.

I hold the plate of cookies out to him. "Want one? They're really good."

"Yeah, I can see that." He deliberates something before grabbing a cookie off the plate, the entire time keeping his eyes on me. He takes a bite and makes an oh-God-these-are-so-good face. "You're right. These are awesome." He licks a drop of frosting from his lip.

I can't stop staring at his mouth.

Dammit, Indigo and the freakin' power of suggestion. If I didn't know any better, I'd swear she did it on purpose.

"I'm really glad you decided to let my friend handle this," my grandma says to me as she sets a mixing bowl into the sink. "I think it'll be best if no one does anything illegal." Her gaze sweeps the three of us. "That goes for all of you."

I almost cave and confess everything to her.

"We won't," Indigo says with an eye roll. "Jeez, give us some credit. We're not that bad."

"I know you're not," Grandma Stephy says, "but when it comes to helping each other out, you and Isa would pretty much do anything for each other."

Indigo and I exchange a smile, and my Grandma Stephy busies herself with cleaning up the kitchen.

"Hey, Grandma, is it cool if we watch a movie?" Indigo suddenly asks her, which seems weird. Indigo rarely asks to do stuff. She just does it. "We thought it might be nice for Isa to sit down and relax for a while."

What? This is news to me. What the heck is she up to?

I try to catch her gaze, but she keeps her eyes on Grandma Stephy.

"That sounds nice," Grandma Stephy says, turning on the faucet. "Maybe I'll watch one with you."

"Sounds cool. But just FYI, Isa is picking, and she'll pick a zombie movie," Indigo says. "Which means a lot of blood and gore and brains. I just thought I'd give you a heads up because I know you hate that stuff."

"Then maybe I'll just have Harry over for a movie night. You guys can watch your movie in the Indigo's room, and we'll stay out in the living room." She gives Indigo a sugary sweet smile. "That way, whatever you've got planned won't happen outside of this house."

Indigo feigns dumb. "Why do you think we have something planned?"

"Because I know everything." She smirks at Indigo. "And I can read right through your bullshit story."

"I was just trying to save you from a night of gore because I know you hate that, but whatever." Indigo turns for the hallway, motioning at Kai and me to follow her. "Just make sure to tie a scarf on your doorknob."

"I don't have to follow your college rules," my Grandma Stephy calls out after her. "This is my house, and I can have sex on the couch if I want to."

I glance at Kai, completely embarrassed. And he seems really interested in his cookie.

"Um, we should go and get the movie going." I cross my fingers I can get him out of the room before my grandma mentions sex again.

Kai nods, looking like he's struggling not to laugh.

We start for the hallway, and I'm about to apologize to Kai for having to hear that when my grandma calls me back. I tell Kai to go ahead and return to the kitchen.

"Is everything okay?" I ask her, opening the fridge to get a few sodas.

She takes out a jar of alfredo sauce from the cupboard. "I just wanted to see how you are doing."

I shrug then shrug again. "I'm tough. I know how to deal with stuff."

"I know you know how to deal with stuff," she says, setting the jar of sauce down on the counter. "But I want to know how you're doing."

Tears burn at the back of my eyes as those emotions I boxed up threaten to break out. "I don't know what you want me to say."

"Oh, sweetie." She hugs me as I start to cry.

We stay like that for a few minutes, with me crying into her shoulder and her rocking me back and forth like she did when I was a child. When I was younger and I got hurt from falling out of a tree or crashing my bike, she was there to tell me everything was okay, and then she would hug me and rock me back and forth until I felt better.

When my eyes dry, I step away. "Thank you. I needed that."

"If you need anything at all, I'm always here, Isa," she tells me. "I know you're not used to having that, but I'm not like your dad. I want you to come to me if anything's bothering you, okay? Even if you just need to cry."

I sniffle. "Okay, I will."

"Good girl." She motions for me to go ahead and go. "Now go and relax with your friends. Just make sure that whatever Indigo has planned isn't going to keep you up super late or require you to sneak out of the house."

I nod and head back to Indigo's bedroom. When I open the door, I find Kai sprawled out on the bed with his laptop open.

"Where's Indigo?" I ask, stepping in and closing the door.

"Somebody called her, and she went into the bathroom to talk to them." He clicks a couple of keys then glances up at me. He takes one look at my face, and his expression plummets. "What happened?"

I sit down at the foot of the bed. "I'm fine. I promise. I just . . . needed a moment."

He looks like he wants to say something, but then he just returns his attention to the computer. His fingers tap against the keys as he stares at the screen.

Curious about what he's doing, I crawl up the bed until I'm right beside him. "So, how bad is it?"

"I have no clue yet." He clicks the mouse a couple of times, and a password box appears on the screen.

I lean over him to get a better look at the screen and my hair falls into his face. "Is that all you have to figure out?"

"Probably not. If I crack into this, more will probably pop up." He sounds strained.

I wonder why. If it's because he's worried he's not going to be able to do it?

"Isa." His voice is soft as he brushes my hair away from his face. "I love you to death and you smell fantastic, but the hover thing is going to make it really hard to concentrate."

"Oh. Sorry." I shift back, giving him some breathing room, questions bouncing through my head. *He loves me to death? I smell fantastic?* "I'm just nervous about this whole thing."

"I know you are." He rolls over, facing me, and props up onto his elbow. "I'm going to do my best to get into these files, but while I try to make that happen, I need something from you."

"Okay." My anxiety goes through the roof. "What is it?"

He tangles a strand of my hair around his finger. "I need you to relax."

I exhale, freeing the tension I had trapped inside my lungs. "I'll try."

He lightly tugs on my hair, a small smile playing at his lips. "I think we should turn on a movie. That way, you'll have something to focus on besides what I'm doing, and if your grandma checks in on us, it won't look like we're total liars."

"That's a good idea." I push off the bed and head to the television perched on the corner dresser. I open the top drawer where Indigo keeps her DVDs and start searching for a good one.

I don't know how, but I can feel him watching my every move, like every one of my senses are connected to him. I'm blaming it on Indigo for filling my head with the idea that he might be in love with me.

"Hey, Kai, can I ask you a question?"

"Sure," he says, sounding reluctant.

"When you went into your house . . ." I sift through the DVDs, keeping my head tucked down, unsure how he's going to react. "Nothing happened, right?"

"What do you mean?"

"I mean, with your dad. I know you were worried he'd be upset with you . . . And you seemed distant when you came out. I just wanted to make sure he didn't . . . do anything to you."

He's quiet for a while, and I start to worry maybe I pressed too much. But then I hear the mattress creak. It's followed by a light thud and then footsteps move toward me. Moments later, his body heat engulfs me.

"You worry about me too much." He's so close I can feel his breath caressing the back of my neck.

"You worry about me the same amount." My eyes are glued on the titles of the DVDs, but if you asked me what they were, I couldn't tell you. I'm way too focused on how his chest is barely touching my back, almost pushing against me, but not quite.

"I don't know about that." He pauses, his breath tickling my skin. Moments later, his fingers touch the back of my neck and he sketches a soft across my skin. "I worry about you a lot."

"W-well, I worry about you a lot." I can't catch my breath. Can't think. Can't feel anything but how hard my heart is slamming against my chest.

"Maybe Indigo's right," he says with a hint of amusement in his tone. "We are really alike."

"Yeah, we both worry too much."

"Yeah, we definitely do."

I scrounge up all the courage I have and turn my head to look at him. He's so close his lips nearly brush mine.

I lean back the slightest bit so I can look him in the eye. "You never answered my question about what your dad said to you."

"He said what he always does. That he's not surprised I screwed up." He steps back, tugs off his beanie, and tosses it on the bed. Then he yanks his fingers through his hair, making the light blond strands go askew. "He kicked me out."

I turn all the way around. "What? Seriously."

He shrugs. "It's been a long time coming, and honestly, I'm kind of relieved. I just wish I had a place to live lined up."

"You can stay here for a while." I place my hand on his arm, trying to comfort him. "My grandma won't care."

He smiles, but it doesn't reach his eyes. "I love you to death for saying that, but I need to find my own place. I'm eighteen years old. I should start taking care of myself."

"No, you shouldn't. You're eighteen, but you're still in high school. You shouldn't have to take care of yourself like this already."

"I could be saying the same thing to you."

"I know."

We exchange a look, or more like a mutual understanding. While our situations aren't exactly the same, we both can understand what the other one is going through.

I note his eyes drifting to my lips again, and I think he's considering kissing me. Indigo's advice plays through my mind, but I'm still not certain I agree with her or if I'm the girl who can handle dating two guys at the same time. I don't even know how to date, let alone be a player.

But I won't lie; I want Kai to kiss me.

He abruptly steps back, cracking his knuckles and breaking the moment. "All right, time to try and make some magic happen."

He returns to the bed, and his fingers start pounding against the keys. I put in a random movie and lie down on the bed beside him, keeping some distance between us, mostly because I'm not sure what he wants. Or what I want. Confusion is laced through my every thought, and I wish I could clear the haze from my head.

A couple of minutes later, Indigo walks into the room.

"I hate to do this to you," she announces as she opens a dresser drawer. "But I have to bail out on you for a few days. My mom just called. Apparently, my dad took off with his secretary again. She sounded drunk, so I'm going to head home and check on her."

"What do you mean he ran off with his secretary again?" I ask. "How many times has this happened?"

"Too many times." She scoops up a stack of clothes, drops them on the floor, and then gets a suitcase out of the closet. "He's been doing this for years, and my mom stupidly takes him back because she has no self-esteem at all and doesn't think she can do better." She unzips the suitcases and shoves the clothes inside. "I thought the whole family knew about this."

"You know my family's never really talked to anyone in the extended family," I remind her, reaching for a pillow. "Lynn's always thought she was too good to associate with anyone."

"True." She moves the open suitcase over to the vanity and uses her arm to push all the makeup products off the edge so they fall messily into the suitcase.

"You've always been the worst packer," I remark as I tuck the pillow under my head.

She grins at me. "It's a gift. Not everyone can be this talented in messiness."

I laugh, but then put on my serious face. "Do you need me to do anything?"

She shakes her head. "Nope." Her gaze deliberately travels in Kai's direction. "Well, you could just kiss—"

"I can go and get your hair stuff out of the bathroom." I leap from the bed, grateful Kai is busy and doesn't seem to be paying attention.

She grins like the Cheshire cat. "Yes, go and do that."

As I walk out of the room, I mentally wish upon a shooting star that she won't say anything weird to Kai while I'm gone.

When I walk into the bathroom, I begin gathering her shampoos and hairsprays. As I'm picking up her brush, my phone buzzes. I set the stuff down and fish out my phone from the pocket of my pajama pants.

Kyler: I just wanted to see if you are okay.

Me: Yeah, I'm fine. Thanks for checking up on me.

Kyler: I told you I would. I was going to call you, but I'm stuck at the gym still, and my trainer will have a shit fit if I make phone calls. I miss talking to you, though. I can't wait until next weekend.

It takes me a second to figure out what he's talking about. The date.

Me: Me, either. Hopefully, I'll have the perfect zombie movie picked out. Just enough blood and guts that you'll get the full experience.

Kyler: Can't wait. ;)

Me: Ha, ha, I bet.

Kyler: What? I really can't. I'm super excited about this. I even spent the afternoon at the ice-cream shop trying to find a new concoction for you to try.

Me: You did that without me? That sounds dangerous.

But honestly, I'm kind of touched.

Kyler: It was definitely interesting. Let me just say that bubble gum and chocolate ice cream is a no go.

Me: It doesn't sound too bad to me. Your taste buds are just too picky.

The phone suddenly rings, and Kyler's name flashes across the screen. I press talk and put the phone to my ear.

"I thought you said your trainer would have a shit fit if you called," I say, leaning against the bathroom counter.

"He will," he replies. "But it's worth it to hear your voice."

"There you go with the rom-com lines."

"Yep. I saved that one just for you."

"Gee, thanks," I say sarcastically.

"Anytime. But really, I just wanted to make sure you are okay. My dad and Kai got into this fight, and I guess he kicked Kai out. He looked so upset when he walked out of the house. It made me think of you and how hard this has to be for you, having to move out of your house and being on your own."

"Well, I'm not on my own. I'm living with my grandma and cousin . . . You were at the house when Kai got kicked out?"

"Yeah. I tried to talk my dad out of it, but he's a

stubborn man." He pauses. "You act like you already knew about the fight."

I fidget with a bracelet on my wrist. "I do."

"How?"

"Um . . . Because Kai's here with me."

"Oh." The silence that follows seems to last forever. "So he's, like, staying with you?"

I think about lying to him, but I'm all lied out for the day. "He's just staying on my grandma's couch until he can find somewhere to live."

"Oh." Another pause and I just start to think he's irritated when he says, "I'm glad he has somewhere to stay. I was worried he'd end up sleeping on a park bench or something."

"He's fine," I assure him. "I won't let him leave until he has somewhere else to stay that isn't a park bench."

"If he does try to leave without having anywhere else to go . . . Will you promise to call me?"

"Of course."

He seems so concerned about Kai, but with how much the two of them argue, I find his response strange.

"Hey, would it be okay if I picked you up for lunch tomorrow?" he asks. "You get, like, an hour lunch break, right? We could hit up the drive-in or something."

"Yeah, sure. That sounds nice." But I cross my fingers I'm not crossing that line Indigo was talking about yet. I don't want to hurt anyone, and I can't ignore the voice in the back of my head telling me I just need to pick one of them.

"Awesome . . ." He trails off as someone says something to him.

It's a girl's voice and I feel myself cringing with jealousy. I hate my reaction and remind myself that we're not dating, that he can talk and hang out with girls like how I talk to Kai. He's not mine. And besides, maybe his trainer is a girl.

Then I hear her say my name, or more like sneer it, and my jealousy turns into confusion.

"Hey Isa, I'm sorry, but I have to go," Kyler says to me. "That was my trainer chewing out my ass. If I don't get off the phone now, I'm gonna have to run an extra mile tomorrow morning."

"Okay."

He says goodbye and then hangs up, leaving me even more confused.

It makes me question why I feel this way. It's the second time I've felt confusedly jealous over Kyler and a girl and I've only hung out with him twice. Is that how stuff is going to be? Am I ever going to get over my insecurities when I'm with him . . . My thoughts drift to Kai and how easy things are with him . . .

Shaking the thought from my head, I take the hair products with me as I return to the room.

When I walk in, Indigo is almost finished packing. I drop the hair products into the suitcase and she zips it up.

"Call me if you need anything," she says, hugging me good-bye. Then she whispers in my ear, "And I mean anything, especially if you get confused over guys."

When I nod, she steps back and leaves the room, wheeling her suitcase behind her.

I dither for a moment in the doorway, wonder if I should have Kai and I move to the living room. It's intimidating being in a room with him. I don't know why it is. I mean, we slept on the same couch together the other night. But this is a room with a bed and walls and a door, and it feels so . . . intimate.

But then I hear my Grandma Stephy talking to Harry, and I decide to quit being a chicken and lie down on the bed beside Kai.

The corners of his lips quirk, but he doesn't look up from the computer. "For a second, I thought you were going to pussy out."

"Why would I pussy out?" I ask, adjusting the pillows. "We're just hanging out."

"Because we're alone in a bed. Think of all the possibilities." He winks at me.

I shake my head, like "Oh, Kai." But deep down, I'm thinking about the possibilities, as well. And dear God, my mind can create some pretty creative ones.

"You're cute when you blush," he says before redirecting his attention back to the computer. I try to pay attention to the movie, but my mind's elsewhere: on my mom, Lynn, my dad, Hannah, the blue car, Kai, Kyler. The list is endless and makes me wonder if I'll ever be able to relax again.

The next thing I know I'm suddenly being woken up from a very deep sleep by a loud buzzing. I'm thrown off. I don't even remember falling asleep to begin with. I was so awake, so worried I thought I'd never be able to sleep.

It takes me a second to process my surroundings through the darkness. I'm in a bed, moonlight is filtering through a window, and my legs are tangled with someone else's.

My attention whips to the person lying beside me, panic setting in. Then I remember what happened right before I fell asleep.

Kai had shut down the computer for the night and was lying down beside me to finish the movie. When I wouldn't hold still, he pressed his forehead against mine.

"You're so restless," he said.

"I know." I sighed. "I'm sorry. I just have too much on my mind or something."

Amusement danced in his eyes. "I have a cure for that."

I was a little afraid to ask. "Oh yeah? What?"

He grinned and then started singing "Lullaby" by The Spill Canvas to me in the softest, most soothing voice ever.

"Go to sleep, Isa," he said, adding his own words in. "Or else I'm going to kiss you."

I giggled as my heart leapt in my chest. I wanted to say something snarky to him, banter like we normal do, but I was too flustered. I didn't think I could fall asleep with how awake and wired my mind was, but I must have passed out only a minute later, because that's the last thing I can remember.

But how my grandma let us fall to sleep together in the bed is beyond me. My guess is that she got caught up doing . . . stuff with Harry.

Kai's sound asleep on his side with his hands tucked under his head. He looks so adorable and relaxed, his lips slightly parted as he breathes in and out, his hair sticking up in all sorts of directions. The urge to run my fingers through his hair surfaces. I want to touch him really, really badly to the point that it might make me a creeper. And watching him sleep like this makes me even stranger.

Before I even know what I'm doing, I start to reach for him. But then my phone buzzes, nearly startling me to death, and I realize that it's the same buzzing that woke me.

Yawning, I pick my phone up from off the nightstand and read the message, figuring it's probably from Indigo, telling me she made it home okay.

Unknown: You're going to get what you deserve.

Unknown: Just you wait.

"What the crap?" I rub the tiredness from my eyes then reach over and turn the lamp on before reading the message again.

Kai stirs beside me, his eyelids opening and blinking against the light. He takes one look at my face and goes from groggily waking up to waking-the-fuck-up.

"What's wrong?" he asks, sitting up.

I hand him my phone. "I just got this message."

Kai reads the message and his jaw clenches. "This has to be Hannah. God, she's such an evil bitch."

"But how did she get an unknown number?"

"It's not that hard." He sets the phone down on the nightstand. "And they're pretty easy to trace. I'll look into it tomorrow."

I chew on my thumbnail. "I hate to say this, but if it is Hannah, I'm kind of worried over what she has planned."

He slips his arms around me and guides me with him as he lies back down. "I'm not going to let her do anything to you." He tucks his arm underneath my head and plays with my hair. "I stopped her from spreading rumors once; I can do it again."

I want to believe he has that kind of power, but . . ."What she's the one who stole the papers out of the car? What if she knows my mom murdered someone, and she tells everyone at school?"

"That's not going to happen," he promises me. "I won't let it."

I want to ask him how, but he kisses my forehead, silencing me.

"Get some sleep," he whispers then reaches over and clicks off the lamp.

He settles beside me, holding onto me for dear life and making me feel safe.

I wish I could hold onto the moment forever, but I know, come morning, I'll have to wake up and face reality.

Chapter SEVENTEEN

ISABELLA

The next couple of days are surprisingly uneventful. With all the drama that happened over the weekend and the threatening text messages, I expected all hell to break lose. But nothing happens.

On Monday, I borrow the car Indigo usually takes to work to drive Kai and me to school. Kyler texts me that morning, telling me he has to cancel our lunch date. While I'm not crazy bummed out, it still kind of sucks because, in a way, I feel like my dream of wanting to date him is slowly fading.

Tuesday and Wednesday breeze by in a flash and before I know it, it's Thursday. I haven't seen any sightings of the mysterious blue car, but that still doesn't mean I've forgotten about it. I keep waiting for it to pop up somewhere and the worry has me on edge.

On Thursday afternoon, I work on homework while Kai tries to crack into the flash drive. Indigo still isn't back from her parents and since my Grandma hangs out with her friends a lot, usually Kai and I have the apartment to ourselves. It gives him plenty of time to mess around on the computer without my grandma getting too suspicious.

He's managed to crack a few of the codes, but more always pop up. I really start to question what could be on there. Why Big Doug would put so much security on a flash drive that supposedly only holds information about my mom's case.

Between trying to crack codes, Kai spends time trying to track down the unknown number that messaged me.

"I think they might have used a burner phone," he says to me, flopping back in the couch with frustration written all over his face. "I don't know what else to do."

"Maybe we should take a break," I suggest when I notice how exhausted he looks. The bags under his eyes reveal that he clearly hasn't been sleeping well. While some of the cuts and bruises have faded, he still has a few along his hairline and beside his eye. "We could take a time out from this and do something else."

He shakes his head, being stubborn. "No, I need to do this for you."

I nibble on the corner of a cookie. "Kai, it's not going to be the end of the world if you don't break into the flash drive. I mean, you said that Big Doug said my mom got an appeal . . ." I swallow down the pain, always do when I think about her. "Eventually, the information on that will be out in the open."

"But I don't want you to have to worry." The passionate look he gives me makes me melt back in the chair. "I want you to have some peace of mind through all of this."

He's been giving me that look a freakin' ton over the last few of days. Which makes me believe even more that he needs a break.

"Sorry, I'm acting so crazy," he says when I give him a please-chill-dude look. "I just wish I could figure this out. If Big Doug were here, he'd be able to figure it out like that." He snaps his finger.

"If Big Doug was here then we wouldn't be doing this to begin with." I stuff the rest of the toast into my mouth, dust the crumbs off my hands, and pick up my phone as it buzzes.

I hesitate before opening the message. It's something I've been doing ever since I got the threatening text.

> *Lily: Hey! Just wanted to check in and see if you were still interested in that job. My manager's about to hire some idiot who I'm pretty sure came to the interview blazed out of his freaking mind.*

"Who's Lily?" Kai asks, reading the message from over my shoulder.

"I met her when Kyler and I played flag football," I say. "She's Wes's little sister . . . Not sure if you know who Wes is."

"Yeah, I know who he is. He's an asshole." Kai sweeps my hair away from my shoulder and rests his chin there. "I didn't know you were looking for a job."

"I wasn't really looking. Lily just suggested I work there. She seems really nice . . . I don't think she's actually friends with Kyler."

"I don't think so either. At least, I've never heard of a Lily." He pauses. "What's going on with you two?"

"Who? Me and Lily?" But I know he's not referring to Lily.

"You and my brother." He pauses again and I can feel him studying me. "You haven't mentioned him at all. As far as I know, you haven't talked to him since Saturday. And just when you said his name now . . . You had a tone."

"I don't know why I did, but I swear, there's nothing going on," I say, but I feel like such a liar.

But nothing really is going on with us. That's the problem. Talking to Kai about my reservations, though, it doesn't feel right.

"I think I'm going to apply for that job," I abruptly announce, swiping my finger across the screen of my phone.

Me: I'm definitely still interested.

Lily: Yay! Can you head over now?

Me: Yep. On my way now.

I glance down at my black jeans with zipper embellishments, my red off-the-shoulder top, and my strappy heels.

Me: Wait. What should I wear?

Lily: Whatever. It doesn't really matter. I mean, he was about to hire a guy as high as a mofo.

I smile at her message, slide my phone into my back pocket, and grab the car keys from the coffee table.

Kai rises to his feet and stretches his arms above his head. "Want some company?"

I nod, heading for the door. "And I want you to take a break so it's a two-for-one."

He grins at me, his arms falling to the side. "Actually, it's a three-for-one because it gives me a chance to spend time with a beautiful girl."

I roll my eyes, but as I step out the door, a goofy smile

plasters across my face.

Kai grabs his grey knitted beanie and tugs it on before stepping outside with me. After I lock up, we head for the car. Halfway down the sidewalk, he places a hand against the small of my back, his gaze skimming the parking lot.

"What are you looking at?" I ask, trying to track his gaze.

His eyes land on a car parked on the corner of the street. "Blue car."

The air gets ripped from my lungs as I spot the blue car with the Superman sticker. I squint, trying to get the plate number when suddenly Kai starts running toward it.

"Kai, no don't!" I shout in a panic.

What if the person in the car is dangerous? What if he gets hurt?

Before Kai even gets close, the car speeds off, the tires spinning and leaving marks on the road. While I want to know who's following me, I'm relieved it drove away before Kai did something irrational that might have gotten him hurt.

"Dammit," he curses, kicking a rock across the grass. "I'm going to lose my damn mind wondering who the fuck it is."

"I know," I say as approach him. "But if we see it again, you have to promise me you won't try to do anything but get the plate number."

He shakes his head, his gaze fierce. "No way."

"Kai," I start, my tone carrying a warning. "I don't want you getting hurt."

"I won't get hurt," he assures me. "They would."

I pop my knuckles against the side of my legs. "I don't want you getting into this mess. You're already too far into it."

His expression softens. "Isa, trust me when I say this mess is mild compared to the trouble I'm in."

"You mean with trying to find a house? Or finding a way your car towed back to Sunnyvale?" I question. "Or this thing with T. Because you still haven't explained to me what that's about."

"And I'm not going to." He slings an arm around my waist and steers me toward the car.

"That's not fair. Why do you get to help me and I don't get to help you?"

"Because you're too pretty."

I let my head dramatically bob back. "That's the dumbest excuse I've ever heard."

"Well, it's true. And I wouldn't be able to forgive myself if something happened to you."

I don't know how to respond. I want to say a lot of stuff, but my heart is racing too wildly. I'm worried my voice will come out all wobbly.

Instead, I get my phone and text my grandma about what just happened. She replies that she'll have her policeman friend look around the apartment the second he gets home.

> *Grandma Stephy: And I want you to stay inside and keep the doors locked until I get home.*
>
> *Me: I'm actually headed to apply for a job.*
>
> *Grandma Stephy: I didn't know you were looking for a job.*
>
> *Me: I want to help out.*
>
> *Grandma Stephy: You don't have to do that, Isa. I'm happy I get to take care of you.*

Me: I still need to work. If for nothing else, to save up for college.

Grandma Stephy: All right, if you want to do that then that's fine. But you keep every penny you earned . . . And Kai's with you, right? I don't want you driving alone.

Me: Yeah, he's right here.

Grandma Stephy: Good. That makes me feel a lot better. That boy would seriously take a bullet for you.

Me: Over dramatic much. J/k ;)

Grandma Stephy: I'm just being protective. Stay safe and get home as soon as you can.

Protective? It feels strange to think about that someone wants to protect me. I glance at Kai, thinking about what my grandma said. Does he really care about me that much? According to Indigo, probably.

When we get to the car, Kai opens the driver's door for me. Normally I'd tease him about trying to be a gentleman, but he hurries to the passenger side before I can.

The car ride is quiet for the most part. It's a cloudy day and by the time we pull up to the store, it's raining.

Before we get out, Kai removes his hoodie and hands it to me. "Put this on and pull the hood over so your hair doesn't get wet."

"Aw. Always watching out for me," I joke as I slip my arms through the sleeves of his jacket.

The scent of his cologne and everything that is Kai engulfs my nostrils. I find myself deeply breathing it in.

Kai gives me a strange look. "Did you just smell my jacket?"

"Um . . ." My cheeks feel like they're on fire. "Maybe."

He sucks his bottom lip in between his teeth, biting back a grin. "Did it smell good?"

I think about shaking my head, but I find myself nodding.

His smile breaks through. "Good." He reaches over and draws the hood over my head, his gaze fixed on me the entire time.

I want to squirm and look away, because it's getting super complicated to breathe, but I can't find the strength to do so. So instead, I end up staring at him with my jaw hanging open like an idiotic.

"Ready?" he asks, leaning away from me.

I nod then fumble for the door handle and get out of the car. Thankfully, the fresh air and scent of rain clears my nerves. I meet Kai around the front of the car, and we walk side by side into the store.

The door dings as we enter and I draw the hood off my head as I take a look around. The place is very disorganized, the shelves are a mess, and the posters on the walls are hung crookedly. But there's some pretty cool stuff around; record players, books, jewelry.

Lily is sitting on the cluttered front counter, reading a book. Her hair is pulled in a sidebraid again and she's wearing sneakers, holey jeans, and a plaid shirt over a black T-shirt.

She looks up when we walk in. "Yes. You made it." She bounds off the counter, her gaze going right to Kai. "And you brought a friend."

"This is Kai." I motion at him. "He's Kyler's brother."

"Oh." A curious look crosses her face then she lifts a brow, looking at me like *explain*.

I'm sure the look is coming from the fact that only a week ago I met her while I was with Kyler. I don't want to attempt to explain it to her in front of Kai. And besides,

I don't have a clue how to explain it.

"Ready?" she asks me, letting the look drop.

I nod, shuck off Kai's jacket, and square my shoulders.

"Good luck," Kai says to me as I hand him the jacket.

I smile, but I'm nervous as I was the first day I went to school with my new makeover.

"You don't need to be nervous," Lily says as we wind around a few boxes and shelves, heading for a closed door at the back of the store. "Glen's chill. I'm sure he'll hire you on the spot."

Her words seem crazy. Hire me on the spot. Yet they end up being true. Glen is chill. Like, way, way chill and hires me after asking me three questions.

1. Do I like secondhand items?
2. Do I know how to work a register?
3. And when can I start?

While I don't know how to work a register, I lie, figuring I'll have Lily give me a quick demonstration.

"So?" Lily's practically bouncing on her toes when I exit Glen's office.

I let out a breath of relief. "He told me I could start next week."

She squeals and gives me a quick hug. "Yes. I'm so glad I don't have to work with the pothead. He kept staring at my tits like the entire time." She backs away from me. "I'm going to go get you some forms you need to fill out. I'll be right back." She disappears into the office before I can even get a word out.

I head back to the store area to go tell Kai the news. I find him sifting through a box of old records with his head tucked down, the beanie still on. I pause, noting how adorable he looks reading the titles. And while I love Kai's hair and everything, he can pull off the beanie look really well.

As if sensing me staring at him, his gaze suddenly lifts and finds me. "So?"

I shrug, a faint smile lifting at my lips. "I got it."

He heads toward me. "That's a good thing, right?"

I nod, meeting him in the middle of the store. "Glen, the manager, seems really chillaxed." My gaze sweeps the disorderly store. "Maybe a little too relaxed, but whatever." I wander toward a display case and stare at the necklaces, bracelets, and rings inside it. "There's a lot of cool stuff in here, though. I think the place just needs cleaned up and then it'll rock awesome . . ." My breath hitches in my throat as I feel him move up behind me.

"You're going to be okay, right?" He sweeps my hair to the side, his arms circle my waist, and he rests his chin on my shoulder.

It's the second time he's done this today and again, my heart flutters like a cracked out hummingbird.

"Why wouldn't I be all right?" Hell to the yeah, my voice came out even. Mental high-five for me!

"Just with everything going on." He pauses and oh my God, his lips brush my neck. "I don't want you to stress yourself out."

"You say that a lot." My voice cracks. Epic fail for me.

"That's because I worry." His lips touch my neck again.

My eyelashes flutter. I freakin' can't breathe.

"Remember that night we licked each other?" he asks suddenly.

I splay my palms to the top of the display case as I try to catch my breath. "I only did it to you because you did it to me first. It felt like we were acting like dogs or something."

"Hmmm . . . dog's huh? Interesting . . ." His response confuses the crap out of me, especially when he just starts singing along with the Avril Lavigne song playing through the store stereo.

"You and your music . . ." All the rest of my words are lost as his tongue slides up the side of my neck. I start to open my mouth, to tell him no more licking while we're in the store, when his lips find my earlobe.

He bites, gently grazing his teeth against the sensitive spot of flesh. My palms press harder against the display case as I struggle to keep my legs underneath. My knees knock together and my eyelids involuntarily shut.

"Does it feel like we're acting like dogs now?" he asks with a hint of amusement in his tone.

I want to nod, fire a comeback, tell him that now's not the time to play, but my mind blanks out.

A soft breath escapes his lips as he shifts his head down and sucks on the side of my neck. His teeth follow, softly nipping.

My mind is spinning, and my heart is an erratic hot mess. I'm worried I'm going to pass out, which means I should tell him to stop, right?

"Does that feel good?" he whispers, his breath caressing my neck.

Shake your head, Isa!

I dazedly nod and focus on my breathing as he dips his head in for another bite. It feels so amazingly good. Better than a freakin' roller coaster under a sky full of fireworks while eating a bagful of cotton candy. My heart beats wildly in my chest, and all I can think is *erotic, erotic, erotic.*

I probably would've let him do it until my neck was covered with hickeys, but I push him away as I hear a door shut from somewhere inside the store.

Kai's wild eyes are on me as I spin around with my hand pressed to my neck.

"Here's those papers." Lily strolls out of the back area of the store and presents the papers to me like a present. "You can fill them out now. Or just bring them in on your first day."

"I'll just bring them in on my first day." I cringe at how breathless I sound. "I really need to get home. I've got a bunch of homework.

"Okay." Her gaze shifts from me to Kai.

Kai scratches at the back of his neck and offers her a stiff smile.

Lily stares him down for another moment before she looks back at me and smiles. "Let me know if you need any help with any of the questions."

I thank her, then Kai and I walk out of the store and get into the car. For half the drive, neither of us say anything. I want to say something, ask him what was with the crazy, totally out-of-the-blue, completely mind blowing, most erotic moment I've had. But just thinking about saying it aloud makes me nervous.

But finally, Kai looks at me. "So, we're okay, right?"

I nod truthfully. Kai and I are more than okay. At least I'm more than okay with what just happened. "Yeah. Of course."

"Good." He seems like he wants to say more, but he turns and settles in his seat, leaving me confused.

My confusion doubles when he reaches over and removes one of my hands from the wheel. I wonder what he's doing until he laces our fingers together then places our hands on top of the console.

I have no idea what the move means. What I do know is that what I felt in the store when he kissed my neck was explosions and fireworks like an insanely whirly rollercoaster. It's how I've always pictured kissing would be like. It makes me realize the almost kiss with Kyler was definitely missing something. It makes me wonder what actually kissing Kai for real will feel like.

It makes me really excited to find out.

Chapter EIGHTEEN

ISABELLA

By the time we get back to the apartment, my Grandma Stephy has dinner ready. The three of us sit down and eat while she informs me that her police friend didn't find the car anywhere nearby. I'm not surprised. I have a feeling whoever is messing with me will only be found when they want to be.

After I eat and clean off the table, I head down the hallway to go take a shower.

Kai's already sitting on the sofa, pretending to do his homework when really he's trying to crack into the flash drive. He catches my eye as I pass by and the look he gives me makes the spot on my neck where he bit and kissed me tingle.

"Are you sick?" my Grandma Stephy steps in front of

me, blocking my view of Kai. "You look flushed."

"I'm fine." I don't sound find. I sound like a girl who was just thinking about her neck getting bit by a hot guy.

She presses her palm to my forehead. "You don't have a fever." She removes her hand. "I think you should take it easy for the rest of the night. And tomorrow too. Come home right after school. Do something easy like watch a movie. You've had a rough week."

"I can do that," I say, running my hand over my neck. "I still need to do some homework, though. Midterms are coming up."

Her gaze drops to my hand on my neck. "What is that?"

My fingers tense. "What's what?"

She leans in, examining my neck closer. "Those marks on your neck."

I inch away from her. "I don't know what you're talking about."

"Isabella Anders," she warns. "You're a terrible liar. Who did it? Was it that Kyler boy you were always rambling about or was it . . ." She gives a suspicious look at Kai.

Kai appears deeply engrossed with something on his computer screen, but I can tell he's on the verge of laughing.

Glad he thinks this is funny because I sure don't.

"Um, I'm going to go take a shower." I whirl around and run like a madwoman for my bedroom to get some clothes and escape whatever she's about to say next.

"Just make sure if you're doing anything, you're doing it safely!" she shouts after me.

I slam the door and lean against it.

I love my grandma to death but man, she knows how to embarrass me.

I give myself a couple of minutes to collect myself before tiptoeing out to the bathroom to take a shower. By the time I sneak back to my room, exhaustion is catching up with me.

I climb into bed even though it's early. I haven't been sleeping very well. Every time I close my eyes, I either dream of the blue car, or of Lynn finding a way to get me arrested, or of my mom with blood on her hands.

As I reach over to turn my lap off, I notice I have one missed call and text. I almost don't look at them, worried they'll be from whoever sent me the threatening message. But I force the fear aside and pick up my phone.

Both are from Kyler.

Sighing, I open the text.

> *Kyler: Just wondering what's going on with you. I haven't heard from you since Monday. Been thinking about you a lot. Are we still on for Saturday?*

I read the message a second time, feeling clueless on how to respond.

This thing with Kai . . . Kai and that kiss . . . Kai and the way he holds me . . . Kai and the way he calls me beautiful . . .

I need to say something to Kyler because I don't think I want to hang out with him on Saturday, not after what happened with Kai. But I don't know exactly what to say.

I text Indigo about it because she'll know what to do. After twenty minutes goes by without a response, I give up and put the phone down, figuring I'll text Kyler in the morning after I've talked to Indigo.

Then I shut my eyes and sink into my nightmares.

By the time I'm getting ready to head out the door for school the next morning, Indigo still hasn't responded to my message.

"Grandma, have you heard from Indigo?" I ask, slinging my bag over my shoulder.

She glances up from rinsing dishes in the sink. "I heard from her a couple of days ago. Why?"

I hitch my thumb around the handle of my bag. "I texted her last night and she still hasn't answered."

I catch something flash in her eyes. Fear? Worry?

"I'm sure she's fine." She scrubs a plate with a sponge. "She's probably just busy taking care of her mom."

I think she might be lying, but let it go for now because I have to get to school.

I head out the door with Kai and the second we step outside, he reaches over and laces his fingers through mine. He does it so casual as if it's the most natural thing in the world. Me, I feel like the most unnatural, awkward girl that's ever walked the planet. My palms are probably sweaty, and I'm almost positive my hand is shaking. I want to pull away just so he won't notice, but there's no way I'm going to.

"So, did your grandma say anything else about your neck?" he asks me after we've gotten into the car and I'm pulling onto the road.

"Yeah, this morning she brought it up again." I feel embarrassed just thinking about it.

He glances at his phone then starts typing in a message. "What'd she say?"

I put on my sunglasses. "I don't want to tell you."

He gives me a sidelong glance. "Why not? Was it bad?"

"Of course it was bad. You heard her last night. Times that by ten and that's how much worse it was."

He works really hard not to laugh. "Just tell me what she said."

I shake my head. "No way."

"Oh come on." He sulks. "I promise I won't laugh."

"Yeah, right," I mutter. "You'll laugh and I'll get embarrassed." When he remains pouting, I sigh. "You have to cross your heart that you won't laugh."

He draws an X over his heart with his finger and then quietly waits for me to tell him.

Man, I can't believe I'm about to do this. He's never going to let me live this done.

"She . . . gave me a . . . condom," I mumble the last part.

He smashes his lips together and moves his fisted hand over his mouth, his shoulder shaking as he struggles to hold back a laugh.

"You promised you wouldn't laugh," I remind him.

It takes him a moment, but he manages to compose himself.

"She's funny," he says. "Your grandma, I mean."

I flip on the blinker to pull onto the main road. "In a good way, though."

"Definitely in a good way." He sketches his finger over his bottom lip as he contemplates something. "But the real question is, did you keep the condom?"

Shaking my head, I reach over and lightly swat him on the arm. "You just couldn't resist, could you?"

He laughs wickedly. "Of course not. Embarrassing you is one of my favorite things." I narrow my eyes at him, but he keeps on talkin'. "Want to know my favorite thing?"

"No," I say then admit, "Kind of."

His eyes light up with mischievousness. "Sucking on your neck."

My fingers instinctively float to my neck and the humor in his eyes fades as his gaze follows the movement.

His Adam's apple bobs as he swallows hard. "Isa, I think—" His voice cuts him off. Grunting in frustration, he opens the message. "Dammit, I was hoping he would," he says to himself.

"Who's it from?"

"A friend of mine. A couple of months ago he had a room for rent. I was hoping it still was available, but it isn't." He sets the phone on his lap and crosses his arms, the stress he's been carrying around for days returning.

"Have you heard from your parents at all?" I dare ask.

He shakes his head, staring out the window. "They won't call me, Isa. They're glad I'm not their problem anymore."

I rack my mind for something else to talk about, something that will bring him out of his funk, but suddenly, he sighs and turns toward me.

"I'm sorry," he says. "I shouldn't be complaining to you."

"You're fine. With your parents kicking you out, you're allowed to complain."

"Yeah, but . . . you're dealing with all this shit with your family and I'm sulking because I'm eighteen and have to start taking care of myself." He carelessly bangs his head against the headrest behind him. "And cracking into this flash drive. . . . I just really wish I could do it. It's getting so frustrating. I've even started dreaming about passcode boxes."

I force myself to grow a pair of lady balls and I reach over and take his hand. "I know it's been stressful. That's why you need to stop worrying about it so much."

"Not as stressful as it's been on you. I just want to do

this for you so I can, I don't know, give you a silver lining in all of this madness. I want you to not have to worry so much and feel safe. I want you to," he shrugs, "be happy again. I miss your smile."

"I still smile," I say, but on the inside all I can think is, *wow, that's the most ridiculously sweet thing I've ever heard.*

"Not as much as you used to." He starts stroking my palm with his fingers. "I can tell it's wearing on you."

I shudder from his touch. It feels deliciously good, like melted chocolate and whip cream and sprinkles. "And vice versa."

His lips lift to a lopsided smile. "I think we should do something fun this weekend. We could both definitely use some fun."

"Sure. I'm down." Wait? Like on a date? Or as friends.

Gah!

Before I can think too much into it, my phone vibrates from in the cupholder. I tap the read-aloud button.

"Message from unknown," the automated voice says through the speaker. "It's game time."

I grip onto the steering wheel. "What the heck does that mean?"

"I have no idea." Anger burns in his eyes. "But I'm getting really sick of this shit. Whoever it is is going to get their ass beat when I find them."

"What if it's Hannah?"

"Then I'll let you beat her ass. I should've let you do it in the driveway last week. I just didn't want you to get into trouble."

He sighs and then messes with my phone for the rest of the drive to school, pushing buttons and mumbling to himself. By the time I'm parking the car, he looks like he wants to bash it against the dashboard.

Me, I'm a beehive of nerves, worrying stinging at me

from every angle as I replay the message. Game time? What does that mean? Is it a threat? A threat for what?

The second I step foot into the school, I get the answer. Almost everyone stops what they're doing and gawks at me. I start to shrink behind Kai, wondering what's going on when I spot papers in peoples' hands and hundred scattered across the linoleum floors.

I bend down to pick one up at the same time Kai does. He starts to read it at the same time I do.

"No, Isa, don't read it," he sputters, snatching the paper from my hand.

But it's too late. I've already read enough. It's an article of my mother's crime with a photo of her at the bottom. And copied to the corner of the page is a photo of me taken while I was at the park that day I played basketball with Kyler. The flash I saw . . . It makes sense now . . . Someone took a photo for this.

My hands start to tremble as I pick up another paper from off the floor and note what's handwritten below the photo: *Meet the daughter of a killer. She looks just like her mother, doesn't she?*

That's not all I see. I see that the trial took place in Virginia, that the writer of the article referred to the crime as horrendous. I also see the name of the person my mom was accused of killing.

Jamison Anders.

I suddenly realize why Kai didn't want me looking up stuff on the internet.

I stand there in shock, willing my mind to forget what I just read. But it's right in front of me, on the papers on the floor, over and over again for everyone to see.

I can't breathe. I can't move . . . I don't . . .

The paper is suddenly snatched from my hand, and then I'm being dragged out of the school. I lifelessly follow Kai, letting him haul me to the car. Without saying anything, he lets go of my hand, sticks his fingers into my pocket, and digs out the keys out. He opens the door and gently guides me down into the passenger seat. After he gets me buckled in, he closes the door, climbs into the driver's seat, and starts up the engine.

As he's exiting the parking lot, I manage to find my voice again. "Where are we going?"

"Away." One word, yet somehow, I feel safe.

I hug my knees to my chest and watch the trees, homes, and stores blur by, trying not to think about what I read. But it's all I think about. Every thought I have centers around that name. Jamison Anders. Who is he? An uncle? A grandfather? A brother? There are so many possibilities, and all I want to do is get my phone and search and search and search until I find some answers. But I'm afraid of what I'll find, afraid it'll somehow be worse than what I'm thinking.

"Who is he?" I whisper. "Jamison Anders. Who is he . . . ?" I swallow hard. "Or, I mean, who *was* he?"

Kai grasps the steering wheel tightly, his knuckles turning white. "From everything I've read, I think he was your stepbrother."

"You mean, my half-brother?" My voice cracks.

"No. Before Lynn and your dad married, Lynn had a son. His name was Jamison and your father legally adopted him as his own son. I'm not sure why, though. I think he was a few years older than we are."

"Oh."

Lynn had a son before she met my dad? Lynn had a son my mom killed? Lynn had a son, and now he's gone because of my mother?

Tears sting my eyes. "No wonder she hates me. I represent this person who took away her son. I just don't get . . . why. Why would she ever agree to let me live with her? It doesn't make any sense."

"I know it doesn't," he says, making a sharp left-hand turn. "That's exactly what I thought the second I found out. Why would this woman let the daughter of a woman she thinks killed her son come and live with her?"

"Maybe to make my life a living hell." I hug my knees tighter against me. "Maybe, by torturing me, she's releasing her anger toward my mom."

He shakes his head, slamming the car to a stop. "I don't think that's it. Well, not all of it. When Big Doug gave me that folder, he said something about how he couldn't see why your mom was ever found guilty, which is why I really need to get into that flash drive. I think it might have some answers."

"Answers to what?" I feel so helpless, like I'm falling into a hole and can't find anything to grab on to. "If there were evidence that she didn't do it, then she wouldn't be in jail."

"That's not entirely true," he says, turning off the engine. "There's been cases where people spend years in jail after being charged for a crime, and then new evidence gets found that proves they were innocent the whole time."

"Yeah, I know, but . . . It's hard to think of it that way right now, and it kind of seems like false hope to think that's going to happen." I slip my fingers through my hair, pulling at the roots. "Kai, who do you think did it? Put those papers all around the school?"

"Probably the same person who stole that folder," he answers, his voice barely audible. "And my guess is both were done by Hannah, or someone did it for her."

I let my hands fall to my lap. "The photo on those papers . . . It was taken the day I saw the blue car following me around."

"I figured as much." He slides the keys out of the ignition and opens the door.

When I look out the window, I realize he's driven to the park with the hollowed out tree.

"Come on a walk with me?" he asks, looking over his shoulder at me with hope in his eyes.

I nod, get out of the car, and meet him around front. He threads his fingers through mine, and then we start across the grass, heading for our tree. Once we're situated inside it, sitting side-by-side with our feet sticking out of the entrance, Kai wraps his arms around me and pulls me against him.

"I know everything seems really shitty right now, but I promise you that I'm going to fix this," he says.

I angle my chin up and take in his bloodshot eyes and the dark circles beneath them. For the last week, he's been so worried about this, and it's starting to take a toll on him.

"Kai . . . I appreciate everything you're doing for me, but I'm not sure this can be fixed." I stare at the hole in the tree where our feet are sticking out. I remember a time when we were small enough we both easily fit in here. Now we've almost outgrown this place. It's sad, but it's life. Always moving forward, changing, no matter what you do. "I think maybe it's time to just accept and figure out how to live with all of this. I know you have your problems to worry about; you don't need to worry about mine."

He fixes a finger underneath my chin and forces me to look at him. "If you want to accept it and move on, that's fine. I get it. But I'm going to get into that flash drive so I can figure this out for you. And I'm going to figure out who put those fucking papers around school and make their lives a living hell."

"I don't want you getting into trouble."

"I won't." He winks at me, trying to appear calm, but I can tell he's all worked up. "I know how to pay someone back without getting caught."

"You look so tired, though," I say. "It's starting to worry me. You haven't given yourself time to really heal from the concussion and the broken rib. And the doctor said you need time to heal."

"Tired-shmired." He dismisses my worry. "I can sleep when I'm old. And my rib and head are fine." He knocks his knuckles against his head and the noise causes a tiny laugh to escape my lips.

But the laughter shortly vanishes and thoughts flood my head again.

"Maybe I should visit her," I say more to myself. "My mom, I mean . . . I can do that, right?"

"Maybe you should wait until I find out more information," he says warily.

"Why? I mean, even if it's terrible, I think I still want to talk to her." I realize the truth as I say it. One day, I want to face my mom, even if it's behind bars. While I don't know what I'll say to her, it feels like something I need to do. "I want some answers. I want to know . . . why."

"It might not be that simple." He hugs me closer to him. "She might not want to tell you why. Or she might not have an answer. There's a ton of ways that conversation could go."

"I know, but I think I want to try."

Silence wraps around us. I can feel him looking at me, but I can't bring myself to look at him and see the pity in his eyes.

Instead, I stare at my shoes. I'm wearing a pair of converse sneakers I bought when I was in London. They have grey stripes and studs on them. I remember thinking how different they were from the normal shoes I wore. When I tried them on, I felt different, too: more confident. That confidence let me dream of a different life where I was a different girl who didn't let her family walk all over her, who didn't hide in the shadows, who was happy.

For a while, I had that light—well, sort of. Now I feel like I'm about to tumble into the depths of despair. But I know I can't. I can't go back to that life of feeling insignificant. I have to keep going forward, changing, figuring out a way to live with this.

"I want to talk to her," I tell Kai determinedly. "And I want you to go with me."

I realize the truth of my words the moment I say them. It's crazy how much I need him to go with me. Indigo might have been right. I might not be in love with Kai, but the potential is there. Kai . . . He knows everything that's going on. And I have to ask, *why is that?* Why is Kai the one I tell everything to? Yes, Kyler is sweet and calls me, and I like him, but that's about it.

But the idea of falling in love with someone and someone loving me like that . . . It seems so out of reach, something I could never have. I don't feel worthy of it, and I'm not sure if I could handle it right now. There's too much stuff going on.

I don't know what to do . . . about anything anymore.

Kai brings his hand to my face and guides my head toward him until my cheek is resting against his shoulder. "If that's what you need, then I'm in," he says.

"Thank you," I whisper.

We sink into the quiet. Kai stares at the entrance of the tree, his knuckles brushing across my cheek, seeming lost in his thoughts.

I get lost in my fears: the fear of finding out the truth,

the fear that my mom is guilty, the fear that I'm somehow evil, the fear of falling in love and being loved back. I have so many fears. I just hope I can face them all.

Chapter NINETEEN

KAI

I'm going to crack the damn code on this flash drive if it freakin' kills me. It's pushing two o'clock in the morning, and I've been up for over thirty-six hours straight. I drank, like, four energy drinks, and my blood is pumping so fast my heart feels like it's going to jump out of my chest.

I know I have a million other things to worry about, like getting money to pay T back. I only have two weeks left to come up with a thousand bucks. Plus, I'm eventually going to have to find a place to live because living on Isa's grandma's couch is getting old for everyone.

But I can't think of anything else until I get access to this stupid flash drive. I know Isa's mom's appeal just got approved, and sooner or later Isa will start learning stuff about the case, but I can't stand the idea of making Isa wait to see if her mom is innocent. I want her to have some facts, especially before she goes to see her.

While I think she has every right to do that, I'm not sure it's a good idea. If her mom turns out to be guilty, it might mess with her head. And with this thing going on with the blue car and the flyers at school, the last thing she needs is more stress in her life. She's going to crack. I could see it in her eyes when she asked me to go with her to Virginia. I couldn't say no, though. Not when she was looking me like that—her big eyes pleading with me to be there for her.

I want to be there for her more than anything. It's something I'm quickly realizing: I would do anything for her, even risk my ass getting beaten on a whim that maybe whatever's on this flash drive will be able to erase some of the pain Isa's going through.

I know what that means. I know why I care more about her than I do myself.

I'm falling in love with her.

And that kiss in the store . . . the one on the neck . . . the biting . . . God, she tasted so good. I don't even know why I did it. I promised myself I wasn't going to go there with her, but suddenly all the desire and need I'd been keeping trapped inside me took over. I thought she was going to push me away, but she didn't, and I started to wonder if maybe she wants me as badly as I want her.

But right now definitely isn't the time to be confessing my undying love to her, though. After what happened at school, she couldn't handle me dumping my feelings onto her. I'm going to have to just suck it up and hold it all in, resist the urge to shout it from the rooftop, be a freakin' sap, because yeah, that's where I'm at. I'm fucking whipped. I know it. And I don't really care.

What I care about is getting into these files.

Violently clicking the mouse, I run the password cracking program for the umpteenth time. It flashes a warning at me, and another password box pops up. I about lose my shit.

"Goddammit!" I curse through gritted teeth, keeping my voice low so I don't wake everyone up.

I click on the program again and again. Just when I think I'm about to lose my mind, that I can't take another second of seeing a box pop up, I'm granted access.

"Holy effing shit." I slump back in the chair, letting out an astonished laugh because, honestly, I didn't really think I could do it.

I start opening files and reading through them. The first ten or so don't pertain to the case and contain records of random people, a map of what looks like a large building, and links to some security system.

I'm just starting to wonder if maybe Big Doug left me the wrong flash drive when I find the folder labeled: *The Bella Larose Case*. I immediately click it open and start reading.

I'm not even sure where Big Doug got some of this information. From case records? No, it's way more than that, like he did some research on the case or knew someone who's working closely with it, like maybe the lawyer. He scanned files, forensic records, the detective notes, witness statements, photos. And some of it definitely points toward Bella Larose's innocence.

Tucked away in one of the files is a scanned piece of paper of a list of suspects. It's handwritten and doesn't look very official, like someone was jotting down ideas. One in particular jumps out at me. I blink a few times, wondering if I'm seeing things wrong. But the name stays there, jumping out at me.

Lynn Anders.

I have no idea why someone would think it was Lynn, what kind of evidence they have, or whether it's just some random assumption. All I know is that I have to keep Isa away from Lynn and her family until we find out, especially after that thing that happened at school. I haven't had the heart to tell Isa, but I'm pretty sure that photo on the papers scattered around at school—the photo of her on the basketball court—was taken by someone that was on the basketball court with her. At least that's what it looked like from how close it was and the angle. I'm not sure if there was someone else there that day, but if not, it might mean my douchebag brother took the photo.

Whether it's Kyler, Hannah, Lynn, or someone else, someone's definitely determined to make Isa's life a living hell.

But I'm not going to let that happen.

Coming Soon

THE YEAR OF SECOND CHANCES

About the Author

Jessica Sorensen is a New York Times and USA Today bestselling author who lives in the snowy mountains of Wyoming. When she's not writing, she spends her time reading and hanging out with her family.

Connect with me online

jessicasorensen.com
and on
Facebook and Twitter

BOOKS BY
Jessica Sorensen

Lexi Ashford:
The Diary of Lexi Ashford (Part One)
The Diary of Lexi Ashford 2 (Part Two) (coming soon)

Entranced Series:
Entranced (Guardian Academy, Book One)
Entangled (Guardian Academy, Book Two) (coming soon)

Rebels & Misfits Series:
Confessions of a Kleptomaniac

Honeyton Series:
The Illusion of Annabella

Sunnyvale Series:
The Year I Became Isabella Anders
The Year of Falling in Love
The Year of Second Chances (coming soon)

The Coincidence Series:
The Coincidence of Callie and Kayden
The Redemption of Callie and Kayden
The Destiny of Violet and Luke
The Probability of Violet and Luke
The Certainty of Violet and Luke
The Resolution of Callie and Kayden
Seth & Greyson

The Secret Series:
The Prelude of Ella and Micha
The Secret of Ella and Micha
The Forever of Ella and Micha
The Temptation of Lila and Ethan
The Ever After of Ella and Micha
Lila and Ethan: Forever and Always
Ella and Micha: Infinitely and Always

The Shattered Promises Series:
Shattered Promises
Fractured Souls
Unbroken
Broken Visions
Scattered Ashes

Breaking Nova Series:
Breaking Nova
Saving Quinton
Delilah: The Making of Red
Nova and Quinton: No Regrets
Tristan: Finding Hope
Wreck Me
Ruin Me

The Fallen Star Series (YA):
The Fallen Star
The Underworld
The Vision
The Promise

The Fallen Souls Series (spin-off from The Fallen Star):
The Lost Soul
The Evanescence

The Darkness Falls Series:
Darkness Falls
Darkness Breaks
Darkness Fades

The Death Collectors Series (NA and YA):
Ember X and Ember
Cinder X and Cinder
Spark X and Cinder

The Sins Series:
Seduction & Temptation
Sins & Secrets

Unbeautiful Series:
Unbeautiful
Untamed

www.ingramcontent.com/pod-product-compliance
Lightning Source LLC
Chambersburg PA
CBHW030529310726
48979CB00010B/1851/J

9781939045201